WICKED AND TRUE

SHAYLA BLACK

WICKED AND *True*

ZYRON & TESSA: PART TWO

WICKED & DEVOTED

SHAYLA BLACK

Steamy. Emotional. Forever.

WICKED AND TRUE
Written by Shayla Black

This book is an original publication by Shayla Black.

Cover Design by: Rachel Connolly
Photographer: Wander Pedro Aguiar, WANDER AGUIAR :: PHOTOGRAPHY
Edited by: Amy Knupp of Blue Otter
Proofread by: Fedora Chen

ISBN: 978-1-936596-77-5

ACKNOWLEDGEMENTS

Books don't happen without lots of amazing people to help an author. I have a list of amazing folks to thank for all their hard work on Zy and Tessa's story.

First and foremost, Rachel Connolly. The book definitely wouldn't be as pretty without your cover genius, inside and out. But I appreciate you pushing me harder in some critical areas to make the story even better.

Jenna Jacob, your unending support and the hours of talking, reading, and assuring me I'm not crazy mean the world to me.

William…my husband and the love of my life. This journey is so much better with you by my side in the trenches. I thank you every day for taking a leap of faith with me and making this work.

I'm also grateful to Sierra Cartwright. Your enthusiasm, generosity, and positive spirit really helped me, especially during a rough winter.

Baby, biologically you're my daughter, but you're like a spirit sister, too. You get me, and you get these books. Thanks for always making me smile after a long day and for helping me keep the details straight.

EK, you know who you are, and I've really enjoyed your help, your honesty, and all the long discussions we had about this duet. I needed that as I went out on this limb.

Hugs to you all!

AUTHOR'S NOTE

Dear Reader,

If you have not read Wicked as Lies, please STOP.

Wicked and True is the second part of a duet in the Wicked & Devoted series about demolitions expert Chase "Zyron" Garrett and single-mom Tessa Lawrence. In order to fully understand and enjoy this book, you should first read part one of this duet, Wicked as Lies.

I sincerely hope you enjoy the saga of these two characters I've come to love so deeply, which is why they required two books to tell the full breadth of their story.

Happy reading!
Shayla

Chapter One

January 26

Chase "Zyron" Garrett sat back in his chair in the suddenly too-small conference room and stared at the trio of bosses glaring at him. He wished the BS Hunter, Logan, and Joaquin had just spewed was a punch line, but EM Security Management had a mole, and they very clearly weren't joking.

It's either your bestie or your girl.

You've got two weeks to figure out which one of them is guilty or we're letting both go.

Bastards. Neither Trees nor Tessa was guilty of a fucking thing. Zy ought to know; he'd already spent three months nosing into his best friend's life. He'd come up with zero dirt, proving Trees as innocent as Zy always suspected.

Now they wanted him to seduce Tessa Lawrence, their office assistant, to discern if she was guilty of selling them out. If he didn't, they would fire her, despite the fact she was a single mom who needed her job.

You've got two weeks—max. If you fail, we'll do the same to your fucking ass, too. Now get busy and get it done.

Calling them bastards was too polite. They were assholes.

Zy clenched his jaw and stood. How was he supposed to do what they'd demanded? He loved Tessa. He'd told her as much on Christmas Eve. Her response had been to run away, sure, but he was ninety-nine percent positive she'd left because she loved him, too…but thought their situation was hopeless. After all, they'd never dated or hooked up. Hell, they'd never even kissed because, for the last ten months, a single sticky paragraph in their employment contracts had kept them apart.

As of five minutes ago, it was gone.

I'm going to take her aside this morning and present her with a new contract. Better sick pay and vacation, tighter nondisclosure...and no nonfraternization clause. She'll sign. Then you'll both be off the hook.

Son of a bitch. Zy had waited and wanted Tessa, ached and burned for her. He'd been hoping that somehow, someday they could be more than co-workers and friends, but he'd never imagined that he'd be strong-armed into getting her between the sheets to spy on her. He didn't have to fuck Tessa to know that selling the bosses out was something she'd never do. But he didn't have a choice. Since they'd already coerced him into snooping on Trees, Zy figured he'd repeat the process...just with hot, bust-up-the-bed sex.

But one way or another, he would prove to the Three Stooges that they could one-hundred-percent trust Tessa.

"Get a move on," Logan, the youngest of his bosses, insisted.

Fuck off, douche bucket.

But Zy kept his mouth shut and gave them all a tight smile as he headed for the door.

As he approached, it crashed open. Caleb Edgington, the team's previous commander, charged in looking shell-shocked, like he'd collided with panic and run face-first into death.

"Colonel, sir?"

Hunter and Logan both stood. The quietest of his bosses, Joaquin, rose with a frown.

"Dad?" Hunter approached him.

The older man swallowed. "Your sister..."

Sudden tension gripped the room.

"What's wrong with Kimber?" Logan scowled.

"I received a threat recently. It wasn't specific, just a tube of lipstick and a warning to hand over Valeria Montilla before they took whoever the tube belonged to. I didn't know who—" Emotion choked off the colonel's words. He pressed his fist to his lips, grasping for the fortitude to finish delivering the bad news.

Zy's gut twisted. The man's only daughter, Hunter and Logan's sister...

Another guy came in behind the colonel—big, blond, badass, and totally pissed off. Deke Trenton, Kimber's husband. "She's gone. She dropped the kids off at daycare, then made a trip to the grocery store… and didn't come home. A courier delivered this thirty minutes ago."

They all crowded around as he whipped out a picture of Kimber, her auburn hair tangled, her big eyes red rimmed, with a gag over her mouth, her hands tied behind her back, and a gun to her head.

Holy shit.

"We'll get her back." Despite his face going pale, Hunter sounded resolute. "We'll do whatever it takes—"

"You're fucking right we will," Deke spat. "I want my kitten back. Jack and the rest of the Oracle team are at our office strategizing. Any help you can spare…"

"You'll have it," Hunter promised. "We need to lock down the rest of the wives and kids."

"Fast," the colonel managed. "Before it's too late."

The older man ducked out, looking as if he could barely keep himself together.

Deke didn't look much calmer. "Thanks for whatever you can do."

"Fuck that, she's our sister. We'll devote day and night to saving her."

Kimber's husband nodded, then he was gone, too. Silence prevailed for a protracted moment before Hunter swallowed, collecting himself. He turned to ice in an instant. Logan lived up to his fiery temper, grabbing an eraser from the nearest whiteboard then throwing it violently. His empty coffee mug followed, shattering against the wall.

Before he could toss anything else, Joaquin stepped in. "We don't have time for this."

"I know. I fucking know. Goddamn son of a bitch!"

Hunter and Joaquin jogged out the door, quietly strategizing ways to keep all the others in their family safe. Logan fumed, trying to gather himself, his lungs working like a bellows.

"I'll come with you," Zy offered. "I'll devote all my energy—"

"No. This shit is centered around Valeria Montilla," he said of the deceased drug lord's estranged wife, whom Caleb Edgington and his sons had rescued from her husband almost two years ago. "Now that her safe house has been breached, Trees and Kane are going to relocate her and her family pronto—and we'll be monitoring every step. But none of that will mean shit if you can't nail our mole."

In other words, prove Tessa was guilty and stop her.

Zy bit back an argument. Logan didn't have time for it with his sister in the clutches of a cartel demanding information the team couldn't afford to give. Giving up a client would ruin their professional reputation.

In short, they were utterly screwed between a rock and a hard place.

"I'm leaving," the former SEAL barked. "You're in charge until one of my brothers or I come back."

"Me?"

"Josiah and Cutter have quit, Trees will be on the road to Florida, taking Kane, who just started his first day on the job. That leaves you and One-Mile, and he's too unpredictable to be in charge."

Good point.

"I'll handle things."

With a nod, Logan tore out of the conference room, slamming the door behind him. After some shouting in the hall and more door slamming in the distance, the office fell silent.

Kimber being abducted was a curve ball he hadn't seen coming. No one had.

Zy marched out of the conference room. The rest of the team stood in the middle of the reception area, looking as shocked as he felt. Tessa was clearly more shaken than anyone to learn that her friend had been abducted.

She grabbed his arm. "Do you know anything beyond the fact Kimber has been taken?"

"No. No one does."

"I can't believe this is happening…"

"The bosses will do everything they can to find her." Especially since their case had seemingly put Kimber in the crosshairs.

"What if they can't?"

Her death wouldn't be pretty, but he didn't say that.

Zy was so used to playing dangerous games with dangerous criminals that he sometimes forgot that people like Tessa weren't. And despite the bosses' suspicions, he doubted she had any experience dealing with a cartel.

He just had to prove that…somehow.

"Don't think that way." He wanted to comfort her but wouldn't take her in his arms here. Neither of them needed to give the office any fodder. Despite the fact he worked with well-trained operatives, they gossiped like a gaggle of hens. "The colonel, Hunter, Logan, and Joaquin are the very best at what they do. And I don't know Deke, but—"

"He's scary."

That didn't surprise Zy. As co-owner of their sister organization, Oracle Security, along with the infamous Jack Cole, he figured Kimber's husband had a fearsome motherfucker side. "Then they'll leave no stone unturned to bring her back. Have faith."

"I'm trying." But Tessa was clearly distressed.

He wasn't surprised; she was sweet. She had a practical streak and could have a spine of steel when she needed to. But women weren't typically good at compartmentalizing their feelings. That wasn't a sexist comment, just a general observation. And because Tessa had a tender heart, she'd find it more difficult than most.

"We'll get through this. In the meantime, Trees and Kane are heading out soon. Did the bosses give you any information on that?"

"No."

Of course they hadn't. They thought she was a spy, so why tell her they were sending two operatives to the Sunshine State to secure Valeria Montilla and her son, along with her sister, Laila?

"Let me check with Trees and Kane, see what's up. As soon as I'm done, we'll make their travel arrangements while they go home to pack."

"A-are they going to help find Kimber?"

"No. They've got another gig." Zy hated not telling her what it was, but if he kept quiet and their mission still went south, he could say with total honesty that Tessa hadn't been aware of a single detail.

"What about One-Mile?"

Zy wasn't sure what kind of task to give their resident smart-ass sniper, but he'd dream up something. If ever the quote about idle hands being the devil's playthings applied to someone, it was Pierce Walker—who only tolerated his fiancée, Brea, using his given name.

"I'll talk to him, too. For now, stay near the phone in case the bosses need anything." He stepped closer, resisting the urge to touch her, and dropped his voice. "But I'm here if you need me."

"I know." She lifted her stare to him, and he almost fucking lost himself in her verdant eyes. "Thank you."

She shouldn't thank him. He was going to seduce her for all the wrong reasons. It would ultimately save her. But if she ever found out all the reasons he'd lured her between the sheets, she would hate him forever.

Nothing like having your balls in a vise…

Zy bit back a curse and headed to find Trees, who stood near the coffeepot with Kane and Walker, discussing strategy. "Those fuckers we work for left me in charge."

One-Mile cursed. Trees raised a brow. Clearly, they thought him being temporary head honcho was as ridiculous as he did. Getting those two to follow his orders would be harder than herding cats. The verdict was still out on Kane, but the bosses hired a certain breed of warrior. Zy doubted very much the new guy would be cut from a different cloth.

So he changed the subject. "Where are we with your trip to Florida?"

"We have a problem," Trees finally said. "We don't know exactly where we're going. Valeria came home from a concert last night and realized someone had broken into her safe house. They ransacked it, too. There were signs of a struggle…but her sister and her son were nowhere to be found."

"Logan said as much."

"If Laila got out, she left in a hurry, because her phone, wallet, and money were all still there. But if the cartel took her…"

"If they did, why would they have kidnapped Kimber this morning, demanding to know Valeria's location? They already have hostages they can better use as leverage."

Good point. "Because they want to fish Valeria out fast and they're leaving no stone unturned?"

"Maybe." It was the most likely scenario Zy could see, but Trees obviously disliked not knowing.

That made two of them. "So no one has heard from Laila?"

One-Mile shook his head. "But she has my number. When I left Florida, I made sure she knew how to contact me."

But if she didn't take her phone when she fled, how could she? "Unless you hear from her, we need to come up with a plan. If Laila escaped, every hour she and baby Jorge are floating out there without help or resources is another hour they're likely to be scooped up by the remnants of Emilo Montilla's gang—if they haven't been already. Do we know who's running the show now that Walker put bullets in his head?"

"I made a few friends while I spent a month down there, trying to off the son of a bitch."

That sounded unlikely. One-Mile wasn't usually nice enough to make friends with anyone, but Zy bit anyway. "And?"

"I've heard that some underlings inside Emilo's compound are trying to seize power…but there's also gossip that his father intends to take over and oust anyone who gets in his way."

That made sense. Emilo had been like a gator—lazing on the shore, enjoying the sun, and sinking his teeth into anyone who wandered too close, especially if they dared to question his authority. But he'd been small-time compared to his father. Geraldo Montilla was a legend for his predatory ruthlessness. The man was pure shark.

Zy's guess? Geraldo had given the splinter faction to his son, mostly so Emilo would have something to do, because he'd known his only son lacked the balls to run the larger Tierra Caliente organization. But now that his son was gone? No way would the narcotics king turn over any part of his organization to Emilo's lackeys. "Makes sense. Do we know where Valeria is holed up?"

"No," Trees answered. "I have a number to call, probably a burner phone. When we get to the Orlando area, I'm supposed to arrange a meet point."

"And we're certain she still hasn't heard from her sister?"

"Yeah, but she says she keeps getting calls from an unfamiliar number. She's been afraid to answer it, but I told her she should next time her phone rings."

"Good call." Maybe Laila had found another phone. "Keep me posted."

As the others nodded and stepped toward their desks, a phone buzzed. Zy searched for the source of the sound and zeroed in on One-Mile, who pulled his device from his pocket.

"Walker." The sniper listened to the frantic, high-pitched voice on the other end, then frowned. "Wait. Wait! I don't speak Spanish." He pulled the phone from his ear and glanced at the others. "Who the fuck speaks Spanish?"

Tension gripped Zy. He didn't, but he was more focused on the caller. "Who is it?"

"Laila, but she's crying and too upset to speak English, so I can't understand a fucking word she's saying. Brea will have my balls if I don't help a woman who obviously needs it."

Walker didn't care about staying on the good side of many people, but he'd do whatever it took to keep the pretty, pregnant preacher's daughter happy.

"I do. I'll talk to her." Kane held out his hand.

"Thank fuck." Walker pressed the phone to his ear again. "I'm going to give you to another guy. He's one of us, so he'll help keep you safe." He slid the device into the new guy's palm.

"Find out where she is," Zy murmured.

Kane raised the phone with a nod. "*Bueno*?"

Zy held his breath as the former small-town sheriff exchanged rapid-fire Spanish with the woman. He glanced across the room to see Tessa organizing her desk with a gusto that told him she needed something to do or she would go crazy. If she was this upset about her friend's abduction, he couldn't imagine what all the Edgington men were going through, not to mention the rest of her family.

That gave Zy an idea—one he'd put into motion as soon as Kane finished talking to Laila.

He and the other operators watched, waiting impatiently until the new guy finally ended the call.

"Well?" Zy prompted.

"Laila escaped—with one of her assailants' phones. She's got Valeria's son with her. They ran to a women's shelter. She didn't know where else to go."

The move had been pretty resourceful on her part. The shelter's management wouldn't ask too many questions, and if cartel thugs showed up, the police would be called. "She needs to dump the phone."

"She turned off location services, but yeah, the longer she holds on to it the more of a liability it becomes. She's concerned that she'll be without any way to contact her sister once she trashes the device."

"Where did you two leave things? Did she tell you where to find her?"

"No. She wanted to know about Valeria. Laila was panicked because she's been calling her sister, who hasn't picked up."

That explained the unknown calls to Valeria's number.

"I assured her Valeria is fine and suggested she try calling her sister again. I also told her it wasn't a good idea for them to hook back up until we roll into town. I hope she listens." Kane shrugged. "By the end of the call, she seemed calmer...but still not thinking clearly enough to devise a plan, so she said she'd leave that to us. Let's put our heads together, gentlemen."

"Get started," Zy said. "I need to give Tessa something to do before she goes crazy. Back in two."

The others started a low-voiced discussion that Zy tuned out as he approached Tessa, who'd wrapped her arms around herself, trying not to cry. He'd tell her to go home, but sending her there to stew alone would be worse.

"Why don't you pick up some things to feed Kimber's family and take them to her house? Otherwise, Deke will be trying to feed the kids when he's really distraught and should be out looking for his wife..."

She frowned. "Don't you need me to make arrangements for Trees and Kane to travel wherever they're going?"

"They're big boys who know how to work a website. What they can't do is comfort Kimber's family in any way that's remotely compassionate or helpful. You can."

"What about you and One-Mile? If you need anything—"

"We'll handle it. Just take care of her family. You know, make sure they have enough food for dinner, give them comfort or a shoulder..."

"Of course. I can do that."

"Call me if you run into any issues."

She grabbed her purse and her car keys. "I will. Let me know if you need anything, and I'll come back."

He should let her go now. He shouldn't get any closer to her or let himself fall any deeper. But he couldn't stand her leaving without touching her. "Are you okay?"

"I'm rattled. I guess I always thought that friends, family, and employees were too far removed from the danger you guys deal with all the time."

Zy shook his head. "Why do you think Cutter and Josiah were both so quick to get out once they realized they were getting married?"

"It just never occurred to me." She shook her head. "That probably sounds stupid, but..."

"No." Naive, maybe. But Zy couldn't blame Tessa. She'd never put herself in the path of danger for an objective designed to keep others safe. She answered phones. She coordinated supplies. She kept the office running smoothly. Despite the bosses' suspicions, there was no reason she would know about this shit. "You shouldn't have to think about this, especially given everything else you've been dealing with."

Like her father's recent passing and her ex-boyfriend's threats.

She sighed. "I'll be back."

As she turned to leave, he wrapped his fingers around her arm. It was the kind of incidental contact he often had with people. But no one else made him burn and shudder with desire the way he did every time he touched her. It was fucking inconvenient to want Tessa so much right now, but this just proved that nothing—not time, conflict, barriers, or tragedy—could put a dent in his need for her.

"Hey, did you, um...by chance, talk to Joaquin this morning about anything?"

The little furrow between her brows told him no. "He messaged me, saying he wanted to meet, but then everything happened and..."

Zy wasn't surprised, but he was bitterly disappointed. Despite this morning's shit show, he wanted Tessa so fucking bad he could almost taste her. "Once you have, we'll talk."

Later that day, Tessa hit the SEND button on her email back to Joaquin. Her hand shook.

It was done. She had officially agreed to the new—and better—terms of their updated contract.

One without the clause that had kept her and Zy apart for ten agonizing months.

She swallowed as she stood, still half-dazed. She'd always thought one of them would have to leave their job before they could explore their feelings. Of course, she was happy the bosses had removed the barriers between them. And yes, she was impatient to be alone with Zy. Obviously, he'd known this was coming.

Her question was…why had the trio of hard-asses they worked for suddenly relented? Zy had appealed to them multiple times, always to have his requests fall on deaf ears. Why had they suddenly changed their minds?

Maybe it didn't matter. Maybe she should stop questioning this new development and start enjoying it.

Maybe…but something tugged at her.

As she went through the day, she tried to focus on Kimber's family. She spent the rest of the morning shopping and cooking, then all afternoon with Kimber's sisters-in-law, Kata and Tara, as well as their kids. Joaquin's wife, Bailey, stopped in, showing her hint of a baby bump, looking as rattled as the rest of the women. Tessa had tossed an early dinner in the oven, played with the children, and offered a shoulder to anyone who needed it…at least until Deke had come in and shooed her out so he could get everyone into hiding.

Tessa didn't blame him. Even now, she felt the urge to head for her daughter's daycare and hug Hallie breathless. Instead, she settled for calling to check in on her almost one-year-old, then heading back to the office to see if she could lend a hand. And yes, to see Zy. According to Joaquin's email, the whole staff had received a new contract with similar terms, since it had been revised to "reflect the direction in which the current owners felt best for their business."

So…after keeping her and Zy artificially apart since the day they'd taken over the team from the colonel, they suddenly didn't care if she and Zy started hanging out? Dating? Having sex? Falling in love?

With a frown, she entered the office only to find Trees and Kane had already caught their flights to wherever they were headed. Zy and One-Mile were holed up in the conference room, on speakerphone with someone. She couldn't hear the conversation, just muffled voices and the occasional curse.

When she peeked in to ask if they needed anything, Zy rose and walked out, shutting the door behind him before insisting that he and One-Mile were all good and to go home. He'd talk to her later.

Did that mean she'd see him tomorrow…or tonight?

Tessa still wasn't sure as she picked Hallie up from daycare and drove back to her duplex. Not while she fixed dinner, bathed her daughter, sipped a glass of wine, half watched the news, and stared at the clock. Not while she read her baby a story and wrestled the fuss-bucket into her crib. Not while she paced her living room before deciding just shy of nine o'clock that a shower might help calm her and clear her head.

More than once, she picked up her phone to call Zy…before ultimately putting it down. Maybe he was still with One-Mile, organizing some rescue operation. Maybe he was helping the others look for Kimber. Or maybe he was thinking about what this change in their contracts meant for them. But there was no way this wasn't on his mind.

Between this worry and her concern for Kimber, Tessa had no idea how she would ever sleep tonight.

A sudden, firm knock on her front door had her whirling around. Her breath caught. Her heart stopped.

With her stomach twisting in anticipation, she flipped on the porch light and peeked out the peephole. Today had proven that anyone associated with EM Security in any way needed to be careful. But as she'd suspected—and hoped—Zy stood in the circle of murky light on her porch, in a white tank, a black jacket, and faded jeans.

He looked like a man on a mission.

With her heart thumping, she eased the door open, not caring that her face was bare, that her hair was twisted in a messy bun, or that she was wearing plain green cotton pajamas without a stitch underneath. She was just happy to see him.

"Zy. What are you doing here?" Her question was silly. That wasn't what she'd meant to ask, but she was so damn nervous. She knew precisely why he was here. Unless something had happened? "It's getting late. Is everything okay?"

"Did you really think that, after today, I wouldn't come?"

"No."

"Is Hallie asleep?"

"She fought some, but I got her down about thirty minutes ago."

He nodded. "Good. Can I come in?"

Tessa hesitated. She'd yearned to be with Zy for lonely, seemingly endless months, ever since she'd lost her heart to him. She wanted him so badly right now she could cry. But if they crossed this line from friends to lovers, it would change everything. "I don't know if that's a good idea."

"Did you get a new contract today?"

Slowly, she nodded. "Joaquin emailed it to me."

"Did you sign?"

"Zy..."

"Did you?" He wouldn't stop, wouldn't rest, and wouldn't give up until she answered.

Tessa gave in. "Yes."

"So did I, first thing this morning. The restrictions keeping us apart are gone."

"They are, but—"

"There are no more buts, Tessa."

"How did you know?"

"The bosses told me."

"Why?" She couldn't think of a single reason they would have told Zy they'd presented her with a revised agreement that no longer precluded her from having any non-work contact of a sexual nature with him.

"Because when they changed mine, I asked about yours. You know the reason."

"I do."

He wanted her every bit as badly as she wanted him. At the thought, heat flashed through her, making her aware of her peaking nipples and the sharpening ache between her legs.

"Can you think of a single reason I can't come in, strip you down, and make love to you? Tell me right now."

His demand made the heat clawing up her body rush to her cheeks. Her heart thudded even harder. "Did you mean what you said on Christmas Eve?" *Do you love me*?

She needed to know. If she didn't have Hallie to think about, it wouldn't matter if Zy only wanted to take her to bed for the night to scratch the itch he'd been fighting all these months. She would risk using her body to tempt him into opening his heart to her. But she had too much responsibility to throw caution to the wind now.

"Every word," he vowed.

Tessa dragged in a shaky breath and studied his face. He meant that.

God, she loved him so much.

She hadn't told him yet. She'd been afraid the admission would set fire to the powder keg of desire between them. She'd also been terrified he would break her heart.

She stepped back and opened the door wider. "Then there's no reason at all. Come in."

Her breathy answer seemed to still the air and stopped time between them.

A visible shudder wracked Zy's body. "Do you want me?"

"I always have."

"I've wanted you, too, baby." Something needy and tormented twisted Zy's face as he stepped over the threshold, kicked the door shut, locked it, then took her shoulders, dragging her against every hard inch of him. "So fucking bad I can't stand another second of not touching you."

Chapter Two

Zy stood in Tessa's little foyer, gripping her tight against him. His lungs worked hard, breath sawing in and out, as he searched her face.

"I can't stand it, either." She slid her palms up his chest to clutch his shoulders. Her eyes burned hot as she trembled in his arms. "Kiss me."

"Fuck, yes."

He took her face in his hands. Tessa's lush lips were mere inches from his, and all he could think about was covering them with his own while he stripped off everything that shielded her body from his stare. He ached to carry her to bed, work every inch of his cock into her, and indulge in all the fantasies he'd had of her seemingly forever.

Tonight. He'd give himself that long to drown in Tessa, in their pleasure. Then he'd have to focus on proving her innocence so the trio of paranoid fuck-bags they worked for didn't fire her. Yes, he hated that tonight was only possible because they had forced his hand. But right now, he only cared that Tessa belonged to him.

"Baby…" he breathed as he brought her closer and seized her nape, tilting her head to meet his descending mouth.

Their lips connected. Finally. Right there in her tiny entryway, the impossible happened.

She gasped. His body jolted. Everything stopped—breath, thoughts, heart, and time.

Fuck, she was so soft. He was greedy to have all of her.

Zy shoved her lips apart and surged into her mouth. She was warm and sweet like honey. He wanted to drown in her, die with her. Need soared. His cock turned to steel. His impatience climbed.

Damn it, if he couldn't keep it together now, how was he going to give Tessa the kind of ecstasy that ensured she'd never look at another man? Never want to leave him?

His crumbling restraint shouldn't shock him. Before he'd even walked through her door, this need had been a fever boiling his blood. But now that he'd laid his mouth on hers... Game over. Their kiss had torched his good sense and sent his best intentions up in flames. The way he burned for her was unlike anything he'd ever felt. The simple touch of her fingers clinging to his arms as her little whimpers filled the air was like kindling on a roaring blaze.

Would they even make it to the bed? Zy wasn't optimistic.

His lips never left hers as he urged her from the foyer to the living room. She took baby steps backward and pushed his coat off his shoulders. He shrugged out of it, not caring when it dropped to the floor, landing somewhere near the shoes he toed off while unfastening his jeans and deepening their kiss.

Even with their tongues tangling and his clothes melting away, he wasn't close enough to her.

Zy lifted Tessa against him, cupping her ass and grinding her against his cock as he took ground-eating steps to her softly lit bedroom. She didn't protest, simply hooked her legs around his hips and rocked against him with pleading moans he swallowed with his bruising kiss.

Fuck, he loved sex...but this? It was paradise wrapped in candied fantasy. It was pleasure stacked on top of ecstasy and soaked in bliss. He'd only kissed Tessa, but already he felt speechless and half-dizzy. His brain had all but stopped, his thoughts skewing to nothing but the million ways he ached to please her.

Zy raced to the bed, setting her on her feet beside it and breaking their kiss. It was the last goddamn thing he wanted, but he needed information. Problem was, when he looked down at her, all rosy and unfocused, her lips plump, parted, and waiting, he nearly lost all restraint.

"Zy..." She lifted her hand to his chest.

The brush of her fingers through his shirt blasted him with heat.

"I know, baby. But before we go any further, you need to tell me two things. How long has it been?"

"Oh...um." She closed her eyes, lashes skimming her cheeks, before she blinked up at him, looking so vulnerable. "About a year and a half."

He'd suspected that. It had been way too long for him, too—by his own choice. He hadn't wanted any woman except Tessa.

"And how careful do we need to be? I'm clean but—"

"We don't. After I had Hallie, my doctor put me on the pill to regulate my cycle."

"Thank fuck. For almost a year, all kinds of shit kept us apart. I don't want anything between us ever again."

"Same, starting with this." Tessa grabbed for the hem of his T-shirt.

Zy was faster. He took hold of her too-big pajama top and yanked it over her head. As he'd hoped, she wasn't wearing a damn thing underneath it.

And holy shit…

Zy's mouth went dry. Tessa's tits were a work of art—pale and round with stiff candy-pink nipples, standing pert above her narrow rib cage that flowed into her small waist. He wanted to cup the soft mounds, see them in his hands, suck the pretty, rigid tips until they swelled and she cried out and begged him to fuck her. He wanted her naked.

But he needed her in his arms.

Zy crouched at her feet and gripped the waistband of her pajama pants.

"Oh, my god. Is this really happening?" Her voice dripped breathless excitement and longing as she raked her fingers against his scalp and gripped his hair.

Yeah, this felt like a dream to him, too. And he didn't want to wake from it.

"It fucking is." He jerked her pants down her hips savagely, baring her thighs, stopping only when the spring-green cotton puddled around her feet. "Step out."

She did, her audible breathing torqueing up his anticipation. Her fingers tightened in his hair. And he didn't care because he couldn't stop looking at how fucking beautiful she was.

Her baby-pink toenails were like dollops of frosting on the confections of her delicate feet. Her dainty ankles gave way to lean calves, dimpled knees, and curvy thighs that made blood rush to his cock. But it was everything she hid between those gorgeous legs he couldn't stop staring at.

Other than a modest dusting of dark blond curls at the top of her pussy, she was bare. And wet. And swollen. Her visible desire sent his need surging.

Zy knew he should go slow, build her desire, tease her until she couldn't stand it anymore. But he'd waited too long and he needed her too much.

Banding his palms around her middle, he lifted her onto the bed, then reached behind his head to tear off his shirt as he followed her down, pressing her onto the mattress with his body. While he tossed the T-shirt aside, he pressed his bare chest to hers, hissing at the heat of their melding skin, before he captured her mouth again.

Tessa flung her arms around him, tilting her head to offer him total access to her mouth as her hips swayed under him in supplication. She let out a needy little whimper.

Fuck, if she kept that up, he'd plunge straight inside her and keep at her until she screamed.

Fighting for patience, he peeled her hands from his shoulders and pressed them flat to the bed, holding them down with his forearms. "I'm trying to go slow. You're tempting me too much."

"I don't need slow. I just need you."

Her words threw gasoline on his blazing need. "We've waited a long time for this. I don't want to rush you. I don't want to hurt you. I don't want to leave you a fucking shred of doubt that I will give you more pleasure than you've ever had, and I want to do it every day of your life."

He wanted her to know—to feel in every part of her body—that she was his.

"Oh." She looked stunned and flushed and beyond beautiful. "You've already succeeded. I've never been more aroused in my life."

Was she kidding? He'd barely touched her. And she thought she was ready?

No. Hell no. Not even close.

"Don't move."

"Okay," she promised with a shaky nod, her exhalations loud in the otherwise silent night. "But I want to give you pleasure, too."

"You already do, baby, just by being with me."

"No. More than you ever imagined."

That would be a tall order considering how many fantasies of her he'd indulged in since they'd met, from his first time masturbating in her shower to thoughts of her last night, lying in his solitary bed, so hard for her he could barely breathe.

He'd never imagined then that he would finally be free to kiss her, unclothe her, penetrate her, and pleasure her. Make her his. Now, her entire body was open to him, and the night was theirs.

Zy smiled as he brushed a blond curl from her face. "You will. I promise."

Then he took her mouth, barging past her pillowy pink lips to taste her kiss again. When she was breathless, he began working his way down, still pinning her to the mattress with his forearms over her wrists. His mouth was on the move, skimming the graceful line of her jaw, gliding up her neck. She cried out with a head-to-toe shudder and a sweet flush. With a feral smile, he laid his lips behind her ear and exhaled. Her hands tightened into fists and she arched beneath him in a silent plea.

In the next heartbeat, he inhaled her musky female scent. It carried vanilla and a hint of something citrus—orange, maybe?—that urged him to breathe her in again and again until she melted his senses.

With his nose full of her, he descended from her neck to her collarbones, laving them before he dropped to the swells of her chest. She was so soft here, the skin like gossamer. The valley between her tempting mounds lured him. There was no way he couldn't rake his taste buds over her skin.

Tessa's body tightened. She let out a harsh breath. She fought to lift her arms from the bed, but he held her in place, tormenting her with his lips as he edged closer to the jutting nipples she arched his way, seemingly desperate to have them in his mouth.

Who was he to say no?

He grabbed both her wrists in one hand, pressing her deeper into the mattress as he took her breast in his palm and lifted it to his thirsting lips. He tasted the tip with a greedy lick before opening his mouth and sucking as much of her onto his tongue as he could.

Tessa jerked. Her cry became a wail. Her nipple turned to stone, and he sucked even harder, grazing her with the edge of his teeth.

Under him, her legs moved restlessly, wrapping themselves around him. She fought to free her hands and plant her lips on him. But he held her in place with a firm grip, switching his attention from one breast to the other. If possible, she tasted even sweeter here. He pulled hard on her. She sucked in a needy breath and gave up trying to escape. Instead, she arched and twisted as if trying to give him more and grabbed at the hand covering hers.

Beneath him, her legs parted, allowing his body to slide between.

Just where he wanted to be.

A flush crept up her peachy-pale skin. She closed her eyes in ecstasy, her body tightening. The pulse at her neck pounded. Her swollen lips parted, tempting him every bit as much as the gorgeous breasts he gorged on.

"Zy…"

He released her nipple and squeezed it, delighting in her soft gasp. "What, baby?"

She wriggled and cajoled. "Now."

Soon, but… "Not yet."

Tessa opened her eyes. "Haven't we waited enough? Is something wrong?"

Their gazes fused, and he felt a zing inside him, at a place so deep in his chest he'd never felt it. He'd never even known it existed.

His heart?

"No, baby. Everything is so right. You feel it, don't you?"

She nodded, then nibbled her lip. "Then why…"

Would he torment her and refuse to plunge inside her immediately? "Because we only have one first time, and I'm going to make sure you never forget it."

"I already won't because it's you."

Fuck. Women who said things like that were usually mentally picking out china patterns and choosing monogrammed towels. In the past, he would have taken his quick orgasm and run. Not with Tessa. That was the closest she'd come to telling him she loved him. And it turned him on almost more than he could stand.

"You're making it hard to resist you."

"Because I don't want you to."

There were a thousand ways he wanted to touch her and a million ways he wanted to take her. Right now, all he could do was close his eyes and try to bring his runaway heartbeat under control.

But it was no use.

"Fuck." He rolled to her side and positioned his mouth just above her nipple, then covered her soaking pussy with his greedy fingers. "Get ready. This is going to be fast."

"What?" The word trembled from her lips, but the question came too late.

He'd already dragged her taut tip in his mouth with a savage suck and plunged a pair of fingers between her folds. He began working them inside her. Oh, holy shit, she was tight. He got dizzy just thinking about how much patience it would take to ease his way inside her and how perfectly they would fit once he did.

As he finally wedged his fingers as far inside her as he could, Tessa let out a low moan, planting her feet flat on the mattress and bucking up to meet his searching touch. With one hand, she gripped the sheet. With the other, she dug her nails into his back.

Zy looked at her, lost in the passion he heaped on her—and he nearly lost all restraint.

His impatience mentally yanked like a rabid dog on its leash, but he jerked it back and focused on Tessa, on her pleasure, hooking his fingers inside her to rub the smoothest bit of flesh behind her clit. All the while, he settled his thumb over the little nubbin and started a teasing counter-stroke.

Instantly, she gasped. Her eyes flew open wide. Her body tensed. And her pussy clamped down on him. The little bead under his digit was as hard as a diamond. "Zy!"

"You're getting close, baby." He didn't ask; he knew.

"Yes, but I want to touch you, taste you…"

He wanted that, too. "Later. The first time will be hard and fast. I can't help it. I fucking need you."

"Yes!" she cried as he took her nipple onto his tongue again, sucking it deep as he traced fevered circles on her hardening clit.

She kept tensing, tightening, clamping down as her breathing quickened, her color flushed, and her pulse drummed. She was seconds from orgasm.

"Oh, my…Zy. Zy!"

Her body was seizing up, and that was his cue.

He pulled his fingers free, shoved his jeans around his hips, slid between her legs, and fitted his thick crest against her slick opening—and started pushing in. Sweat already slicked his back as he locked his fingers with hers, then drilled his stare into hers as he did the same to her body, one strong, driving thrust after the next, punctuated by her little whimpers and pleas, until he was fully seated inside her.

Hell, the feel of Tessa around him was the most perfect ever. He'd fucked women for a decade and a half in all corners of the world, of all shapes, sizes, and colors. And right here, right now, he knew this one had been made for him.

He was never letting her go.

Zy used his knees to spread hers wide while he anchored his elbows against the mattress for maximum leverage. Then he pushed harder into her, plunging in and bottoming out, wishing he could go even deeper and lose himself inside her forever.

Under him, she met him thrust for thrust, lifting to him, twisting and welcoming, spreading frantic kisses across his shoulder and up his neck, her teeth tugging at his earlobe with just enough sting to make him sizzle. She mewled restlessly, urging him on.

And he was on fire. Every nerve ending, every inch of his skin. Down in his gut and inside his heart, he burned for this woman. And he fucked her like it was the first and last time he ever would. Like only she mattered. He wanted her to understand on a visceral level how much he desired her and always would.

The second they were forced to leave this bed, he was going to find the nearest jeweler so he could put a ring on Tessa's finger and call her his every day, every night, for the rest of his life. No way would he let her slip through his fingers. Whatever she needed, whatever it took, whatever he had to do, she would be his.

She tightened again, and he felt her pussy begin to flutter around him. "Zy! Oh, my god. Please. Please. I can't... Don't stop. I—"

"Yes," he ground out, thrusting into her faster and faster. "Fuck. Fuck, yes. Oh... Tessa. Baby!"

She screamed in his ear, her pussy clenching and spasming on him as he let go with a harsh, hoarse cry, gripping her hands tight, rattling the bed, and showing her absolutely no mercy.

Pleasure pinged inside him, filling every corner of his body, flooding his cock...and inundating his heart. He gripped her hands tighter, shoved his elbows deeper into the mattress, and used his knees to propel himself even harder. A low growl of shocked ecstasy rattled from his throat as he released deep inside her.

Suddenly, he wished she wasn't on the pill. He wished even more that he had every right to plant his seed in her womb, hold her while she slept, and call her his wife.

Slowly, the blackness in his vision receded, his heart rate slowed, and his breathing returned to normal.

And only one thing careened through his overwrought brain. "I still love you, baby. Move in with me."

Tessa clutched him, pressed her lips to his, and burst into tears.

The following morning, Tessa rolled over and sent a bleary-eyed glance at her alarm clock. It would go off in ten minutes. That's how long she had to figure out what to say to Zy.

He'd asked her to move in. She hadn't seen that coming...but she should have. He'd talked about it before and he'd told her that he loved her. Lord knew she was beyond tempted to say yes. She might not have said the words to Zy yet, but she loved him, too.

His warmth and woodsy, masculine musk lured her closer. She pressed her body to his, nuzzled his neck, and inhaled him. His scent filled her nose and swam in her head. God, how was she supposed to think straight when she was this close to him?

Tessa couldn't get enough of the man, couldn't stop wanting every inch of him—all steely, well-forged muscle wrapped in downy-warm skin in the body of a sex god. She didn't even know the words to describe how good he made her feel when he touched her. He'd definitely been indefatigable all night. She'd lost count of the number of orgasms he'd heaped on her, especially when he'd been determined to prove that his oral fixation hadn't been mere pillow talk.

Today was Tuesday and she had to work, but to have all the pleasure he'd given her, Tessa would gladly give up sleep. But even if he hadn't made love to her over and over last night, resting wouldn't have been in the cards because Zy had given her too much to think about.

Caution urged her to stop and thoroughly consider his proposition. Moving in together was a big step. Sure, he'd been great with Hallie the week he'd stayed with them, but her daughter was almost a toddler now. She slept through the night, but she was far more active, requiring constant supervision every waking moment of her day. She was mobile and inquisitive. And she got attached to people very easily. Last week, one of her daycare workers moved to another position, and Hallie had cried for hours, stomping out her displeasure. Tessa could only imagine what would happen if the little girl glommed on to Zy and then he moved on to greener pastures.

Of course Hallie had recovered. All it had taken to make her smile again had been a happy song and a stuffed sparkling unicorn.

This hesitation isn't about Hallie; it's about you.

Tessa inched away from Zy and stared out at the cloudy morning. When her ex-boyfriend, Cash, had abandoned her, she'd been devastated—and she hadn't even loved him. She'd just been pissed that he'd run out on her and afraid she wouldn't be able to handle single motherhood. She'd since proven otherwise to herself—and the world. But Zy was another story. She loved him so much her feelings scared her.

So much that she hadn't told him how she felt.

How would she recover if she moved in with the man she loved, then he decided that shacking up was more permanence than he wanted? Or that being a daddy figure was more responsibility than he could handle? Tessa wasn't sure how she'd make it. Then again, what would happen if she turned Zy down? He'd have every reason to leave.

And it was entirely possible he'd had everything to do with the sudden changes in their contracts. The more she thought about it, the more she wondered… The bosses would never admit they'd caved, but it seemed possible Zy's insistence had convinced them to relent. What happened if he'd gone to all that trouble for her, and she refused to commit?

He'd be gone. And who would blame him?

Suddenly, Zy wrapped his arms around her and brought her against his body. "Morning, baby."

His voice sounded rough and smoky, exactly like he'd been on the all-night sex bender he had been.

"Good morning." Her voice sounded overused, too. Must have been all that screaming. "I should get up."

Just like she should scrounge up some coffee for Zy, grab a shower, and start waking Hallie for breakfast.

But all she wanted to do was lie here with him for one more stolen moment.

"You okay?" He held her tight.

"Why wouldn't I be?"

He chuckled. "I could feel you thinking."

"Sorry."

Zy kissed her forehead. "It's okay. I don't need an answer right now."

"Thanks for understanding. There's a lot to consider."

"There is. But you should let me plead my case again. You know, just in case you need more persuading."

He rolled her to her back and slanted a kiss across her lips, urging her legs apart. She shouldn't let him. They didn't have time. But Tessa melted beneath him as he scooped her backside in his hands and pushed inside her. She was tender and swollen, but it didn't matter. She still welcomed him with a shudder and a gasp.

After a night of sex, her whole body was hypersensitive. But all Zy had to do was look at her, and she came alive. Her nipples beaded, her sex flooded, and she tingled everywhere. She didn't see how she'd ever stop wanting him.

Last night, he'd shown her what pleasure really meant and left no part of her untouched. Today was starting no different.

Zy eased inside her so slowly she wanted to cry, but no amount of writhing or moaning changed his pace. He withdrew in an even more molasses stroke, driving her crazy. Tessa pressed her lips to his feverishly and dug her fingers into his shoulders, trembling and whimpering and giving all of herself to him. Again. She couldn't help it. Refusing Zy when he set his mind on pleasure was impossible.

"That's it, baby..." he growled in her ear as he lifted her hips and impaled her in another unhurried stroke before he dragged his way out, leaving her struggling to breathe as she climbed toward another helpless peak.

"Zy..." she panted. "Zy, please."

He gripped a fistful of her hair and tugged just hard enough to force her head back. He took advantage of her arched neck, sliding his lips down the column before he dragged his tongue up over her throat and chin, then finally covered her mouth, prying it open for his next kiss. Eagerly, she parted her lips wide for him, just as she did her legs when he pressed his way inside her again with another thrust that left her gasping, straining, and clawing.

But he wasn't satisfied. He never was until he made her a trembling, pleading mass. She felt that relentless part of him now, searching for weaknesses he could exploit, for ways to make her yield all of herself. He wouldn't give up until she did.

"If you're looking for mercy, I have none. I want you to come."

She was almost there, now too far gone to form words. Instead, she nodded frantically, thrashing and bucking against him in a fevered cry for more.

"I know you're close. I'd love to keep you on the edge until you beg me..."

His words sent a shudder down her spine. Her eyes widened. That sounded both horrifying and wonderful.

"But we've got a busy day, so I'll settle for one last back-clawing scream."

God knew he could wrench it from her. He'd already proven that over and over. "Zy…"

"But not yet." He hooked his arms under her thighs, spreading her even wider and leaving her completely vulnerable. Whatever he wanted to do to her, he would.

And she would happily let him.

His strokes picked up speed. God knew the friction was already about to unravel her. She tried to move with him, get the last bit of stimulation she needed to vault over the peak, but he held her at his mercy, open for his pleasure. She couldn't do anything except hang on for the ride, knowing that orgasm would only come when he decided to give it to her.

The tension stretched on. Despite how tender she was, she ached for the pleasure Zy dangled just out of reach. He kissed his way across her shoulder, nuzzled his face in her neck—then slammed his way deep inside her until her bed frame creaked, until she couldn't catch her breath, until the climax she wanted went from unattainable to inevitable.

She keened again, her throat almost raw, as she splintered into a thousand pieces for him. She tensed and jerked, riding ecstasy that somehow, unbelievably, outdid all the orgasms he'd given her over the past ten hours. Or did she just think that because her body sang with the kind of head-to-toe bliss she'd never experienced until Zy?

He crashed into her, the tendons of his neck standing out, sweat trickling down his temples, and his eyes looking so blue above his five-o'clock-shadowed face.

"I love you," he ground out roughly as he slammed home again and let go with a harsh cry and a tremor that wracked his body.

I love you, too.

Panting, he collapsed onto her, absently kissing her shoulder. "Holy shit. I'd love to call in sick. Work is overrated."

Despite her sated afterglow, Tessa laughed. "I wish…but we can't."

Everyone would know why. And even if the bosses had finally allowed them to explore their relationship, those three definitely hadn't given them permission to slough off their jobs because they'd rather have sex.

The sounds of Hallie grunting and working up to a cry began drifting through the baby monitor on her nightstand.

"Duty calls, huh?" He grinned at her. "Guess I can't blame it on the bosses this time."

Her heart flipped over. She was so in love with Zy and wanted to tell him how she felt so badly. But if she said the words, he would assume that she wanted to move in with him. He'd expect it, even.

Tessa wasn't ready for that.

"Pretty much."

As if to reiterate the fact she needed to get out of bed, her alarm clock went off next, playing a Keith Urban song.

Zy laughed and rolled to his side, pressing a kiss to her lips. "No rest for the wicked, I guess."

"None. You poor thing."

"Yeah. I guess we should get up. You want me to make you some tea before I head out?"

It was sweet of him to ask, but… "You're leaving?"

"I need a shower and a change of clothes."

"Of course." If he showed up in what he'd worn yesterday, One-Mile would definitely notice. "I'll see you at work. Don't worry about the tea. I got it."

"All right." He pressed another kiss to her lips, this one lingering, telling Tessa without a word that he didn't want to go. "Did I, um… persuade you any?"

To move in with him? "Well, you're very persuasive; I can't lie about that. And I'd love for you to persuade me again, any time you want." She kissed him and cupped his face. "But what you're asking of me…it's a big step. I need more time to think."

His jaw tightened. "It didn't take you long to let Cash through your door."

"But that's just it. Well…first, we weren't living together romantically. I was giving him an opportunity to be a father to his daughter." She'd needed the money, too. She still did. Rent was due in four days. She'd probably make it this month, but it would be tight… Next month? She'd have to figure it out then. "And second, I was too impulsive with Cash. Thankfully, when he left it didn't affect Hallie. Then again, he never paid any attention to her. But you would."

"Hell yeah. I want us to be a family, Tess."

She wanted that, too. But she needed to be sure. "Then give me more time."

"How much?"

"I don't know." How long should it take to decide what might end up being the rest of her life? "A week?"

Zy didn't say that he didn't like her answer, but it was all over his face.

"It's not that I don't want to say yes," she assured him. "It's that I want to say yes so much it scares me. And we found out barely twenty-four hours ago that our contracts weren't going to keep us apart for another…"

"Eight hundred eighty-seven days. I was counting."

"I was trying not to. Moving in together isn't something we should do on a whim, and after last night… It was great." *Understatement of the century.* "If we take that step, I want to be sure it's not just for the sex but for the right reasons."

"I get it." He sighed. "It's easier for me to jump in because I only have myself to worry about."

"Exactly. Hallie and I come as a package deal."

"I know, baby. I'd love her, too."

His words melted Tessa's heart. "We'll talk about this more tonight."

"All right." He groaned and pulled away from her, rising to his feet.

She hustled out of bed and dragged on her pajamas, then dashed to the thermostat to turn up the heater. This January seemed chillier than the last. Or maybe she just felt that way because she hated the cold… and Zy wasn't next to her anymore.

Before she could make her way to Hallie's room, he stopped her, now dressed, and pressed another kiss to her lips. "I'll see you at work."

She nodded. "I'll be there by eight."

"Well, I'm the boss right now, so if you're a little late, I won't tell." He winked.

"But Kimber needs us. Did you hear anything last night?"

Sobering, he shook his head. "I checked my phone a couple of times. Nothing. I'll make some calls and have an update by the time we meet at the office. Okay? I know she's your friend, but try not to worry."

Too late. But she gave him a little smile. "Thanks. I'll see you soon."

Chapter Three

At three minutes after eight, Tessa slung her sedan into the lot, yanked her keys from the ignition, grabbed her purse, and hopped out of her car. Despite Hallie being a little cranky this morning—she blamed teething—Tessa was surprised she'd almost arrived on time.

As she shoved her keys in her purse, she looked up to find a stranger approaching. Early thirties, wearing casual clothes and a ball cap. Someone from the Oracle team, maybe? It seemed likely that they would incorporate Zy and One-Mile into their tactical planning to rescue Kimber. If the operation required a demolitions expert or a sniper, they were the best.

The man nodded her way as he cut through the parking lot, heading straight for her. He came closer, and something about him set her on edge. She assessed him again. He was too clean to live on the streets and his smile looked too ready to belong on a thug.

At least that's what she thought until she got a good look at his cunning dark eyes.

Tessa hustled for the door.

"Sorry if I startled you. Tessa Lawrence?"

He knew her name? "Who wants to know?"

"We have some mutual friends."

Was he from Oracle after all? "Who?"

The stranger waved her question away. "That's not why I'm here. You have two thousand dollars in your bank account. You owe twelve hundred dollars in rent and another one eighty-five for daycare. Your car payment is another three-fifty. Then you have to buy groceries and—"

"What do you want?" *And how do you know so much about me?*

"To talk to you. We can help each other." He pasted on his friendly smile again.

Every instinct she possessed told her not to believe it. "I'm okay."

"You're falling a little more behind every month. What will you do when you can't pay your rent anymore?"

"I don't think that's any of your concern, Mr.... Who are you?"

"It's not important. I'm here to make you a proposition. There's ten thousand dollars in it for you—cash. Today. It will take maybe ten minutes of your time and—"

"If you're suggesting for even an instant that I give you sex for money, then—"

His hearty laugh cut into her righteous speech. "I'm not, Ms. Lawrence. You're pretty, and maybe you're a tiger in the sack. But you're not worth ten grand. I can't think of a single woman who is. This is strictly business."

Now Tessa was even more confused. "Then what do you want for that amount of money?"

Her guess? It was illegal, and she wasn't interested.

"Information. That's all. You're in a position to know some things my associates need to. Once you provide that, I'll give you cash. And if you like the arrangement, it might be something we can continue, as needed."

She narrowed her eyes, not liking the sound of this. "What kind of information?"

"We're looking for someone."

Valeria Montilla? Even if that wasn't the case, Tessa didn't like his vibe, didn't like this conversation, and didn't like the direction this encounter was heading. "I can't help you. And you shouldn't come back."

She bustled toward EM's door—but he was faster, gripping her by the arm. "Listen, it's not in your best interest to say no. Trust me when I tell you we have ways of...persuading you to comply."

The uneasiness roiling in her stomach turned to fear, especially when she realized they stood alone on the shadowy side of a building in a light industrial area. The place next door was abandoned. And the alley behind them was too close for comfort.

Tessa tore her arm free. "Don't touch me."

"I don't think you understand, Ms. Lawrence. We're trying to be nice here, but—"

"Hey!" Zy shouted from EM's door as he pounded down the steps, then strode across the parking lot. "Who the fuck are you? Get your hands off her. If you want something, you deal with me."

The stranger cursed under his breath, then released her, sidled behind her, then shoved her into Zy's path before he sprinted down the alley and disappeared behind the fence.

"Are you okay?"

She nodded. "Fine."

"Go inside."

Tessa feared he intended to chase that guy. "Zy..."

"Go!"

He took off running, looking as if an all-out sprint was second nature to him, assisted by his long legs. She watched him go, her heart in her throat.

What was this stranger capable of? Did he have a gun? Would he use it to stop Zy from chasing him? The thought terrified her.

Tessa stood frozen in panic. If she dashed inside for One-Mile's help, it would probably come too late. If she called the police, it would take them too long to arrive. And if she chased after them herself, Zy would be furious, not to mention she ran the risk of leaving Hallie an orphan. What the hell was she supposed to do?

Before she came to an answer, Zy returned from the alley, panting, looking frustrated and furious.

"What happened?" she asked. "Did he get away?"

"He had a head start and a waiting vehicle. He was halfway gone by the time I even started chasing him. What did he say to you? What did he want?"

"I-I'm not sure."

"He must have said something."

"He was looking for information about someone but—"

"Who?"

"He never actually said. He'd just finished saying that it would be in my best interest to tell him what he wanted to know when you walked outside."

"In your best interest how?"

"He didn't get around to explaining that, either. But he knew everything about me, even how much money I have in the bank." She shivered. "It was creepy."

Raking a hand across his short stubble, Zy sighed. "I fucking don't like this. And you don't have any idea who he was?"

She shook her head. "I've never seen him before. He didn't look familiar to you?"

"Nope. I'll ask One-Mile if he's seen anyone hanging around lately and look at the security cameras to see if we caught a better angle of him. In the meantime, you shouldn't walk to and from your car alone."

That was no problem. She didn't want to. "So what do we do now?"

"Carry on with our day, I guess. We have a shitload to accomplish. Let's start by making some phone calls and seeing if there's been any progress on the Kimber front. And I'll take a look at the security cameras and let you know if this guy looks familiar. And until we know who he is or what he wants, I won't let you out of my sight."

Tessa exhaled in relief. She always felt safer with Zy. "Promise?"

He glanced around to make sure no one was watching, then reached for her hand. "Baby, I'm not going anywhere."

After another long day at the office, full of one frustration and dead end after another, it was nearly time to quit. Tessa had gathered her things, and Zy was following her to her car when his phone rang. He pulled it from his pocket. Hunter.

Shit.

"It's the boss. I should take this," he told her as he scanned the area around her car, finding it clear. Only One-Mile's Jeep and his bike were in the vicinity.

It bugged the hell out of him that someone had accosted Tessa in the parking lot. It bothered him even more that the stranger knew so much, including where to stand to avoid their parking lot cameras capturing a full-frontal shot of his face. But Zy would have to unpack that later.

"I can wait for a few minutes."

"Go get Hallie. I'll watch you walk to your car."

"Okay. I'll go home and start dinner. If you can eat with us, come on over."

"I'll let you know." He watched Tessa make her way to her vehicle as he answered the call. "Garrett."

"Hey."

In that one syllable, Zy heard his boss's exhaustion and worry. "How are you doing? Anything new?"

"No. Whoever has my sister grabbed her from the parking lot at the grocery store. It looks like they followed her there, pulled up beside her in a van, and grabbed her as she stepped out of her SUV. The plates are registered to a stolen truck in Texas, so we have nowhere to go from there. They tossed her purse into her front seat, phone and all, like they knew Deke would trace her to the store and find a dead end. No prints on anything. The only sign of Kimber since is that fucking picture with a gun to her head and a demand to know Valeria Montilla's location."

"I'm sorry, man. Tell me how I can help."

"Nothing you can do. Whoever has my sister seems to have a sixth sense about who we'll call and where we'll look next. It's fucking frustrating."

Zy smiled at Tessa when she got into her little sedan safely and drove away with a wave. "If you think of something I can do—"

"Make progress on finding our mole. Anything new?"

Renewing the argument that neither Trees nor Tessa would sell them out would fall on deaf ears. "I'm working on it. I need more than a day."

Hunter sighed again. "Yeah, but we don't have a lot of time. Hear anything new from Trees? He tried to call me earlier. I missed it."

"I talked to him this morning. Last I heard, he and Kane had come up with a plan to separate. They'll each bring one of the sisters to Louisiana because anyone looking for Valeria is probably looking for two women with a toddler, so changing the optics should help."

"If that's the plan, then tell Kane that he takes Valeria and no communicating with Trees about location. End of conversation."

Because, according to Hunter, Trees might still be guilty. *Ugh...*

"Okay. But they're having trouble connecting with Laila. She's reluctant to leave the shelter, and Valeria refuses to leave the state without her son."

"It's a shitty fucking time to get stubborn, but it's her kid. I get it."

Zy knew Hunter meant that. He would do anything for his son, Phoenix.

"I know what my assignment is." Even if it was bullshit. "Anything you want me to get One-Mile working on?"

"Not yet. Until we know who the fuck we're dealing with, there's no one to shoot. But tell him to stay ready. If this is going where I fear, he may be taking another trip to Mexico."

No surprise there. "You got it."

Zy almost told Hunter about the asshole in the parking lot, but his boss didn't need more on his plate. He'd already tasked One-Mile with helping to track down Tessa's stranger. If Hunter needed the sniper's services to rescue Kimber, Zy would have him back-burner this mess. But he didn't like this thug threatening and rattling Tessa.

"Thanks."

"You all need anything else? Tessa volunteered earlier to come cook for everyone and play with the kids again if—"

"Tell her I appreciate it, but they're all in hiding now. Dad, Logan, and I are staying visible. Everyone else these motherfuckers could use against us is somewhere safe." He sighed again. "I just realized they're in the safe house we prepared for Valeria and her family. Shit."

Yeah, shit. "I know Trees and Kane were hoping to pull out tonight."

"Which would put them back in town tomorrow. Fuck. I can't think of any place—"

"Don't worry about it now. I'll talk to Trees later. We'll put our heads together and come up with something."

"If there's any chance he's guilty, I don't want him involved in that decision."

"He isn't. I would swear my life on that."

Hunter hesitated, then cursed. "We'll talk about it later. I gotta go. Dad thinks he might have something new."

"Keep me posted."

"You got it."

Zy ended the call with a sigh. He hoped something broke for the Edgington family soon. Kimber was the glue that held the family together with laughter and love. The colonel and the bosses would all be devastated if they lost her for good.

Fuck that. It was early days, and no one was giving up. Instead, Zy pocketed his phone and headed inside, making his way around the maze of walls, desks, and equipment. Finally, he maneuvered his way to One-Mile's corner of the world.

"What's up?" the sniper asked.

"You see anything in those parking lot cam images? That guy look familiar?"

Walker shook his head. "No. I even zeroed in. He positioned himself just right to—"

"Avoid our cameras. I know." Zy cursed.

"And she has no idea what he wanted?"

"That's what she said."

The bosses would probably point out that's what someone with something to hide would say, but Zy knew Tessa. If she didn't know, she didn't know.

"Thanks for trying, man."

"Sorry I couldn't do more. You need anything else before I head out?"

Zy shook his head. "Just talked to Hunter. They've got nothing new. I'll keep you posted. But don't go far. You never know when we'll have to bounce."

"Nothing new about that." The sniper stood and grabbed his keys. "But unless the world is fucking ending, I'm not available on Valentine's Day."

It seemed totally unlike One-Mile to be sentimental. "Because it will be your first with Brea?"

"It will, but no." He gave a wry smile. "That's when we're getting married. I let her pick the date."

"And that's the one she chose?" Zy snickered. "It's kinda cute."

Walker laughed with him. "Yeah. What are you gonna do? Happy wife, happy life."

Only because Brea made him a very happy man in return. "Her father warming up to you?"

"A little better every day. At least I think he's convinced now that I'm not going to bust into his house and tear up the joint before I beat the shit out of him." He shrugged. "It's progress."

Zy wasn't shocked. Walker looked like a mean, tattooed motherfucker. "Congrats."

"Thanks. And now I have to get the hell out of here. Brea and I have another birth class tonight."

"That's cool. You must be excited." It was crazy that the sniper would be a father by late spring.

"Try terrified."

Zy raised a brow. "You, afraid? Seriously?"

He scoffed. "Once you've rolled around on the floor with a bunch of pregnant, hormonal women, talking about everything that could go wrong during birth, tell me how confident you feel about your balls staying attached."

Then, with a tip of his head, the sniper was gone, leaving Zy alone.

Since they all had keys to the office, he could secure the place just fine...but it would be absolutely weird to lock up because all the bosses were gone. This business wasn't just their livelihood. They'd all put their hundred percent into it, and the fact they weren't around was another indicator of the gravity of the situation.

With a shake of his head, Zy shut down his laptop, locked up, and headed out to Tessa's place. He arrived a few minutes later and entertained Hallie while she tossed together some tacos, beans, and salad. After he set the table, they sat, Tessa feeding Hallie before he took over for a bit to spell her.

Like the first time he'd stayed with these two, being here felt natural. They fell into a family rhythm, and he imagined being with them every night, every weekend, enjoying life together. He'd already called a jeweler this morning about rings. He had an appointment tomorrow afternoon. After that, he'd hopefully have something to put on her finger.

Once she agreed to move in with him—and he wouldn't rest until she did—how long before he should pop the question? How long before she'd be ready to say yes?

Fucking soon, he prayed. He wanted this. He wanted her and Hallie and to expand their family. And he wanted it right now.

"You okay?" she asked.

"Yeah." He'd love to tell her what was on his mind, but she wasn't ready to hear it.

"What did Hunter say? Any progress?"

"No, but they're trying everything they can."

Tessa frowned with worry. "They must be frantic."

Zy had heard the fear in Hunter's voice, but he didn't want to alarm her any more. "Of course they're concerned, but they're doing what they always do, following clues and working angles. Something will turn up."

"Do they need more help with food or supplies? What about the kids? I could take them off their hands for a bit."

He shook his head. "They've got everyone on lockdown at an undisclosed location, just in case. The fewer people who know where the better."

"Ah, that makes sense." Tessa shook her head and forked in another bite of salad. "Hey, I wonder if that guy who accosted me in the parking lot this morning wanted information about where they're hiding."

"Maybe." It had crossed his mind, too. "If that guy shows up again, you let me know. I'll make it clear that he needs to leave you the fu—the *F* alone."

Tessa smiled and followed his stare over to the baby, chewing happily on tortillas, carrots, and teeny bites of chicken. "She doesn't understand you yet."

"But she will. Easier to clean up the language now. It gives me time to get it right since I'm bound to…*F* it up."

"You're so cute."

That's why you love me, he almost said. But did she?

Zy wasn't entirely sure, and it bothered him more than he wanted to admit.

"I'm glad you think so," he said instead. "Do you remember anything else that guy said?"

She paused, seeming to mentally replay the conversation. "It all happened so fast, I'm trying to remember everything he said. He told me they had ways of making me comply, so that was unnerving."

Hell yeah, it was. "It's basically a threat."

"That's how I took it, too."

"But he didn't say what they would do if you refused to cooperate?"

Tessa shook her head. "He just indicated they were trying to be 'nice' in offering me money for the information they sought. The whole conversation was maybe thirty seconds. By the time I realized what he was saying, you came out and broke it up."

Damn it. Zy wished like hell he'd stayed out of it long enough for Tessa to hear the stranger's whole spiel, but he'd seen what seemed like a player with swagger trying to horn in on his woman—and he'd lost his shit.

"Don't give it another thought. If he's smart, he won't be back."

"I hope you're right. It was weird."

She'd obviously been unsettled by the encounter, so Zy took her hand. "I'll look out for you, baby. I promise."

"I know." She sent him a soft smile. "Thanks."

Suddenly, Hallie shrieked and pounded her palms on the tray of the high chair.

Tessa laughed. "That's her way of saying she's done with dinner and wants attention now."

"Yeah? How about I do the dishes so you can play with her?"

"Actually, she needs a bath. We're running a little behind schedule tonight." Tessa stood and lifted Hallie from her high chair. "I want to get her into bed. Because someone didn't fall asleep on time last night and was a bit fussier than usual this morning."

She kissed the little girl's head and headed to the bathroom, flipping on the light and talking to her daughter in a happy singsong tone that earned her a baby giggle. Listening, Zy smiled as he started clearing the table.

Twenty minutes later, they met back in the living room. Tessa carried a clean Hallie, looking flushed and tousled from wrestling her rambunctious toddler in the steamy water.

"You're looking very pretty, young lady," he said to the girl whose wet brown curls framed her pink-cheeked face.

She smiled, her big green eyes lighting up.

"She's so happy," he remarked to Tessa. "You've done great with her."

"There were days I wasn't sure I had it in me, but I'm happy now. Even with all the Cash drama, I don't regret anything about her coming into my life. And I can't believe she's going to be one in just over a week."

Time had flown.

"Think she'd let me hold her?" He hadn't pushed the issue because she'd always been a little leery of men, but if he was going to be any sort of father figure, he needed to start now.

"Worth a try. If you can rock her a little, maybe read to her some, that will give me a chance to boot up my laptop and send Joaquin some paperwork he asked for."

Zy frowned. In the middle of helping to locate his stepsister, Muñoz wanted some shit from the office? It didn't make sense, but then again nothing about this situation did. "Sure."

Ten minutes later, Tessa strolled in as he stood to settle Hallie in her crib.

With an indulgent smile, she reached for her baby. Zy handed her over, his heart flipping when she kissed the little girl's forehead. "I love you, Hallie-bean. Sleep good."

The baby's eyes fluttered open for a moment, then she sighed and fell asleep.

A smile of motherly tenderness softened Tessa's face as she set the girl in her crib and backed away. "She's exhausted. She'll sleep straight through the night, I'll bet."

"Good." He wrapped an arm around Tessa's waist and led her out of the girl's bedroom.

"Yeah. I'm exhausted, too. Someone kept me up last night." She gave him a playful poke in the ribs.

"I'm not apologizing for that."

"I didn't ask you to."

"Nice to know." He took her in his arms, settling her against his body. "Because I'd like to keep you up again tonight."

"Oh?" Her smile turned flirty. "What if I don't want to be up?"

"Too bad." He grinned, then pressed his hard cock against her softness. "I'm…up."

She sucked in a breath. "Clearly, you are."

"Wanna see more?"

She bit her lip. "I think I do."

"Excellent." He dipped his head, angling his lips over hers. "I've missed you like hell all day."

Then he covered her mouth with a groan as he took her pale curls in his fists and tugged. She sighed into the kiss and gave herself over to him in the span of a heartbeat. She talked about not being sure she could trust him with her heart? Bullshit. The way she dropped all defenses as he kissed her took trust. And when he delved into her mouth, seeking out the darkest, sweetest depths, she offered no resistance. She gave him everything he asked for and surrendered even more.

She had feelings for him, maybe even deep ones. But something—probably a need to be completely sure before she committed—held her back. He could be patient. Tomorrow, he'd have her engagement ring and he'd wait for her to be ready.

Until then, he had no problem telling her he loved her…and using his body to show her just how much.

Zy broke their kiss long enough to strip off his shirt as he walked her into the bedroom. He caressed her under the cozy sweatshirt and found her braless. Excitement splintered through his system as he cupped her mounds and thumbed her nipples, finding them hard and waiting.

Fuck yes. He was never going to get enough of this woman—but he'd happily die trying.

He reached for the hem of her top. Zy had told himself that he'd go slow tonight, savor her, show her that he could make it all about her until she squealed and begged and cried. But damn if he wasn't sweating and fevered, needing all of her the second he touched her.

Then his phone rang.

Cursing, Zy hoped like hell it was spam when he pulled the device from his pocket. A quick glance told him he wasn't that lucky. "It's Trees. If he's calling me now, there's a problem."

"You two usually talk every day. Why would today be different?"

He was having trouble stringing an answer together when the too-big sweatshirt slid off her shoulder to reveal her pale skin that gleamed everywhere the soft lamplight hit it. But if he wanted to prove she wasn't their mole, he had to keep a lid on Trees's whereabouts. That way, when this shit went south—and he feared it would—he could tell those assholes they worked for that she wasn't the problem.

"He should be in the middle of something a lot more urgent than talking to me right now." He pressed the button to take the call. "Hey, man."

In front of him, Tessa frowned as if she didn't appreciate his answer, but she didn't say anything, just cocked her head silently, seemingly waiting for him.

"Hey," his buddy said over the phone. "Since you're in charge, I figured I'd check in with you."

"Yeah." He looked Tessa's way. "Give me five?"

"Sure." She disappeared into the bathroom, flipped on the light, and grabbed her hairbrush.

That seemed like a waste. He was just going to mess it up…but he'd have fun doing it.

"You talking to me?" Trees asked.

"Sorry. Talking to Tessa." Reluctantly, he jogged out of the bedroom, through the living room, then stepped onto the back patio to be enveloped by the chilly winter night. "What's up?"

"Did you finally take her to bed?"

"If I had, why would I tell a nosy prick like you?" He laughed.

Trees joined in. "So that's a yes. Was it everything you thought it would be?"

"Let's put it this way: I have an appointment to look at engagement rings tomorrow."

"You're that sure?"

"One hundred percent."

"Wow. Congratulations, man. That's awesome."

"Well, even if I buy a ring tomorrow, she's not going to say yes right then."

"A little gun-shy?" Trees asked.

"Yeah, that's what she says. And I get it." He just didn't like it. "But you didn't call to ask about us. What's up? You and Kane get everything worked out with the sisters?"

"Finally." He sighed. "It was a fucking long, scary-ass day. But yeah, we're on the road now. And I need to talk to you."

It sounded serious, and Zy's gut seized. "What's up?"

"Kane and I connected with Valeria, and she got her son back. They left a few hours ago in a minivan. He plans to drive straight through. But I got word that the safe house they had for Valeria isn't available anymore, so where do you want us to go?"

Good question.

"I'd ask one of the bosses," Trees continued, "but with everything they have going on, I didn't want to come to them with more problems."

"Yeah. Let me…call Cutter. He's a local boy, and he and Shealyn are back from their honeymoon."

"And from what I heard, her sister's wedding to Josiah got derailed by violence two days ago. They might be busy."

"Well, we're likely to have another situation like that on our hands if Cutter doesn't spare me five minutes."

Trees sighed. "True. Yeah, call him, then let Kane know."

"What about you and Laila? Where will you go?"

"I rented an RV. We're posing as a married couple on vacation, seeing the country before we have a baby."

"You're serious?"

Trees sighed. "We stopped to pick up supplies before we headed out of Orlando, and some chatty tourists started talking to us in the grocery store, so I made up a story. Laila was clinging to me like she was terrified. She literally expects Emilo's henchmen to jump her at any moment. They messed her up."

Zy had heard the same from One-Mile, who'd talked to Laila when Emilo had held him captive a few months back. "She feels safe with you?"

"As safe as she feels with any man, but it's not much. I told her I was a friend of Walker's. It helped. He's apparently the good guy since he politely declined to rape her."

"Jesus. So what's your plan?"

"We're going to make our way back slowly, make sure Valeria gets situated into whatever safe house you can find for her. If it looks good, like no one is watching it, then I'll take Laila out there. If it gets hit… my plan B is to take Laila to my place."

"Well, it's secure enough."

"It should be, yeah. There's just one problem." Trees dropped his voice. "Laila is so damn sexy, I can barely keep my eyes—and everything else—off of her."

Falling in instant lust was so unlike Trees, it took Zy aback. "Does she suspect?"

"There are only so many ways to hide an erection like mine."

True. Trees wasn't just tall; he was built big everywhere. Zy knew because, thanks to Uncle Sam, they'd been in close quarters for years, often in places where privacy was next to nil. "Do you need to speed up your trip?"

"And what happens if I do and Tierra Caliente figures out where Valeria is hiding? Laila will be collateral damage. After the hell I suspect she's been through, she deserves some fucking safety, man."

Zy couldn't argue with that. "Yeah. Okay, let me see what I can toss together. You keep on keeping on, and I'll touch base with Kane soon."

How the fuck he'd find a place that quickly, Zy wasn't sure, but it was time to get to work.

Which meant that making love to Tessa would have to wait.

Fuck.

"Great, buddy. Thanks."

"Talk to you tomorrow."

"Don't hang up," Trees insisted.

"Something else going on?"

"Yeah…" His buddy sounded mighty reluctant to say what.

"Talk to me."

"Are you sitting?"

Oh, shit. "No, and I don't have time to now. What the fuck is happening?"

"When Laila escaped the house in Orlando, she couldn't get to her phone, which was charging in her bedroom. But she managed to knock out one of her assailants and—"

"How the hell did she do that? Because if you're attracted to her, I know she's a tiny thing."

"Fuck, I hate that I have a type," he grumbled. "Yeah, she is. And she knocked the son of a bitch out by surprising him with a loaded diaper pail to the face."

The situation wasn't funny, but Zy couldn't hold in a laugh. "She sounds resourceful. Bet that guy thought it was a shitty fight."

"Yeah. Laila is…something," he said barely above a whisper.

"Where is she now?"

"Sleeping in the back. Finally. That's why I wanted to call you. At our last stop, we pulled into a gas station to fill up. Thankfully, when Laila got her assailant's phone, it was unlocked and she had the presence of mind to change the passcode. I was going to wipe the thing clean but—"

"Get to the point." He had a safe house to find pronto.

"I browsed the phone while we were filling up. This guy was Tierra Caliente, and you won't like how they're communicating."

Zy froze. He had a terrible notion where this conversation was going. "Don't say it."

"I don't want to, but I have to, man. They're using Abuzz."

He groaned. "Fuck."

"You have to call your dad."

And tell him that a cartel was using his platform—one of the fastest-growing social media apps in the world—to help them do their dirty work?

"Why? I don't owe the bastard anything." But that was a knee-jerk reaction, and Zy knew it as soon as he spewed the words.

Trees sighed. "I know, but people are using *his* platform to coordinate illegal activities and violence."

Which was very clearly against Abuzz's terms of service. That should absolutely infuriate his father. Phillip Garrett was all about being a good global citizen, especially when that meant protecting his multibillion-dollar baby. The man had proven over and over that he cared more about Abuzz than pretty much anything…

On the other hand, people were being hurt because of this bullshit. If the cartel's communication was flying under the radar of the platform's bots and monitors, Zy knew he'd have to reach out and make sure his father stopped it.

Fuck.

"What do you think are the odds that my dad will respond to a text?"

"And not call you in the first two minutes to ask a million questions, then chew your ass out for taking a perilous job blowing up shit, rather than the cushy executive desk he wanted to give you?" Trees snorted.

The thought gave Zy hives. "I was afraid of that."

Why did his dad have to be a sharp, tech savvy, fucking brilliant businessman?

"I wish I had a better answer for you, but… Sorry, man."

Trees meant well and he was trying to help. "It is what it is. You did me a solid by telling me. If we can shut down this line of the cartel's communications, they should have a more difficult time finding Valeria."

"Exactly. When was the last time you guys talked?"

Zy winced. "Just before I boarded my flight in Qatar. I had him pull some strings to get me on a flight out of the Middle East before I got arrested, and predictably he reamed me out."

"You blew up the communications facilities they were constructing."

"Because every son of a bitch they hired to help with that endeavor was on the take and—"

"I know. But the optics of his own son blowing up the facility he was helping to fund to ensure that poor people in rural areas would have reliable means of communicating wasn't good."

"That isn't what they were doing in that place. They were only going to make the rich richer by building a substandard facility that was a hazard, pocketing the extra cash, then gouging the poor with exorbitant rates for piss-poor service."

"Your dad didn't see it that way."

"Whose side are you on?"

"Do you really have to ask that question? I'm just trying to give you his angle so you're prepared. How did you two end that last chat? I'm guessing it wasn't on good terms."

"I hung up on him." And he'd dodged every call since.

"Well, you need him now. Time to make nice."

"Tell you what. Let's trade jobs. I won't be tempted to nail Laila, and my dad doesn't hate you," he joked.

Trees laughed. "No can do. The bosses put *you* in charge. And your dad is afraid of me."

He was, and the first time Phillip had met Trees, all big and bad and tattooed, Zy thought his dad was going to piss his pants. "An even better reason for you to talk to him."

Trees scoffed. "He won't even take my call. Man up, dial his digits, and get this shit taken down. When I pull over to get some shut-eye, I'll send you screenshots so you can be specific with him."

"Thanks, man." Zy hated what he had to do, but he appreciated the information that might help him finish this mission sooner.

"Just trying to help."

He knew. "Stay safe, check in, and keep your dick in your pants."

Trees sighed. "The first two? No sweat. The last one... No promises."

CHAPTER Four

Zy headed back into the house and frowned. It was still and dark. And when he poked his head into Tessa's bedroom, she lay in bed wearing a pair of silky blue pajamas with a book open on her chest, fast asleep.

He'd be lying if he said he wasn't feeling the effects of a whole night of sex himself. Exhaustion nipped at him, but he pushed it aside. He wasn't making love to Tessa tonight, and he hated to wake her. And sadly, finding a safe house for Valeria and her son in the next five hours and calling his dad were more pressing than his hungry cock.

With a sigh, he kissed Tessa softly.

She sat up with a startled gasp. "What? What's going on?"

"Nothing. You fell asleep."

"Oh. Sorry. You were on the phone for a while, and—"

"I totally understand."

"You coming to bed?" She propped herself up on her elbows and searched his face.

Even in the moonlight, she looked tired, dark circles bruising her under eyes. He couldn't be a selfish bastard tonight. She needed to rest. And he had other priorities.

Zy shook his head. "I have to head out. That was Trees, and he needs some mission support. It's urgent. If I get any sleep tonight, it will be late, so I'll do it at my place. And I'll see you tomorrow, okay?"

"Sure. Be careful and stay safe."

Would she be worried if she didn't care about him? Maybe love him at least a little?

"I will. Night, baby." He kissed her softly.

"Night," she mumbled, then lay back on the pillow.

She was asleep again before he even left the room.

Zy let himself out of the house, locked the door behind him, hopped on his bike, and sped through the chilly night back to the office. It was late, but not obnoxiously so for a call. The instant he set foot in the office again, he flipped on the lights and the coffeemaker, prowled to the conference room, propped his feet on the table, and called Cutter.

The former EM Security operator, now married to the TV star he'd once protected, answered almost immediately. "Zy?"

"Yeah. Hey, congrats on your marriage, man."

"Thanks. Sometimes I can't believe my good fortune."

No shit. Shealyn West had made *People*'s most recent Sexiest Woman Alive list, and she'd fallen not for her on-screen movie-star boyfriend but for a regular Joe who wasn't famous and wasn't rich. But Cutter was real. Zy really respected her choice since he'd grown up in the land of the plastic.

"I'm sorry to bug you this late."

"It's not that late for me. I'm in LA. Just arrived a few hours ago."

Cutter was starting his new life with his new wife…and he didn't need the old life dragging him down, but Zy wasn't sure where else to turn for a quick answer.

"And I know you must have a million things to do." Including his gorgeous bride. "So I'll keep this quick. I need a safe house somewhere around Lafayette. And I need it in the next few hours."

"That urgent?"

"Life-or-death. And I don't know the area the way you do."

Cutter sighed. "I have some thoughts. Gimme ten."

"If you can come through, my life won't be the only one you're saving."

"Want to tell me about it?"

If he was still a team member, Zy wouldn't hesitate, but the EM brothers had left him in charge, and he wasn't going to risk sinking their ship by having loose lips. "I can't."

"Sorry. I wasn't thinking. Of course you can't. I'll get right back to you."

The line went dead. Zy barely had time to make a cup of coffee and text Kane to be on standby for further instructions when his phone rang again.

"That was quick, Bryant."

"Like you said, I'm more familiar with the area. So I've got two choices for you."

"You're a miracle worker. Lay them on me."

"My best friend, Brea—"

"You mean Walker's fiancée?"

"Yeah." And Cutter didn't sound thrilled. "Her father has been a widower since Brea was a baby, and he's finally getting remarried. His girlfriend is willing to give up her home and stay with 'friends,' meaning Preacher Bell, for a few weeks."

Valeria and her sister would be in hiding for months, maybe even years. But in a pinch, this temporary solution might do. "Tell me about it."

"Three bedrooms, two bathrooms, single story. Quiet neighborhood. Nothing flashy about the house. She's a schoolteacher, been widowed a long time. No children. Almost no one drops by, and she assures me she can handle the few who do."

"And second?"

"My apartment. I didn't see the point of breaking my lease when it was half over. It's not far from your place, so you can keep a discreet eye on them. Plus, a Lafayette SWAT member and his wife, a homicide detective, moved downstairs from me a few months back. Not much slips past them."

"You got the two-bed, two-bath unit with the balcony?"

"Yep. They're welcome to take the desk out of the spare room and set it up as a bedroom."

Zy weighed his options and made a quick, gut-level decision, not that he informed Cutter. No reason to tell him anything that could drag him into this cartel shit. "Where could I find the key to either place?"

"How about I call Brea and have her give both keys to Walker. Hell, they're probably together anyway. Connect with him, and he'll hook you up."

"Thanks, man. I owe you."

"You don't. You and the team have helped me and Shealyn out so much, not to mention the fact her sister told me you and Trees were mighty instrumental in getting them out of that shit with the crazy cult."

"Maggie is being nice. We just hung around and made sure nothing went south."

Cutter scoffed. "Maggie is never just nice. Between you and me, I got the sister with the sweeter disposition. Maggie is Josiah's problem now."

Maggie was every bit as beautiful as her sister, and Zy was pretty sure Josiah welcomed the challenge of taming his bride-to-be. "That, she is. But seriously, if I can ever do anything to help you or your wife..."

"I'll holler. And if you find yourself out in crazy California, call me."

"Are you going to be okay in LaLa Land? I mean, earthquakes, fires, mudslides, and murders. Hell of a recommendation."

"Yeah." Cutter sounded like he knew he needed to have his sanity checked, then he laughed. "When you put it like that..."

Zy joined in. "Holler when you're back in town. The team will want to see you, and we'll grab a beer."

"I'll be there for Brea and Walker's wedding on Valentine's Day—unless she comes to her senses and tells him to take a hike."

Not likely. "When's that baby due again?"

"Thanks for the reminder. I've got two words for you. They start with an *F* and end with an *off*."

They chuckled before they hung up. Then Zy made a quick call to Kane to verify that they were still on the road and still planning to arrive tonight, probably about three a.m. That gave him just under four hours remaining to grab the keys, scope the place out, put a few groceries in it so they wouldn't have to venture out where anyone who might be in the cartel's pocket could see them, then hand everything over to Kane. He'd deal with Trees and his attraction to Laila later.

After he made the dreaded phone call to his father. Fuck, he'd almost rather cut off an arm. But lives were on the line, and that was way more important than all the grief he had with his dad.

Sighing, he found the contact and hit the button.

"Chase? Is it really you?"

Ugh, he hated being called by his given name. It reminded him of his childhood and all the crap he'd been through. Sad when the first-world problems of his upper-class upbringing seemed every bit as bad as life in a war zone. "Yeah. It's me. I need to talk to you."

"Oh, now? After you've declined every one of my phone calls for… what? Eleven months?"

"I had nothing to say."

"Well, maybe I did. Starting with your juvenile stunt with the C4 in—"

"Next time, hire people on the straight and narrow. Your 'business manager' was actively looking for cheap, in other words substandard, products so he could keep the difference. After paying all the appropriate officials to keep his shit on the down low and sharing the extra cash with his buddies, of course. The place would have crumbled sooner rather than later, and I did you a favor by taking it down before people died inside the building. You're welcome. But I didn't call to hash out ancient history."

"Fuck, how did I raise such an arrogant prick?"

I learned from the best. "Tell me I'm wrong. If you can do it with a straight face and a clean conscience, I'll take it down a notch."

"It wasn't your judgment to make. You might have tried calling me first to tell me—"

"Oh, I did. But you were always just a little too busy to listen to my concerns. What was her name, by the way? I'll bet she was younger than me."

"Chase Phillip Garrett, shut your fucking mouth. You don't talk to me that way."

"Sorry, Dad. That worked when I was fourteen. Not so much anymore. Do you want to know why I called or do you just want to yell at me?"

"Your mother and I are getting divorced. We're announcing it Monday."

About damn time, but… "How many pretty pennies will that cost you?"

"Worried about your inheritance?"

Zy scoffed. "Nope. I'm doing just fine on my own. I'm not remotely interested in your money."

"You don't want to be a billionaire when I pass on? Theo does."

"Yeah, well…I'm not willing to lick your ass for a pile of cash."

"God, you're so stubborn, abrasive, not at all shy about being annoying as fuck."

It's better than being a greedy, ass-kissing sellout. "You're welcome."

"This conversation is going nowhere. Let's end it."

"As soon as I've said my piece. In the course of an op, I intercepted a phone from someone in the Tierra Caliente cartel. Heard of them?"

"Not really."

"Murderous, drug-running, lowlife criminal thugs." Come to think of it, Dad would probably appreciate them. They shared the motto *Anything for a buck…*

"Why tell me this?"

"They're using your fucking app to coordinate drug deals, abductions, and murders. You might want to put a stop to that before the press gets wind of it."

Phillip scoffed. "I know you didn't call me because you have any interest in saving my ass or my business."

He was right about that. "I called because my bosses' sister got kidnapped by these assholes, and maybe that wouldn't have been possible if you'd stopped flapping your jaws on the financial cable shows long enough to enforce your terms of service."

His father fell quiet. "Can you prove this?"

"I've got screenshots." Trees had sent them not long after they'd hung up.

"Send them to me. I'll deal with it."

"'Dealing with it' doesn't mean just erasing those posts or groups. It means obliterating their accounts and banning these people for life."

"I can't take steps like that without careful consideration and investigation. I—"

"Don't start this bullshit. Why can't you ever, just once, do what's right?"

"Stay out of my business and I'll stay out of yours."

"I'd love to, but—"

"What the fuck makes you think you're better than me? You've done plenty of questionable things, like blowing up a perfectly good building that would have helped a whole bunch of poor people in a war-torn region."

"Because I consciously choose to do the right things for the right reasons. I kept that building from destroying more lives than it could ever have helped. I don't shove my nose up a bunch of globalist tycoons' asses for a buck. And I would never fuck my friend's underage daughter for a thrill."

"It was consensual."

"Kendra was a minor. Legally, she couldn't consent, and you goddamn know it. And it's also possible that you not stopping the cartel from planning their illegal shit on your platform directly resulted in her being kidnapped once upon a time. How's that for fucked up?"

"I'm a grown man—and your father. I don't need you telling me what's right and what's wrong."

"I think you do. You've gotten it wrong for as long as I've been aware you're a shit. We can sit here and exchange insults all night or you can promise you'll look into this and expunge these assholes from your platform."

"You realize they'll just communicate in some other way you won't be able to track?"

Maybe. "But we won't be making it easy for them, and it won't be your liability."

His father sighed. "Where are you? Months ago, Dr. Waxman said he spoke with you at Kendra's wedding in Louisiana."

"I'm not far from there." And not for anything would he tell his father that he was planning to propose to the most amazing woman, buy a house here, raise her daughter and the other kids they would share, and have a goddamn happy life. Phillip Garrett would only laugh before he tried to shit on all that.

"Making what? A lot less than the two million a year plus bonuses and perks I offered you before you left the Middle East."

Zy sneered. "I tried working for Daddy. It didn't end well. I don't need the money, and I'm not coming back to Cali. Anything else before I hang up?"

"I don't like having this enmity between us."

Wow. That was his dad's form of an apology. Talk about way too little way too late. "We've all made our choices, and I sleep just fine at night with mine."

"Your mother would probably appreciate hearing your voice. She's rented a house in Sonoma. I'm sure she loves it there since it's so close to all the wine she uses to self-medicate."

And who do you think drove her to that? "I'm in a crisis right now, but I'll reach out to her as soon as I can."

"You don't have to keep risking your life for people who can barely pay you."

"You just never fucking understand. Not everything is about money. You've said before that you can't figure out what makes me tick? There you go. Once you get that, maybe we'll see eye to eye. Until then, I don't have time for this insult-fest. Congratulations on your divorce."

"Chase, don't you—"

Zy hung up before his father could finish the sentence. What else could they possibly have to say?

Shoving the unpleasant conversation aside, he gulped down his now lukewarm coffee, killed the lights, and headed out to run errands. A few phone calls and a few stops later, he managed to get everything set up in the temporary safe house, and Kane promised that he'd text when he, Valeria, and the baby got settled. Tomorrow, they'd figure out their next steps with the late drug kingpin's estranged wife and how the hell to keep her safe until the bosses could return and resume the mission.

When he finished everything, it was nearly one thirty in the morning. Zy would have loved to return to Tessa's place, undress, crawl into bed with her, then slip inside her body until she wrapped her legs around him and came for him. But she deserved her rest, and he suspected she needed more time and space to consider his proposition.

But tomorrow…he'd begin the first official phase of Operation Mrs. Garrett. Hopefully by then, he'd have a ring in his pocket and he'd be finding all kinds of creative ways to persuade her to say yes.

Tessa rolled over as her alarm clock played a vaguely familiar ballad. The electronic digits told her it was time to start the day. Damn it, she'd been sleeping so well…but she would have slept better beside Zy.

Well, if he'd let her sleep at all.

With a little smile, she stretched and reached for her phone to see if he'd left a message. Nothing, but that didn't surprise her much. Whatever he'd been working on last night had seemed both important and involved, and he probably hadn't wanted to wake her up.

As much as she'd love to hear his voice, she resisted the urge to call. She'd see him in the office soon, and if she got on the phone with him, she wouldn't pull herself together for work on time. Hallie might be happy for the extra sleep. The child hadn't stirred all night, but they had a schedule to maintain. Sundays were for lazy mornings. It was only Wednesday.

She slid out of bed and showered, put on a light touch of makeup, then hopped into her slacks and a warm sweater. She was zipping up her boots when she frowned. Hallie was still asleep? By now she was usually either fussing or making noises in her crib as she played. Poor baby must have been really worn-out last night.

Tessa gathered her phone and her purse, got all of her baby's things together for daycare, so she'd only have to change and dress the girl before tucking her into her car for their short drive. As soon as she'd wrangled everything, she started the teapot and shoved a piece of bread in the toaster. If Hallie was going to give her a few extra minutes to eat, Tessa intended to take advantage of it.

Five minutes later, she wiped her mouth and cleaned up her mess, tossed Hallie's things into the car, then headed into her daughter's room with a smile.

Instantly, she knew something was wrong.

It was freezing inside. The window was open. The screen had been slashed and was flapping with the wind. What the hell?

Her heart began pummeling her chest as she groped for the light switch and flipped it up. "Hallie?"

Nothing. The crib was empty.

She blinked. No. This wasn't happening. Her baby was here somewhere. She had to be. But Hallie was too little to climb out of her crib, much less open a window and cut the screen.

Fear strangled Tessa. She couldn't breathe. Terror burned her veins. Panic punched through her chest and ripped out her heart.

She flung herself to the crib and looked for anything that might tell her what had happened. All she saw was the empty mattress. One of her daughter's favorite stuffed animals had been discarded at the bottom of the crib. But no sign of her baby.

Oh, my god… "Hallie!"

But she heard nothing in return except the eerie echo of silence.

Hallie was gone.

No. No! There must be some simple, logical explanation.

There was. Last night she'd slept like the dead, so she hadn't heard a thing. And someone had taken her daughter.

Who? And why would anyone want her baby?

The dark-eyed man in the ball cap who had accosted her yesterday streaked through her memory. The one with the smooth voice, shrewd eyes, and repugnant words. Had he taken Hallie?

We have ways of…persuading you to comply.

Tessa screamed. Tears flowed. Irrationally, she yanked the mattress from the crib and tore away the blankets, hoping against hope that Hallie lay underneath. Instead, she caught sight of something flat and white that had blended in with the pale sheet.

Shaking, tears stinging her eyes, she lifted the piece of paper.

WE HAVE YOUR DAUGHTER. IF YOU WANT TO SEE HER AGAIN, GIVE US THE INFORMATION WE WANT TODAY. TELL NO ONE OR THE GIRL WON'T MAKE IT TO HER FIRST BIRTHDAY. WE'RE WATCHING YOU. WE WILL CONTACT YOU WITH INSTRUCTIONS.

Tessa gaped. Her gut told her that who or whatever that stranger yesterday had represented? Those people had kidnapped her baby girl. Lifted her through the window and stolen her to God knew where… and left everything behind except the pajamas she'd been wearing. Oh, god. They hadn't even taken diapers, toys, or food with them. How would they take care of Hallie?

Did they even intend to?

Panic froze her, but she couldn't stop shaking. Grief stabbed her chest. The pain was more than she knew how to bear. How could anyone do this? Hallie was just a baby. Innocent. Sweet. She hadn't hurt anyone.

Tessa's stomach threatened to heave. She forced it back. Hallie needed her. She had to think. What was she going to do?

Call the police? No. Officers would come. The kidnappers had said they were watching. They would know. And they would hurt her baby.

What about Zy and the rest of the team? They could help. They handled situations like this for a living. She was lucky to work for people with the know-how to rescue her baby. They could end this nightmare.

But before she even reached for her phone, she stopped.

If the kidnappers were watching, was it possible they had eyes and ears everywhere, even inside EM Security Management? Oh, god, maybe they did. Several of the firm's recent missions had gone horribly wrong. Zy had been injured just before she'd met him. One-Mile had been captured and nearly killed by a ruthless cartel. She'd overheard whispers that the enemy seemed to know in advance when, where, and how the operatives were coming. Was information somehow leaking from EM?

It wasn't impossible.

Tessa wasn't willing to take the chance that if Zy and the bosses planned a rescue for Hallie, the enemy wouldn't find out and make good on their threat. And she would never see her precious daughter again.

She couldn't live with that.

Besides, were there even enough operatives available to save Hallie? The bosses and most of the company resources were tied up finding Kimber.

Oh, god. Had the same criminals who had taken her friend taken her daughter, too?

Probably. These hard-core animals were willing to do whatever it took to get what they wanted. Hallie meant nothing to them. Her baby being at their mercy terrified Tessa.

She didn't dare cross them. She would never be able to live with herself if her failure to follow simple instructions resulted in her daughter's end.

Tessa was in way over her head. But she didn't see any choice except to play by the kidnappers' rules—at least for now.

Sucking in a shuddering breath, she reached up to close the open window. Her hand shook uncontrollably. Despair threatened to close in. But she had to stay strong and keep it together. If Hallie had any chance of staying alive, and if she ever wanted to see her baby again, she had to make the right choices.

That meant she had to stop the bawling threatening to take her to her knees. That meant she had to tell the daycare that Hallie was with family for a few days. She had to go to work and do her best to act as if her world wasn't falling apart. She had to close herself off from everything and everyone. As of now, she only had one concern and one goal: to recover Hallie.

Whatever these people wanted, Tessa vowed to give them. As long as she got her baby back alive, whole, and well, she'd do whatever they wanted.

Chapter Five

An hour later, Tessa stared at her computer screen, waiting for some word—any word—from the kidnappers.

Around her, One-Mile was on the phone, his growl an indistinct mumble muted by the whirling of her thoughts. His voice was like sandpaper abrading her nerves. She wanted to curl into a ball and make the world go away.

God, she couldn't take this. The pain of missing Hallie was literally killing her.

Pictures of her baby covered the walls and desk. Her daughter's bright, smiling face and innocent eyes flooded her with anguish. Tessa barely managed to hold in her sobs. She'd already had a terrible cry in the car on her way to the office and had to repair her mascara so no one would know. But Zy had known anyway. He'd seen her puffy eyes and red nose. When he'd asked what was wrong, she'd said she had allergies and turned away.

If she'd had any feelings to spare, she would have been gentler when she replied to him.

But she didn't. And right now, she didn't have enough emotions left over to worry about his. All her concern was for Hallie.

"I'm going to lunch," Zy said. "I'd ask you to join me, but I need to run a personal errand."

Why was he telling her? Unless his errand was to bring her daughter back, she really didn't care. "Okay."

"You want anything? A burger? A sandwich?"

She shook her head because even trying to carry on a conversation was painful. "Thank you."

"Text me if you change your mind."

She wouldn't. Food was the last thing she wanted.

Tessa wished she could throw herself into Zy's arms, tell him everything, and beg him to bring her baby back. He would do it—or die trying. He loved her and he adored Hallie, so he would give it his all.

But she'd already been over this in her head. She couldn't.

Tessa knew her standoffishness might ruin the relationship developing between her and Zy. But she truly couldn't look at him and pretend everything was all right. Worse, she felt useless because all she could do to save her daughter was sit and wait for her kidnappers to reach out. She had no illusions; if Zy ever found out she'd kept something as major as Hallie's kidnapping from him, he would think she didn't trust him. He would feel betrayed. There might not be any coming back from that.

"I will," she murmured.

"Baby." His voice dropped as he tucked a strand of hair behind her ear. "Are you sure you're all right? Did I say or do something to upset you? I hated being away from you last night—"

"It's not that." Her voice croaked.

God, she was barely talking at him, and he was trying to take responsibility for her grim mood? If she didn't already love him, she would love him so much more.

But some irrational part of her wanted to blame him for Hallie's abduction, too. If work hadn't called, if Zy wasn't so good at his job, if he hadn't answered his phone, he would have been at her place last night. He probably would have heard someone rustling around her daughter's bedroom and stopped them before it was too late.

But that was unfair. Hallie was her responsibility—and her heart. *She* had been the one to fall down on the job by sleeping like she didn't have a care in the world.

How stupid she'd been. How reckless. Now she was paying.

"All right. I'm a phone call away," Zy assured. "Let me know if you need me."

I need you so much. "Thanks."

Then, with a last worried glance over his shoulder, Zy was gone. Tessa desperately gripped her mouse, as if it could keep her from falling into a black hole of despair, and tried to keep herself together. But she had no idea where her baby was or if she was okay. She would be starving by now. She was long overdue for a change. She wasn't happy in unfamiliar surroundings and would need someone to comfort her. What if someone had left her alone in a room without any food or supervision or…

"I'm out," One-Mile said. "When my fiancée suggested we meet for lunch, I gave her the address of a motel. Once she figures that out, she'll clobber me…or put me in a great mood. If I'm not back in an hour, you'll know which."

Tessa closed her eyes. How great it would be not to have a care in the world. "Bye."

"Hey, you okay?"

"Fine."

He frowned. "When women say they're fine, men should watch their balls. What did Zy do?"

"Nothing," she said truthfully. "He's great."

It's the rest of my life that's falling apart.

The sniper snorted. "If you say so. Listen, I suck at commiserating. On a scale of one to ten, my ability to empathize is negative eight, but Brea is great. If you need a friend—"

"There's nothing she can do." And Tessa doubted his fiancée would be thrilled that One-Mile had offered up her ear without her consent.

"All right. But if you change your mind, let me know."

I can't. "Thanks."

With a nod, he tossed his keys in the air and headed out the door. Then she was completely alone in the office.

Less than a minute later, her phone rang.

Tessa dove into her purse and scrambled to retrieve it. She glanced at the display. Private caller? Normally, she'd think that was spam and send the call to voicemail. Today, she answered. "Hello."

"You've done a good job so far, Ms. Lawrence. Nice and quiet."

Instantly, she recognized that voice. It was the man in the parking lot yesterday. "What have you done with my daughter? Bring her back —now. She's just a baby and—"

"You weren't listening yesterday. Now you are."

He was tearing her world apart and putting Hallie at risk, and he thought he was clever? "You son of a bitch. I—"

"Name calling? Since I have your baby, I think it would behoove you to be nice."

And if she didn't, he could hurt Hallie. Tessa squeezed her eyes shut and gripped the phone, trying to keep her head and trying not to sob. "You're right."

"Very good. I'm assuming you'd like to get down to business so you can have your daughter back? Am I wrong?"

"No," she gasped out. "You're not. But how do I know she's okay?"

"She's being well cared for."

"I want proof."

"Let's make this work for both of us. You tell us what we want to know, and I'll send you proof that your daughter is fine."

Everything inside Tessa rebelled. "You said that if I told you what you wanted to know you'd return her to me."

"Our timeline is…fluid. We have a few things happening at once, so it will take a bit to work out all the details. And we'll need your help for that. But once it's resolved, absolutely."

"How long will that be? She needs her mother and—"

"How long depends a lot on you, on the promptness and quality of the information you give us."

Tessa closed her eyes and stopped fighting. No matter what she had to do to get Hallie back, she'd do it. "You said you wanted information about someone?"

She wasn't sure who they would want to know about and how she was supposed to find out whatever they wanted to know, but she was resourceful and desperate. She'd make it happen.

"Our situation has changed, and we're in need of something even more vital now. Some event occurred in your office. Your bosses are gone and frantically looking for something or someone. Explain."

Tessa hesitated. Of all the things she'd imagined the caller asking, that hadn't even been on the list. It also told her that the person on the other end of the call didn't have anything to do with the people who had taken Kimber. If it had, they would already know what was going on at EM Security Management.

She was guessing, but it seemed logical that whoever had abducted her bosses' sister, demanding Valeria Montilla's location as ransom, blamed Emilo Montilla's wife for his death. Who would do that? His family? The criminals who had previously made a living from his cartel? Maybe either. Or both.

But if that was true, then who had kidnapped Hallie?

"Well, I—"

"Not on the phone. You'll send all your answers to our questions to this email. Write it down carefully." He recited the address and had her read it back. "Don't use your company email."

Did he think she was stupid? "Of course not. And once I've answered this question, you'll give me information about my daughter?"

"Absolutely."

Then the line went dead.

Guiltily, Tessa looked around the office, but she was still alone. No one would see her betray her employer.

Is it really that much of a betrayal? They're only asking questions that might end up being public knowledge at some point anyway.

True, but rationalizing didn't help. She still felt guilty, but she swallowed it down for Hallie. She launched her email app on her phone and tapped out the address she'd been given. She drafted an answer, deleted it, and started over several times. Finally, she settled on a reply that provided the most thorough yet neutral information she could think of.

```
Kimber Edgington was abducted on Monday morning.
The ransom demand is a current client's location.
EM Security Management has refused to betray this
client and is now attempting to locate Kimber to
rescue her. That's all I know.
```

With a trembling finger, she sent the email off. Within minutes she had a reply, demanding clarification. So she did her best to answer. No, they weren't entirely sure who had abducted Kimber. The client in question was late drug dealer Emilo Montilla's wife. No, she didn't know where Valeria was right now. No, she didn't know what attempts her bosses had made to rescue Kimber yet because they'd been out of the office and out of pocket, dealing with the situation.

After nearly thirty minutes of back-and-forth with the emails, she received another. When she opened it, her heart caught, then lifted.

The asshole who had taken her baby had provided a video of Hallie. It was date- and time-stamped a few minutes ago. She was wearing a sweatshirt that looked like it belonged on a little boy, but it was clean and warm. Hallie had a bib covering her chest and was picking up bites of what looked like chicken nuggets and banana from the tray of a clean high chair.

Tessa replayed it three times, tears welling in her eyes and falling down her cheeks before she paused to breathe and pray. Thank God her daughter was okay. At least for now.

But when she wrote back to ask the kidnappers when she would get her daughter back, she got a two-line reply.

`We need more information. Stay tuned for further details…`

Tessa broke down and sobbed again.

After the high of finding the perfect, dazzling engagement ring for Tessa and dropping a shit ton of money on it, Zy took a call from Kane just as he was leaving the jeweler.

Funny, he'd always thought being the boss would be cushy. Having his pick of assignments sounded great. But the past forty-eight hours had shown him that being in charge wasn't easy. Coordinating the sisters' move across state lines and to a new safe house was proving to be a bitch—and this was just one mission. Often, EM Security had several going at once.

As much as he hated to say it, Zy had a new respect for Muñoz and the Edgington brothers. They had backed him into a shitty-as-fuck corner when they'd demanded he prove either Tessa or Trees was their mole, but he understood. They had so many irons in the fire, and they weren't interested in his feelings, just in getting the job done—and done right. It sucked, but now that he was walking a mile in their boots, he got it. Still hated it, though.

He hadn't had a chance in the past two days to prove anyone innocent or guilty. Twelve days left before the ax fell. Zy knew he needed to suck it up and get a move on. But he had to get Valeria and her son settled first.

He pulled his phone from his pocket. "What's up, Kane? Talk to me."

The guy on the other end sighed. "Don't worry. We're okay. But Jorge has been fussy. He's running a low-grade fever. She thinks he's coming down with something, and neither of us feels safe enough in the new location for me to leave so I can hit a drugstore."

Fuck. Zy wanted to get back to the office and check on Tessa. Something was wrong, and everything in his gut told him he shouldn't let that shit fester. She hadn't said much when he'd pressed her, but her eyes had begged him for something. Comfort? Solace? Help?

He wished he knew what was going on.

Soon. He'd definitely get to the bottom of it. Right now, duty called. "I'm already out, so I can grab whatever you need. Anything else?"

"A sippy cup and some baby spoons. Maybe a bib or two." He heard a woman's voice in the background, then Kane seconded whatever she'd said. "Yep. And some more diapers, size three."

Zy had never shopped for diapers, but he'd figure it out. "You got it."

And once he dropped everything off, he could use it as an excuse to swing by his place, just two buildings over, and finally grab some lunch. His stomach was beginning to think his throat had been cut.

Twenty minutes later, he'd talked to the pharmacist and had a bottle of liquid ibuprofen. He also bought a decongestant with a dropper and some flavored drinks with electrolytes, along with the other things Kane had requested.

At the apartment complex, he parked near his unit so anyone

watching wouldn't see anything out of the ordinary. Not that he had any reason to suspect the dregs of Emilo's organization were on to them, but after this much arranging, he wasn't about to get careless and risk fucking everything up.

The community was made up of working people, and most were still punching their clock at this time of day, so it was no surprise Zy didn't see a single soul, much less one who might be following him.

Quickly, he made his way to Cutter's former unit. Kane answered the door, looking as if he hadn't slept in two days—probably because he hadn't.

An unfamiliar woman who must be Valeria turned to him with a tight smile, then focused her attention on the crying baby in her arms.

Zy handed all the stuff over to Kane. "You good here?"

But clearly he wasn't. Zy would bet the guy had about as much experience with babies as he did.

"For now. But I need some sleep."

Which he couldn't get with a fussing toddler around.

Fuck. So much for his plans to get back to the office and talk to Tessa. "Why don't you go to my place for some shut-eye?" Zy handed over his keys and rattled off his building and unit number. "I'll stay with her."

Kane set the bag on the nearby hall table, looking relieved as hell. "Thanks. Been a few years since my survival training, and I sucked at sleep deprivation even then."

"I can't spare a long time." Zy glanced at his watch. Already two thirty? "I'll spell you for a couple of hours. Hopefully, you can all catch up on your sleep tonight."

Kane said something to Valeria in Spanish. She nodded and sent him a thankful smile, then he was gone.

Zy turned to the woman who had been married to a ruthless criminal. He wasn't sure what he'd expected, but Valeria wasn't it.

She looked painfully young and she was barely over five feet tall. She had ridiculously long lashes, big brown eyes, a slight cleft to her delicate chin, and a wary expression that seemed permanently etched on her face.

"*Hola*." He nodded her way.

"*Hola.*" She bounced her fussing son in her arms to quiet him and sent Zy a suspicious glance.

Of course she didn't trust him. Not only was he a complete stranger, she'd had a rough existence. After all, if Laila was messed up because Emilo's men had used her for sex against her will, they might have done the same to Valeria.

He approached slowly with a smile. "Sorry. *Hola, gracias,* and *un cerveza, por favor* is the extent of my Spanish."

She laughed, despite the little dark-haired baby boy in her arms still listless and crying. "It is a good thing my English is better than your Spanish, then."

"Very much. My name is Zy. I work with Kane."

"Do you mean Preston? He is nice. Very professional."

"Yeah, Preston." It was good to know the new guy was making the right impression.

"He is much better than the very big man who arrived with him."

"You didn't like Trees?" Zy frowned.

"I did not like the way he looks at my sister."

So even Valeria had noticed his buddy's fascination with Laila. *Shit.* "I'll talk to him."

"Please do. My sister is fragile, and if she thinks he will give her safety, she will cling to him. I would not want him to mistake her desire for security as a desire for anything else."

Normally, Zy would have no cause to worry about his pal. But any assurances he gave the woman now would be a lie. "Understood. Here are the things you asked for."

He picked up the bag from the entry table, then deposited it on the counter between them. She took it, sat with her son in her lap, then tore into the ibuprofen, dosing him like a pro. He'd barely swallowed the medicine when she had him back in her arms, against her chest, and she was patting his back. "Thank you. How long before the other man brings my sister here?"

"A few more days. They're taking a longer road and making sure no one followed. I'm checking in with Trees a few times a day. We're doing everything we can to make sure no one from your late husband's organization gets their hands on either of you."

"Laila is only valuable to them if she leads to me." Valeria frowned. "You understand that, no? And she has been hurt too many times by the people in my life. Convincing her and my mother to come stay with me for the summer shortly after I married was the worst mistake of all. My husband took them prisoner to keep me in line. The cartel… they hurt her. Very much. Her life would have been better if I had not begged her to come. So as much as I love my sister, maybe she should not come here."

He'd have to see how the bosses felt about that. "We'll take that under advisement. But our immediate goal is to keep you and your loved ones safe, especially after the difficulties you've had for the past few months."

"I appreciate that you are trying, but I am disappointed. I enjoyed my house in St. Louis. I had never seen snow or known winter until I lived there. I loved it. I felt safe, unlike in Florida. I had a feeling almost immediately that we were being watched. Mr. Edgington assured me that was not possible." She snorted, and he heard bitterness in the sound. "But I was never safe there. Neither was my son. Do you have any children?"

"No." Though he hoped Hallie would see him as a father figure someday.

"Then you do not know what it does to a mother to fear for her child's safety or the lengths she will go to in order to protect her little one."

Valeria was right, and he could hardly blame her for worrying about her son after the difficult life she and her sister had endured at the hands of the Tierra Caliente cartel. "I don't."

"Someday you might. I am sure the same is true of all fathers." Her face softened with empathy. "And siblings. My heart goes out to the Edgingtons. I hate to imagine what they are going through."

Zy whipped his stare to Valeria. She could only know that if Kane was blabbing. Goddamn it, Valeria didn't need to know about this. It would only make her wonder if the protectors she'd hired would sell her out for Kimber's return. But Hunter, Logan, and Joaquin were busy, so he intended to have a chat with the new guy.

For now, he pasted on a smile. "Don't worry. They've got everything under control, and I'm sure the recent chaos and your displacement is temporary. We'll find you a new location and a new identity so you can start over soon."

"I would like that as well." She sent him an acidic smile. "But clearly my old life is not yet ready to let me begin a new one. Excuse me."

With that, she disappeared into the back bedroom and shut the door, leaving Zy alone with a couple of hours to stew.

He checked all the locks and wasn't surprised that Cutter's place was shipshape. One-Mile often called the guy a Boy Scout, as if that was an insult, but Bryant had always seemed prepared.

While he waited, he texted Tessa but got no reply. She should still be at the office. Maybe she was busy? Doing what, he couldn't imagine, but it was possible one of the bosses had called and given her something urgent. He'd figure it out when he got back.

At four thirty, he gave Kane a wake-up call. The guy returned a few minutes later still looking bleary-eyed, but at least he now had some gas in his tank. Unfortunately, Zy couldn't take the time to get on him about opening his big mouth to clients. He wanted to catch Tessa before she went home, and he had to lock up the office.

Zy headed out, stopping by his place to drop off the engagement ring and finally grab some damn food. Then he raced back to the office, arriving a little after five.

Tessa was already gone, damn it. But One-Mile was still around.

"Hey," Zy called to the sniper as he walked through the door. "Anything new?"

"Not that I know of. But I took a long lunch." He flashed a cocky grin. "I got back about three. Tessa headed out shortly after that. Said she had a headache. But, um…"

"What?" There was something One-Mile wasn't saying.

"I don't know how many headaches make a woman cry and look at her phone every thirty seconds."

He'd never heard of that kind of headache, either. Something had upset Tessa. Was her stepmother giving her shit again? Had Cash come back and threatened her? Whatever it was, she hadn't wanted to talk about it, and Zy didn't like that. "Fuck."

"Do you know what's up with her? She says you two didn't fight."

"We didn't."

Walker shrugged. "Then I don't know, man, but I would address that head-on ASAP."

Zy intended to. "Yeah. I'm out. You leaving?"

He nodded. "I can make my last phone call from the road."

"Go. I'll lock up behind you."

The sniper nodded, gathered his keys, and strolled out with the confidence of a man who had everything he wanted in life and his whole future ahead of him.

As Zy followed him out and secured the door behind him, Joaquin rang, demanding he come over to deliver a status update. But when he ended the call and reached his bike, he realized someone had fucking slashed his tires. His money was on the guy who had accosted Tessa yesterday. He'd look at the security footage again, but Zy would bet he'd find next to nothing.

By the time he'd called a tow truck and had his bike hauled to a local shop for new tires, hours had passed, dark had fallen, his stomach was rumbling again, and he was worried as hell about Tessa. She'd started responding to his texts, but only in monosyllables. It wasn't like her.

Finally, he reached Joaquin's. After a two-hour grilling, it was late. But he was free of all his other responsibilities, and he didn't have to give a fuck about anything but Tessa.

At nine p.m. he made it to her place and knocked. It took a few minutes, but eventually she turned on the porch light and answered the door. He was shocked the interior was dark except for the light above the stove. Her hair was askew and she was huddled in an oversized bathrobe, with a red nose and swollen eyes. She looked as if she'd been bawling her eyes out for hours. He wanted to hold and reassure her, but she crossed her arms over her chest—a silent *keep out*.

Tessa was independent, and Zy knew she was used to working out her own shit, but he was done letting her suffer alone.

He took her tense hands in his. "Baby, talk to me. I know something's wrong and—"

"It's a migraine." She swiped the tears from her cheeks and backed away with a sniffle. "I just need a day or two to myself. But thanks for coming."

Tessa tried to shut the door in his face. He wasn't satisfied with her answer and pushed it open again.

"No. I'm going to take care of you and Hallie." When she opened her mouth to object, Zy shook his head. "I want to. Have you taken anything for your headache?"

"I've done all I can," she whimpered. "It's not enough."

Zy frowned at her answer. "Have you eaten? I'll make you another one of my infamous omelets."

"I don't want food. My stomach is too unsettled."

Her answer sounded more like a cry. Zy scowled. "I know your head hurts, but starving yourself isn't going to help. You should try something. When was the last time you ate?"

"I had toast for breakfast."

And nothing since? No wonder she felt like hell. "That's it. I'm coming in and taking over—"

"No. You can't," she screeched as she pushed at him desperately. "You can't turn on the lights or tell me how to feel or reassure me that everything's okay. You're used to playing the hero, running in to save everyone when they need you. This is something you can't fix. Just go."

Everything inside Zy told him not to walk out that door. She might not need a hero tonight, but she needed something. Care? Reassurance? Whatever it was, he doubted it had anything to do with a headache. After all, if the pain in her head was excruciating, how was she able to scream without so much as wincing?

"I'm not walking out when you need me. Did someone upset you? Kathleen? Cash? One-Mile?"

"I'm not upset."

As lies went, that was a whopper. "Baby, you've obviously had a rough day. Talk to me. Let me help you."

"You can't. Please..."

"If you don't want me to feed you or even talk to you, I won't. But you look exhausted." He tried to wrap her in his arms and cradle her against his chest. "At least let me tuck you in, then I'll climb in bed beside you. Nothing else. I won't do anything more than hold you and—"

Tessa burst into tears. "Zy, I can't. Just…go. Please."

She wasn't merely asking to be alone; she was begging him to leave. That was a kick to his goddamn heart. The last thing he wanted to do was walk out on Tessa when she desperately needed a shoulder, but he couldn't force her to accept his help. And she didn't fucking want it anyway.

Frustrated as hell, he held up his hands and stepped back. "Okay. If you need anything, it doesn't matter what time it is. Call me."

"Thanks." She wrapped one arm around her middle. With her free hand, she pushed him toward the door. "But I won't."

God, she was cutting him off at the balls and it was killing him. Why?

This wasn't about him. At least he didn't think so. But what the fuck was going on?

"One more thing before I go?"

"What?" Her voice sounded impatient, like she wanted him to leave…but deep down she needed him to stay.

Zy ached to touch her, but she would only push him away. He didn't understand. Last night, everything had been fine. Hell, great. Tonight, she couldn't wait to be rid of him.

"Are we okay? Did I do something to upset you? If I did, we need to talk about it."

"I can't do this now. I need you to go." Tessa gathered the robe even tighter around her. "And I know you have a key to my door. Please don't use it."

As answers went, it wasn't one. But everything she said scared the hell out of him.

Fuck. She was too tired and overwrought for him to reason with. He hated to leave things between them like this, but she hadn't given him much choice.

"All right. I'll see you tomorrow?"

She nodded tightly. "At the office. Good night."

Then Tessa shut the door in his face, and the dead bolt clicked into place. Zy stared at the closed portal. What. The. Fuck. Had. Just. Happened?

Scowling, he turned and left. It was only a temporary retreat. Tomorrow, he would get to the bottom of Tessa's issue. She was going to tell him what the hell was wrong…no matter what he had to do.

Chapter Six

Zy entered his apartment and slammed the door behind him. Son of a bitch. Every mile he'd put between him and Tessa just felt wrong. He hoped she was in a better mood tomorrow, but he had a bad feeling.

If he slept tonight, it wouldn't be for hours. He was too pissed off and keyed up. Might as well get some shit done.

Yanking his phone from his pocket, he sent Kane a quick text, who answered instantly. No, he hadn't gone to sleep yet, but Valeria and the baby had.

Perfect. Zy set his helmet down, grabbed a protein bar and a beer, and walked two buildings over to Cutter's old place. Kane opened the door almost before he knocked.

"What's up?" He stepped back and let Zy enter. "Hear anything from the bosses?"

"No." That's another thing that worried him, too. The Edgingtons were the best at what they did. He didn't know Jack Cole or Deke Trenton well, but he knew their reputations. Kimber wouldn't still be missing unless these kidnappers were fucking professionals. They probably knew that by now—and were devising Plan C.

"Damn it."

"Hell of a first week on the job for you, huh? A kidnapping and a dangerous transport of a highly valuable client and her baby. And I'm not exactly boss material, so I can't give you much guidance, but I do have a little advice."

Kane shrugged and shut the door behind him. "Sure. Valeria and the baby crashed out about thirty minutes ago, so it's just us. Shoot."

Zy sat on the love seat across from the oversized chair Kane plopped into and took a swig of his beer. "You got the client and her son here quickly and in one piece. That was priority number one, so good job. But that wasn't your only responsibility. This may not have occurred to you, but Valeria shouldn't know anything about the situation with Kimber, especially if she finds out that the ransom demand was her location. You understand why she might worry whether we'd sacrifice her to the very people she's running from to have Kimber back?"

"Yeah," he said as if that was obvious.

"I'm glad you get it. Just be careful. You can't say stuff like that to her—or even around her—anymore."

Kane scowled. "I didn't. Look, I might not have all the fancy experience you and the rest of the team have, but I know better than to run my mouth to someone dependent on our protection. Valeria only needs to know what will keep her safe. And having her doubt us will only make our job harder."

"Exactly." Zy sat back, chewing on his protein bar and washing it down with brew. Together, the flavors were disgusting. "You're sure you didn't say anything to her? That she didn't somehow overhear you?"

"Positive."

"Then I have no idea how she knows, but she does."

"I don't know, either. But it wasn't me. Any chance Laila found out from Trees? Because if she knows, Valeria knows. Those two are constantly talking and texting. They're tight."

Possible…but unlikely. Trees knew the drill, but he'd circle back with his buddy and find out if his dick being in a knot had somehow affected the blood flow to his brain.

One thing Zy did know? Valeria was obviously concerned about her sister if she wanted Laila secreted elsewhere.

Zy nodded and stood. "Thanks for the info."

Kane also rose. "Going already?"

"Yeah. It's almost ten o'clock, this is dinner"—he held up the remnants of his protein bar and the other half of his beer—"and I'm fucking tired."

"If I can do anything to help…"

Zy shook his head. "Just stay with Valeria and the baby until someone says otherwise. If his condition gets worse and he needs a doctor, let me know. No other trouble?"

"No. She's definitely aware that people are after her and her son and she'll do just about anything not to attract attention. On the road, she had some interesting ways to disguise the fact she's young and pretty, which makes me think she's an old pro at people wanting to do her harm."

That didn't surprise Zy. He didn't know the whole story, but he figured that no woman—especially a pregnant one—walked away from her drug lord husband without understanding the consequences and risks. "I'll check in tomorrow."

Kane nodded. "When will Laila roll into town?"

Zy was about to call Trees and find out.

"It's best if you don't know." He nodded toward Valeria's closed bedroom door. "Just in case. Night."

Before Kane could object, he was gone.

On the walk back, he downed the rest of his dinner, tossed the wrapper in the outside dumpster, then ducked into his place. It was getting late, and he'd love to veg out with some sports news before he drifted off, but the day wasn't done with him yet.

After a quick shower, he tossed on some boxer briefs, then slid into bed, propped against a couple of pillows. With a sigh, he reached for his phone.

"What's up?" Trees answered almost immediately.

"Long fucking day. How about you?"

"Not too bad. But long fucking night."

"What do you mean?"

"I'm driving this recreational tank from campground to campground, trying to take our sweet time returning to Lafayette."

"Yeah. Is the plan not working?"

"Oh, it is. We haven't been followed. I'm sure of that."

"So what's wrong?"

"Everything Laila has to wear is meant for Florida weather and seems two sizes too small." Trees groaned. "When I look at her, it's impossible not to see tits and ass and that wide fucking mouth. I stare at it all the time—I can't seem to stop—and my cock is like a divining rod that points only to her."

He tried not to laugh, but it was funny. Usually, Trees could resist any woman. Hell, during basic he'd even had one undress for him, spread her legs, and invite him to fuck her at a party. At the time, Zy thought his buddy had been crazy to decline. Now he understood Trees wanted something real, and he respected the hell out of the guy for standing his ground.

So if his desire for Laila was troublesome, there could only be one reason.

"You like her."

"Fuck yes, I do. She's…sweet. She's thoughtful. She's strong. She's the kind of woman I want to hold and protect while I'm aching to violate and defile her every way known to man."

Zy got it. Despite Tessa's wide independent streak, he often felt the same about her.

Trees sighed. "And after one look, she was terrified of me."

A six-foot-eight man was understandably intimidating to a woman who'd been bullied and used. "Can she hear you?"

"No. She's in the back taking a goddamn shower. She'll only do that when I'm driving."

She refused to be vulnerable while Trees could get to her, and the poor bastard was envisioning her naked. "So what are you going to do?"

"What the hell can I do? I've got to keep driving her around in this hell on wheels for a few more days or until you tell me Valeria is safe enough in her new location and Laila can move in, no problem."

"You can head back to Lafayette now."

Trees hesitated. "You're not kidding, are you?"

"Valeria is convinced that Laila will be in less danger if they don't share the same roof. And I can't really argue. Two women and a baby boy are a lot less common, so they're a lot more noticeable."

"You won't get any arguments from me on that."

"Good. We just have to find Laila somewhere safe. Somewhere no one can get to her. Somewhere she'll be comfortable and have protection. Hey, I've got an idea." But Trees wasn't going to be happy.

"Don't say it…" His pal grumbled.

They'd been friends so long the guy could damn near read his mind.

"I have to."

"Fuck."

"It's temporary. She doesn't have to move in with you. Just…keep her safe at your place until the bosses find Kimber and return to the office. Then they can figure out a permanent place for Laila. And hell, maybe that's not even in Lafayette, so you'd never have to see her again."

But if Trees was already this wrapped up in her, Zy figured it wouldn't be too long before the big guy wouldn't want to let her out of his sight. And heaven help her if Trees decided she was the post-apocalyptic woman of his dreams and future mother of his post-modern disaster children. She probably wouldn't be getting out of bed or seeing daylight for months. And when she got pregnant, she would be his for life.

"I didn't say I didn't want to see her. I said I didn't want to live on top of her."

That's exactly where Trees wanted to be. "I'm calling bullshit."

"Back off. I'm trying to be a gentleman, but there's no fucking privacy here. Even the shower is so small it's impossible to jack off."

Despite all the shit today, Zy had to laugh. "That right? So you're having a…hard time?"

"Shut the fuck up. Do I need to remind you that you had a goddamn hard time with Tessa before the bosses finally took pity on you?"

And just like that, he sobered. "No. Not that it matters right now. She's barely speaking to me."

"What the fuck did you do, not lay her right?"

That wasn't the problem. "The job called me out last night before I could even touch her. She seemed okay, though. Tired but not mad. This morning, she came into the office looking like she'd been sobbing. But nothing I've said or asked is persuading her to open up. She claims she has a migraine…"

"Those suck."

"Yeah, but I don't believe her."

"Why would she lie?"

"I don't know." It was a question Zy hadn't been asking himself because he'd been too frustrated about the way the night had gone down. But maybe he should have.

"Hallie's not sick?"

"Tessa would have said so. Whatever upset her, when I stopped by her place, she refused to let me stay. But my gut tells me she didn't really want me to go. So nothing makes sense."

Trees sighed. "I know you don't want to hear this, but…is there any chance she's guilty?"

"Of what?"

"C'mon, man. The bosses are convinced that either I'm their mole… or she is."

"They're wrong."

"Maybe. But you know I'm clean because you searched my shit."

"One room."

"Then go fucking search the whole place before I get home. You won't find anything, and you know it."

"Yeah. What's your point?"

"You haven't searched Tessa at all. Hell, you've flatly refused to even consider her a suspect."

Trees was right, but everything inside Zy rebelled. "It just doesn't make sense. Tessa is no sort of spy. She doesn't have the abilities or the connections or—"

"That you know of. But be logical. It's not Hunter, Logan, or Joaquin."

"I know. I don't want to go through this—"

"Shut up. It's not you. It's not me. And it's not One-Mile."

Since the sniper had been in rough shape when they'd rescued him last September, no. If he'd been in cahoots with the cartel, they wouldn't have nearly killed him. "I know."

"And it's not Cutter or Josiah. They're gone."

"They are, but it's not impossible that they were involved when they were here."

"C'mon. The Boy Scout? The antiseptically clean former CIA agent? Do you really believe either of them would stoop to this level of shit?"

No, and as much as Zy hated to admit it, they'd been on other missions when danger had hit the fan. But he hated to acknowledge that out loud.

It didn't matter; Trees inferred it for him. "That leaves Tessa, buddy."

"It can't be," he said without even thinking.

"Why not?"

Zy groped for a reply, thrilled as fuck when he stumbled on to one. "Because this shit started when she was on maternity leave. She wasn't even around."

Trees hesitated. "True, and I'm not convinced she *is* the guilty one. I'm just not sure who else it could be. Let me ask you this: what happens if you don't figure out who EM's mole is?"

"She's fired." *So are both of us.* Zy didn't say that, mostly because the bosses were still down an operator. Replacing two more at once would be a bitch and that could buy them a little more time, but Tessa… In their eyes, she was both expendable and easily replaceable.

"Look, when I get back, I'll sit down and perform a thorough, top-to-bottom scan of all the internal systems. I'll even come in on a weekend and scan every single person's computer so I'm not in anyone's way. But until then, you need to prove you can rule her out completely."

"How the fuck am I supposed to do that?" But Zy knew. He'd run a double-cross disinformation mission before.

"Stop playing games with yourself, man. I know you love her—"

"I fucking bought her an engagement ring today."

"Wouldn't you rather know now if you should give it to her?"

Zy closed his eyes. "When do you think you'll make it here?"

"Oh, I'm going to head into town so I can get out of this rolling torture chamber by tomorrow night."

"I'll see you then. And I'll try to have some answers."

The following morning dawned bleak. The sun rose in the sky, but without Hallie, Tessa didn't care. She just wanted to curl into a ball and cry. She certainly didn't want to put on clothes, pretend to smile, and spend all day in the office, where Zy would undoubtedly grill her some more.

But she didn't dare stay home. Her daughter's abductor might want more information from the office. What would happen to Hallie if she wasn't there to pass it on?

Woodenly, she rose and went through her usual morning motions —shower, makeup, clothes. She couldn't stomach tea or food, so she grabbed a bottle of water, then climbed into her little sedan, trying not to look at the empty car seat in the rearview mirror that wrenched her heart.

Despite every muscle seeming to weigh a thousand pounds, she made it to the office on time. When she opened the door, she saw exactly what she'd been dreading.

Zy was waiting for her.

"Morning," she murmured.

It hurt to look at him and know she was lying to him with every breath.

He came closer, gently cupping her shoulder. "You feeling any better this morning, baby?"

Normally, she loved when he called her baby. When he whispered the endearment in a slow caress, he made her feel special. When he growled it low and rough, he made her feel sexy. When he murmured it in that deep, tender tone, he nearly made her cry.

Tessa swallowed against the stupid urge to blurt everything. It might not help, but it definitely could cost Hallie her life. She couldn't risk it. "No. Thank you, but I need to sit."

She shook off his touch and walked to her chair, her laptop in its sleeve as she clutched it against her chest like a shield. When she sat, she could feel his eyes on her, along with the million questions he itched to ask.

Please don't.

But she didn't get that option. The bosses were all gone, and he was in charge. Whatever Zy said went.

"Do you need something?" she asked him in her most professional voice.

"Not right now, no. But I'd like to talk to you at lunch."

That's the time of day the kidnappers had contacted her yesterday. She couldn't be gone if they wanted something. "I'm busy."

Zy's eyes could be warm blue velvet when they touched her with care. With her answer, they turned as cold as the Arctic Ocean. "It wasn't a question and it's not a date. Be in the conference room at noon."

"Anything I need to be aware of this morning? Are Valeria and her son all right?"

"Why do you ask?"

Tessa shouldn't be surprised. She'd been evasive and dismissive to Zy for twenty-four hours. She'd dodged him, his texts, his calls, and his affection. What else could she possibly expect? She'd do almost anything to make talking to him easy again, to have their camaraderie be as breezy as it had been before.

Almost anything…except sacrifice Hallie.

"She's a mother worried about her safety and her child. I relate to her."

"She's someone we've been hired to protect, and that's all you need to know."

As Zy turned away, Tessa reared back. He wasn't merely upset or angry; it was as if he'd turned off his human valve—at least around her. Across the office, he exchanged a fist bump and a joke with One-Mile. He got someone on the phone a few minutes later and seemed to have a perfectly cordial chat.

The second he hung up, he looked at her as if he could look through her.

Tessa jerked her gaze away and went back to clandestinely checking her phone. Still nothing new. She was getting antsy. When would she hear from the asshole who had taken her daughter? What if Hallie wasn't okay?

God, she couldn't think that or she'd lose her mind.

She did her best to pretend to work for the next few hours, copying, filing, answering a few calls, all of which she sent back to Zy.

Finally, at a few minutes before noon, he approached, stopping beside her. "Change of plans. Come with me."

Alarm zipped through Tessa. "Where are we going?"

"Not your problem, but I can't do this alone."

"All right." She didn't have a choice. If the kidnapper contacted her, she'd just have to hope he understood. "Where are we going?"

"The baby store."

Tessa's heart stopped. She couldn't have heard him right. Certainly he didn't mean they'd be going someplace where she'd bought lots of Hallie's favorite things and brought her along a million times, cooing how much she loved to shop with her favorite little girl. It would be torture. "The baby store?"

"Yeah, wherever you buy Hallie's stuff. Valeria needs a few things. I have a list. I don't know what half this shit means."

"All right."

It pained her to grab her phone and tuck the device away, then follow Zy outside.

He held out his palm. "Keys?"

"I'll drive. It's my car."

"And it's company business, so what I say goes. Keys," Zy insisted.

With a sigh, she handed them over. He helped her into the passenger's seat, hovering so close she could feel his body heat at her back and his warm breath caress her neck. She shivered as she sat and watched him come around to the side of the car before slipping into the driver's seat.

He shoved the key in the ignition. "We're alone now. Are you going to talk to me?"

"About what?" She blinked at him wide-eyed, pretending confusion. But she was quaking with terror. She was terrible at keeping secrets, especially from people she loved. Not telling Zy what was going on in her life was damn near killing her.

"Whatever's crawled up your ass in the last twenty-four hours—"

"I-I had a headache, and I still don't feel good."

Zy raised a brow at her.

He clearly didn't believe her. "And you don't want to tell me what I've done that made you push me away?"

"It's not like that." But that must be what it felt like to him.

And his acidic smile said so.

"You still don't want to talk? Fine. Let's just get this done." He tore out of the parking lot and shot down the road.

The silence between them felt oppressive.

"Zy..." she ventured, then set a hand on his taut arm. Tessa remembered that arm around her, his hands skimming her body as his lips worked up her neck to cover her own before he sank deep and gave her scream-worthy pleasure.

"What?"

She didn't want to upset him and she didn't want to lose him. Maybe it was time to take a different approach...

"Please try to understand. It's not you. There's...something going on."

"I figured. Tell me what. We'll fix it."

Tessa shook her head. "This is something I have to work out. I know you want to help me, but—"

"Hell yeah, I do. I love you. It's in my DNA to help you."

Of course. He was a problem solver and a doer, but... "I have to do this alone."

Zy sighed as he rolled to a stoplight and pinched the bridge of his nose. "Why?"

"It's..." She tried to think of an excuse he'd believe. "It's in my head. I've just been through a lot and...I want to be really sure I'm ready."

"You said you were the night we made love. What made you change your mind?"

Good question. If Hallie hadn't been taken and she didn't have to worry about her daughter's abductor watching her, Tessa would be in Zy's arms, eager for the moment they could be alone again.

But that wasn't her reality.

So she grasped at the first answer she could think of. "What happened between us that night was huge. It scared me. I've never felt anything like that."

That wasn't really a lie. Zy had knocked her off her feet and swept into her heart. The whole night had dazzled her senses so much it actually boggled her mind. The thought that she might lose him for good worried her. But she was terrified for Hallie.

"So what are you saying? You need more time to adjust?"

"Yes. A few days." She hoped the abductor would be done with her and release Hallie by then. "I just need to get my head screwed on straight."

Zy took her words in but didn't speak. Tessa wished he'd say something.

Instead, he bolted across the intersection as the light turned green. Three silent minutes later, they reached the store. She would kill to know what he was thinking.

He parked the car and yanked the keys from the ignition—and she felt his frustration rise between them.

Tessa couldn't help herself. She slipped her hand in his and willed him to look her way. "Zy, I care about you and—"

"Do you?"

"Yes." That he might believe otherwise had tears stinging her eyes. "Please give me a little time. Everything now…it's a lot to wrap my head around."

"And you've got another responsibility to think about." He sighed. "I know."

But he didn't seem happy.

Before she could say anything else, he launched himself out of the car and headed toward the baby store, locking the sedan with her fob when he turned to ensure she was out and following.

Normally, he'd get her door, help her up, be the gentleman. His sudden distance told her he was disheartened and exasperated. How was she going to repair it when she couldn't tell him the truth?

Inside the store, he pulled up a list from a text message. She tried not to remember the countless times she and Hallie had been here. She tried not to lose her mind missing and worrying about her daughter so horribly it was a physical ache.

She failed miserably.

Fifteen minutes later, Tessa was hanging by a thread. They had acquired all of the things Valeria asked for. Zy was quiet as they checked out. He was silent as he carried the bags. He was pensive as he loaded the trunk, slid into the driver's seat, and started the car.

He backed out of the spot so quickly it was almost reckless, but his moves were so controlled she'd swear he was a stunt driver.

"So you're not moving in with me anytime soon, I take it?" he demanded.

Tessa really wanted to. She'd tried to be cautious and measured when he'd first asked, but she already knew he was the perfect man for her and would be an amazing father for Hallie. He'd give her more children. He'd provide safety. He'd give her love.

But with Hallie missing, she couldn't say any of that. If he realized her daughter had been taken, he would fuck being circumspect and move heaven and earth—burning down the world if he must—to get Hallie back. Not only would her daughter be gone forever, but she might lose him, too.

"No." She clutched her hands in her lap, staring at her interlocked fingers so she didn't have to see the hurt on his face. Tessa didn't have to pretend to cry; the tears were right there when she realized that Zy would stop investing his heart in someone who wouldn't commit. "I don't think it's a good idea."

He nodded, not saying another word until they pulled up in front of the office, then he stopped and let her out at the door. "Then we don't have anything to talk about until you make up your mind. Go inside. I'll bring your car back before five."

Tessa bit her lip. Her intention to reassure him had blown up spectacularly in her face, and she couldn't do anything to keep him from drifting away, maybe for good. "Please don't be angry."

But that was a losing battle, and she knew it.

He huffed. "Too late."

The next day seemed like a rinse and repeat of the previous day, complete with a too-busy schedule and Tessa's standoffish bullshit.

About two o'clock, a stranger had strolled in. One-Mile had introduced him as Matt, one of his oldest friends. Apparently, they'd spent summers together in Wyoming growing up. Who knew? Certainly not Zy. Hell, he'd had no idea the sniper had any friends at all. Then came the kicker. Apparently, Matt had worked some cold missing-persons cases back home in the past and he had a particular set of skills, whatever that meant. At this point, Zy didn't care. If the bosses had hired him to help find Kimber's trail, that meant they weren't making progress.

Fuck.

By the time he pulled up at Trees's place, Zy was over the day. He turned off the layers of security around the joint, one by one, then let himself inside, carting the groceries and other supplies his buddy had requested. Then Zy turned on the lights, pumped up the heater, and lit a couple of scented candles to air out the musty smell.

Go fucking search the whole place before I get home…

Zy really didn't want to. After another day of wondering whether he and Tessa would even make it until the end of the week, he didn't fucking feel like tearing apart his best friend's house. But since they ran the risk of being out of a job in the next eleven days, he owed it to them all to run down every possibility, even the ones he felt sure would be a dead end. At least he could tell the bosses he'd really, truly turned over every stone.

You haven't searched Tessa at all. Hell, you've flatly refused to even consider her a suspect.

Yeah, and that changed tomorrow.

An hour and a half later, Zy had been through every room in Trees's place, along with his prep bunker. The fucker was so orderly. Everything the big guy stored was aligned, wrapped, dated, and secured. Nothing was ever out of place.

Zy snorted. He was lucky if he remembered to turn on his dishwasher once a month.

In the kitchen, he grabbed a bottle of water, leaned against the counter, and—he couldn't help himself—texted Tessa.

`Can I come over later tonight? We should talk.`

`Please don't. I'm still not ready.`

`Will you ever be or do you just want me to go the fuck away?`

`Zy…`

But that was the only answer he got.

Son of a bitch.

He sighed, tempted to swap out his water for that unopened bottle of vodka he'd seen on Trees's pantry shelf, but he'd never been the guy who drank away his girlfriend problems. He'd never even felt a twinge of distress over a woman before. He'd always snickered at those pussy-whipped saps. But he got it now, and he felt sorry for every poor, brokenhearted bastard he'd ever derided in the past.

He was one of them now.

Since yesterday afternoon, he'd been too preoccupied to eat. Sleep? Fuck no. That wasn't happening. He merely punched his pillow and tried to figure out what was troubling Tessa…and if she might actually be their mole. Splice in a memory of her body beneath him, filled with his cock and crying out in orgasm, and Zy wasn't sure whether pounding his fist into a punching bag or around his nagging-hard dick would clear his head and improve his mood.

In his pocket, his phone buzzed. He pulled it free, disappointed to see the message was from Trees, not Tessa.

`There in ten. Everything ready?`

`Yep.`

`Thank god. I need to be more than a foot away from this woman.`

Or he would fuck her. Zy read the subtext loud and clear. Hell, he'd lived it for months with Tessa, until her shit had hit their fan.

What the fuck was he supposed to do with an engagement ring she seemingly didn't want?

Another problem for later.

He stepped outside to pace the porch—and avoid the vodka bottle—when the big RV pulled into the yard and disappeared around the back of the house, killing the lights.

Of course Trees wouldn't want it visible from the road. Tessa had jacked up his thoughts so much, he hadn't even considered the obvious.

Feeling like an idiot, he jogged around the place and met Trees just as he was stepping from the RV with a long-suffering sigh and a stretch. "Hey. So fucking glad that's over."

"I'm glad for you, man. Good to have you back."

Trees peered at him with the light from the RV's interior. "You look like shit."

"Well, stress, lack of sleep, and your girlfriend looking for the politest way possible to tell you to fuck off will do that."

"No shit?"

He nodded. "It's been one of the worst weeks ever."

"Sorry, man." Trees clapped his arm, then glanced over his shoulder. When he looked back, his face darkened. "Did you bring everything I asked for?"

"Yeah. I had a little trouble. It took a couple of stores to find the clothes you asked for, but it worked out."

Trees breathed a sigh of relief. "I owe you."

Zy heard a rustling inside the RV, then his buddy stepped aside and offered his hand, palm up.

Small fingers laid across his meaty ones as a waif of a woman came down the steps. She was exactly what Zy remembered…yet she wasn't.

Coffee-colored hair hung in waves to her back. A choker with a black bow emphasized the daintiness of her neck. Its tails brushed the swells of lush breasts her tiny black tank couldn't possibly hope to contain. Her denim shorts stretched tight across the flare of womanly hips and were so small they ought to be illegal. She wore no shoes, just a muted toe polish that nearly blended in with her skin. And when Zy looked up at her again, she studied him with old eyes in a face that looked way too young for such knowledge.

"Hi, Laila." He stuck out his hand. "You may not remember me. I'm Zy."

She looked down at his hand, dragging in a breath—for courage?—and shook it. "Hello. Is Señor Walker coming?"

Trees leaned in, looking less than pleased. "She likes him."

"I trust him," Laila corrected.

And she didn't trust Trees. That wasn't a good sign.

Then she stepped off the RV and brushed past them, curling her arms around her tiny middle to ward off the winter evening chill.

"See what I've been dealing with?" he grumbled as she headed toward the house, wincing as she tiptoed over dead branches and crisp fallen leaves with her bare feet.

"Are all her clothes that…brief?" Because even in the semi-dark, it was impossible to miss the fact that half her ass hung out of her too-short shorts.

Trees rubbed at his eyes. "That's her modest outfit."

Holy shit. No wonder Trees's dick was in a twist.

"Well, I brought her sweatpants and oversized T-shirts, just like you asked."

"Thank god. Maybe that will cool things off between us."

Maybe, but Zy wasn't holding his breath. Everything about Laila's appearance had *Trees's type* written all over her.

"Sorry, buddy."

Trees groaned. "Can't you come stay with her for a few days? Maybe by then I can jack off enough to get some of the blood back to my brain."

"Nope. Whatever you do with your meat, keep that shit to yourself. But a word of advice? Don't fuck the client."

"Technically, she isn't the client."

True, but that was a problem in itself. "Valeria doesn't like the way you look at Laila."

"Which is a really good reason for Kane and me to switch assignments. He can watch Laila, and I'll keep an eye on Valeria and her baby. Problem solved."

Except the bosses would never go for that. He was half expecting to be summoned tonight to provide an update. They'd lose their shit if they found out that Trees—someone they considered a potential mole —was alone with Valeria, whose safe houses had been disclosed and breached multiple times in the past few months.

"No can do. What else do you need here?"

"You in a hurry?"

"Not so much me, but I'm assuming the sooner you let her into your place, the sooner she can cover up everything tempting you."

"Good point." He headed for the house. "Anything new?"

Some, and Trees wouldn't like it. "Let's go inside."

His pal opened the back door, letting Laila inside and showing her to the guest room on the opposite end of the house from the master. With a quiet nod that belied her seemingly loud, fuck-me-now outfit, she disappeared.

Trees stomped into the kitchen and plucked a beer from the fridge. "Thank you for picking these up for me."

Before he could open the bottle, Zy stopped him. "It's not cold."

"I don't even fucking care. That woman…"

Was driving him to drink—literally. "You can't imbibe on the job."

Trees gave a long-suffering sigh and put the beer back in the fridge. "Fuck."

"Is she mouthy and difficult?"

"No. She barely speaks, and I swear sometimes I'd do just about anything to know what's running through her head. The problem is, I want to fuck her."

Yeah. Zy understood that perfectly. He'd lived through the excruciating months of wanting the woman he couldn't have. "Sorry."

"I'll deal. What do you want to tell me?"

"Some friend of Walker's has temporarily joined the team to help with Kimber's recovery. Name's Matt. You probably won't see much of him. I met him. He seems okay."

"Even though he's a friend of Walker's?"

"Trust me. I was as shocked as you."

Trees shrugged. "Why wouldn't I like that news? It's fine by me. Hell, whatever they need to do to bring Kimber back…"

"Keep that in mind because what I say next might make you blow a gasket." Zy let out a breath. "The bosses are thinking about using Laila as bait to help get Kimber back. Pretend to set up a hostage swap and—"

"No. Fuck no! Over my dead body. Absolutely not happening. End of conversation."

"It's not my favorite plan, either, but I think they're running out of options and getting desperate. Kimber is a wife and a mother with two small children who need her, and Laila is—"

"Expendable? That's fucking bullshit! She's a human being and she's"—he shook his head—"fragile."

"I know."

"You don't know! She's been bullied, abused, and raped since she was fourteen by the very people who want their hands on her now. You'll have to kill me before I let anyone dangle her in front of a bunch of cutthroats. I'm dead fucking serious."

"Is there any chance such a plan will allow for the capture of those who wish to hurt my sister?"

At the sound of Laila's voice on the far end of the kitchen, Zy froze. Beside him, Trees scowled and cursed. Then they looked at one another. Zy telegraphed to his buddy that she was his woman and, therefore, his responsibility. Trees's expression told him in return that since Zy was the acting boss, he wanted no part of this office bullshit.

Zy shook his head. *Sure, why not heap more shit on my shoulders this week? You wouldn't be the first…*

"It's possible," he finally answered. "But it's risky."

Laila scoffed. "Even breathing around these people is risky—and certainly not a guarantee. My sister has endured too much, and she has her son to consider. I will do it."

"You will *not*," Trees exploded, towering over her with bared teeth and menace.

In the shadow of his thunder, she stood unblinking and uncowering. "You cannot stop me. You brought me here safely, and for that I thank you. But I owe you nothing beyond my appreciation."

"I didn't ask you for anything. But I would consider it a personal fucking favor if you would please give a shit about your safety."

She cocked her head, her big eyes looking so sad. "Unfortunately, Emilo never gave us that choice. And I am certain his father, Geraldo, who is probably running his organization again now that he is gone, will be even less interested in such things."

That was the elder Montilla's reputation, from what Zy had heard.

"Fuck," Trees muttered.

"If the Edgingtons or Muñoz ask me to help set a trap for Geraldo and his goons, I will say yes. My mind is made up."

And Trees wasn't about to stop fighting to change that. "Laila, you'll be bait. Chum. Something my bosses will skewer on a hook and use to reel these bastards in. And if they lose you?" He shrugged. "Oh, well. Not their problem. Do you understand that?"

"Yes. But do you understand I will have no future if I refuse?"

With that, Laila turned away, then paused and looked back at Zy. "I cannot pay you for the clothes on my bed. Please return them."

"It's not a problem. You left your house in a hurry and you weren't dressed for our winter."

"I will not accept your charity."

Then she was gone.

Before he even spoke, Trees looked ready to lose his shit. "See what I mean? She's going to drive me crazy."

Clearly, and Zy didn't envy his pal.

He'd always thought Trees would fall for some pliable female who was a little twisted and conspiracy-theorist, too. They'd have a few kids, prepare for a doomsday that hopefully never came, and enjoy the shit out of a life they lived as off the grid as possible. In his mind, she'd be loving and boisterous, filling in Trees's large conversational gaps. She'd cede to him about important things and make his life hell the rest of the time. And she would love sex.

Zy didn't think Laila was any of those things, but it didn't matter. Trees was already in deep shit.

"Take a breath. One day at a time, okay? You'll get through this."

Trees nodded like he didn't quite believe him and didn't want to argue. "Let's talk about something else. What's up with you and Tessa?"

"I don't want to bore you. I don't understand it enough to explain, anyway."

"She's pushing back?"

"She's pushing me away."

Trees scowled. "I would have sworn that woman loves you."

"I thought so, too, but she's never said that in so many words. And now she's barely answering my texts. Something is…weird. Something is wrong."

"Well, that's definitely not right."

"I don't know. Maybe I pushed for too much too fast. I told her at Christmas that I love her. About three minutes after we got the all-clear to have more than a working relationship, I asked her to move in with me. She says she needs time to think. But it doesn't feel like she's thinking; it feels like she's just putting daylight between us."

Trees frowned. "So what if you've moved fast this week? I don't think you rushing her is the issue. After all, you two have been eye-fucking and exclusive for months. You wanting to start a life with her didn't come out of left field. It's something else."

"Yeah. I was at her place a little bit ago. She actually begged me to leave." The panic in her voice had ripped at his guts. "And she's been lying to me. Sure, about little things like her headache. But still, lying."

"Any chance there's someone else?"

Zy pondered, then shook his head. "No. I think it's me."

And he was worried they were one bad conversation from being over.

"Or…she's guilty and she has something to hide."

"I don't see it."

"Because you don't want to. Keep pursuing her, man. You'll never be happy if you just walk away from her. But while you're doing that…look into her. Take her seriously as a suspect. Do your fucking job."

As much as Zy hated it, Trees was right. Now that he thought about it, Tessa hadn't just sounded panicked; she'd sounded guilty. "I don't have a choice. I guess that's priority one."

And fuck waiting for the right moment. He was starting the next instant he saw her.

Chapter *Seven*

The following morning, Tessa pulled into the parking lot after another horribly sleepless night of wondering how Hallie was or even if her baby girl was alive. She tried not to think the worst…but her thoughts refused to center around anything else.

This had been the absolute worst forty-eight hours of her life. She'd give anything to have her daughter back—even tell the kidnappers every single secret EM Security Management kept. She just needed them to contact her with a demand.

As she pulled up to the office building, she found the small lot surrounded by police cars with flashing lights. Officers held the perimeter. A pair of suits prowled the vicinity, looking grim.

Something had gone horribly wrong. Tessa's heart jumped in her throat.

As she tried to turn in, a uniformed cop stopped her. "This area is closed, ma'am. It's a crime scene."

Now that she was closer and could see beyond the police vehicles, she saw yellow tape cordoning off the area around the stairs to the front door. Zy was there, racing down and around the tape when he saw her.

"She works here," he said to the guy.

The officer nodded, then waved her around the area and into a spot near the adjacent building, just beside the alley.

Her pulse raced, heart beating against her ribs as she climbed from the car.

Zy met her halfway.

"What's going on?" she asked, staring between the busy parking lot and his bleak expression.

"A jogger came down the sidewalk about five thirty this morning and saw a trio of dead bodies piled at our door. None have been ID'd yet."

Fear gripped Tessa's belly. Dead bodies? Oh, god. Had her kidnappers decided the baby was expendable? "Anyone you recognize?"

She heard her voice shaking. Zy did, too, and cupped her shoulder in a gesture meant to calm and comfort. Apology twisted his expression.

No. No, it couldn't be. Don't let anyone have hurt my precious baby girl.

She dropped everything in her grip and clutched his arms. "Zy…is it anyone we know?"

He cupped her face and shook his head. "No, baby. No one we know. Three men, all late twenties or early thirties. But I was here shortly after the bosses arrived. I saw them before the coroner came. It was"—he swallowed—"bad. They were tortured."

Her relief that Hallie wasn't among the bodies was quickly stamped out by the terrible thought that whoever had killed the men might hurt her daughter next if she talked. "Oh, god."

"Don't cry, baby." He comforted her with his embrace. "Don't cry."

"How can I not? They dumped the bodies here, at our office." And Tessa couldn't help but worry that was a message meant for her, to show her what could befall Hallie if she didn't keep her mouth shut.

"I know, and once the coroner is able to identify the victims, maybe that will tell us why."

"It's not random."

"It's not." He sighed. "Walker and Matt, the temporary guy, are inside avoiding all this shit. Let's go."

"Were you waiting for me?"

"Yeah." He retrieved her things, slipped an arm around her, and walked her toward the door, trying to block her view of the crime scene with his big body. But it was no use. Tessa craned her head to look behind him—and saw far more than she'd bargained for. Missing eyes, missing fingers, missing genitals.

Tessa jerked her stare away. Her stomach bucked. She clapped a hand over her mouth to hold in both a scream and the urge to be sick. She couldn't imagine that happening to her baby or she would lose her mind.

Zy cursed and hustled her inside, shutting the door behind him before plastering her against the surface with his body, palm over her head as he leaned in. "Why did you look?"

"I couldn't..." *stop myself.* She'd had to make sure none of those bodies belonged to Hallie. She had to know what message her kidnappers were trying to convey.

It made her sick.

Yes, Hallie was seemingly alive—for the moment. And Tessa hadn't known any of those men. Still, she felt the urge to sob. Once, they'd been someone's son, someone's brother, someone's friend. Maybe even someone's father. They'd had the worst possible deaths imaginable. Her heart hurt for them and all they'd endured. But terror for Hallie, for what could happen to her baby if she broke down and screwed up, gripped her throat.

Blinking up at Zy, she tried to keep herself together. She wished things were different and that she could tell him everything. Today proved that was impossible.

"Couldn't what? Talk to me."

Tessa shook her head. "It was just shocking."

Zy didn't look convinced. "Are you sure that's it? Nothing else upsetting you? You haven't been yourself lately."

Of course she hadn't. But she swallowed her scream. It wasn't his fault that someone had taken her precious baby and ripped her heart from her chest.

She had to get it together and force her anxiety down a notch. All this worry for Hallie would do absolutely nothing to save her. She had to focus on things that would.

"I know. I'm sorry. I was hoping today would be better." When she'd woken up without Hallie again, she'd known it wouldn't. "But seeing the bodies..."

Zy sighed and brought her closer, caressing her back. For a brief moment, she propped her head on his solid chest and buried her face in his neck, inhaling him and trying to suck in his strength. "I should have called and told you not to come."

"I needed to." If this had anything to do with Hallie's kidnapper, he'd probably be calling soon. "But thanks."

Tessa trembled as she forced herself to pull away and head to her desk. By the time she tucked away her purse and her lunch, she looked up to see Zy watching her with a frown. With concern, yes. But today, she saw something else.

She didn't really want to look at that expression too hard. She was afraid of what that meant for her, for them.

Then One-Mile stepped up to her desk, a rugged cowboy type beside him, hat in hand. "Hey, Tessa. This is my buddy Matt. He's going to do some temporary work for the bosses. He needs one of the spare computers."

She wondered what kind of work and why. Normally, she'd care enough to ask. But she heard her phone vibrate and all but dove for her purse. Sure enough, there was her private caller again.

Second ring. God, she needed to answer this. It was so hard to breathe and smile at Walker's friend when she felt so frantic. "Hi. Nice to meet you. Let me take this call, then I'll be right with you. It's daycare..."

Matt nodded, then slid his hat back over his wavy brown hair. "Of course. Thank you, ma'am."

Third ring.

As he walked off, she looked up to see Zy heading to the back of the office. "I'll be in the conference room."

Then he was gone, and she was alone...sort of. But going out front to answer the call was out of the question. She needed to answer now.

Fourth ring.

"Hello?" she gasped out.

"I was beginning to think you weren't going to answer. That would have been very unfortunate." The stranger from the parking lot again.

"I'm in the office. It's a busy place. How is my daughter?"

He laughed. "Un-uh. You know the drill. Information first, then your reward."

"Forgive me for being jumpy about the three mutilated bodies in front of our office this morning."

The man paused as if he hadn't expected that. "Tell me about them."

He didn't know?

"The police and the coroner are here. I-I didn't get a good look. They were all young men. All..." *very horribly dead.*

"I'll call you back."

"Wait—"

But it was too late. He was gone.

Tessa closed her eyes. Why had she assumed he knew about the corpses and opened her big mouth? She'd much preferred the smug, didn't-have-a-care-in-the-world kidnapper to the panicked, out-of-control one. Now that she'd stupidly rattled him, would he take it out on Hallie?

Her hands shook as she tried to go about her morning like nothing was out of the ordinary. She hooked up her laptop to her monitor and opened her company email. Joaquin had sent her a list of things to do today—people to email, copies to make, clients to bill. None of that would take too long or require her to think too much, thank goodness. She could barely spare any thoughts for anyone but Hallie.

As she sent him an email promising to take care of all of the items quickly, her phone began to buzz again. Tessa lunged for it and answered immediately.

"Yes?"

"Change of plans."

"I need to know if my daughter is okay."

"You'll get a full report when we get full information. If you want it, you will do two things immediately. First, take a picture of the crime scene with the bodies."

"I don't know if they're still here."

"You better see to that first, then. And second, what are EM Security's plans to rescue Kimber Edgington? We need details."

"I haven't seen the family in days. They're planning elsewhere and not saying anything to the staff." At least that's what Tessa thought. Or had they been telling Zy something he wasn't supposed to share? "B-but I'll ask some of the operatives, see if they know something I don't."

"You do that. I want some answers in half an hour or less."

Then the caller was gone.

Tessa dragged in a ragged breath and told herself to keep it together. She couldn't take a few minutes to herself. She couldn't go to the ladies' room and have a cry. She had to suck it up and get busy. Her breakdown would have to wait until she'd gotten some word about Hallie.

Gripping her cell, she opened the camera app and cracked the door. She encountered a female officer, who turned to her with a scowl.

"Ma'am, you can't be out here."

She nodded, not looking at the crime scene as she pointed her phone in that direction and pressed the button a few times, hoping she caught a usable shot. "I-I left something in my car."

"It will have to wait. I'm sorry."

"Of course." Tessa tried to smile as she ducked back inside.

Quickly, she opened her photos and scanned the five she'd taken. Yes, there were three bodies visible. Some pictures were better than others, but she wasn't looking at details. She couldn't do that again.

Trembling, she turned on the recorder on her phone and tucked it in her pocket, then headed for the conference room. On the way, she saw One-Mile and Matt, who watched her expectantly. Shit, she'd forgotten to get the cowboy a laptop.

With a harried smile, she held up a finger, silently asking them to give her just a minute.

They nodded, and she let out a shaky breath while trying to collect her wits. She wasn't sure how she was going to ask Zy for information he wasn't at liberty to give—if he even knew—but she needed to come up with something quick.

Pressing a hand to her knotted belly, she knocked softly, then pushed her way inside. Zy sat in the big chair at the head of the table, feet crossed on the massive wooden slab, and replied to the speaker-phone. "I think you're right, and we need to think about all the possible angles. What's up, Tessa?"

She shut the door behind her—and was still blank. She masked the moment by clearing her throat and smoothing down her skirt. "Am I interrupting something important?"

"Talking to Trees. Did you need something?"

"Actually…yes. Can I bug you for a minute?"

"Sure." He gestured to the seat beside him. "I'll call you back, buddy."

"Yeah. It's gotten too quiet here. I should see what the fuck is going on."

Zy chuckled. "I think it would be wise not to let that...situation get out of hand."

"I don't know that you should be laughing, man. Just remember that. Talk to you later."

Tessa frowned. "What was that about?"

He smiled smooth as silk. "Rodent problem."

What? She'd never heard either of them talk about mice or squirrels, but whatever. They seemed to have a million inside jokes, and this was probably one of them.

"I wanted to talk to you." She folded her hands on the table in front of her and stalled for time to gather her thoughts.

"About?"

Then the most obvious tactic occurred to her. "Kimber. She's my friend. She didn't do anything to make a drug cartel mad. And I worry...if they came after her, what's to stop them from coming after any of us?"

Her question took Zy down a notch. He lowered his feet to the floor and leaned in, slowly putting his hands around hers. "I won't lie and say I wasn't shocked by what happened to Kimber."

"Why her? Just because she's Hunter and Logan's sister? They wanted to hit low?"

Zy shook his head. "It's a lot more complicated than that. This mess started when the colonel, Hunter, Logan, and another contractor all went into Mexico to rescue Kendra Waxman from Emilo Montilla. Remember her? The bride at the wedding we worked last June?"

"I remember."

"At the same time, they rescued Valeria Montilla. She was pregnant. I guess Emilo didn't appreciate it."

"But he's not alive to care anymore. He's been gone for weeks, and they only took Kimber a few days ago. So who would do this?"

Zy sighed. "That's part of the difficulty here, knowing who to go after. Emilo's death left a power vacuum in that splinter of the cartel. We think there are two factions vying for control. We just don't know which is responsible for abducting Kimber."

Tessa tore her hands free and sat back in her seat, her mind racing. Whichever side had taken Kimber, the other side had taken Hallie to force her to spy.

Oh, my god…

"Either way"—he went on—"they took Kimber because she's important to *all* the players. Hunter and Logan because she's their sister and they continued to dog Emilo to his dying day and one of their team members took the asshole out. But they struck at the colonel, taking his only daughter as punishment for leading the mission to rescue Valeria in the first place. And they hit at Deke, taking his wife, because they've been working a separate op that involves Tierra Caliente. The message is…you take one of ours, and we'll take one of yours."

She didn't have to pretend to tremble as she lifted her hand to her mouth. "What are we going to do? These aren't good people. We need to get Kimber back. I've tried not to panic for days, but—"

"Panic doesn't serve any of us. I promise you, the bosses are doing everything they can. Matt is here to help. They're running down every single clue."

"But what if it's not enough?" Tessa demanded, realizing that she was talking about her daughter more than she was asking about her friend. "Tell me they have *some* plan."

Zy shook his head. "I'm sure they're working on it, but…"

She almost came out of her seat. "But?"

He gripped her hands again. "But I'm not supposed to tell you anything. There's a plan, absolutely. It's going down soon. You know they're not the kind of men to do nothing, right?"

"Right." And once they did, what would that mean for Hallie? "Can you tell me anything? I'm so worried. It's part of the reason I've been acting so crazy. All this danger… I'm not used to it. I can't sleep. I can't eat. I'm a mess."

Slowly, Zy nodded. "Tell you what. Yeah, there's a plan. I'm going to head out early today, visit the bosses. They want to bump heads before plans are final. I should know more tonight."

Tonight? That was forever away. "Can we talk once you know?"

"Absolutely, baby. I don't know how much I'll be able to tell you, though..." He looked her up and down with eyes so blue she almost lost herself in them. "I miss you."

"I miss you, too," she said in total sincerity. She missed his smiles during the day. She missed his kisses as they left the office. She missed his possessive touches when he tumbled her into her bed, tore her panties away, and shoved himself deep. But most of all, she missed just being close to him.

Then Tessa had to look away to think again so she could start plotting how to make him tell her everything. She'd never felt so alone.

Somehow, she held herself together as she rose to her feet. "Let me know as soon as you know something."

"The minute I do," he promised. "Any chance you're rethinking moving in with me?"

"All the time." Her voice broke on the lie.

"Good. We'll talk about it later, too. I gotta get back to it." He nodded at the speakerphone.

"Okay." Tessa hated to leave. She didn't have the information the kidnapper wanted, but she could certainly go back with something. Maybe that would be good enough for now. "Talk to you soon."

Zy nodded as she let herself out. On the other side of the door, she turned the recorder off, then raced to the storeroom where the spare computers were stored. She pulled the most updated from the pile. Cutter's machine, she thought. Trees had already gone over it with a fine-tooth comb. It should get the job done.

She took it to Matt with a stiff smile and an apology. "Sorry for the wait. Oh, here's the power cord."

"It's no problem. Thank you, ma'am." Matt tipped his hat.

If she hadn't been falling apart and already in love with Zy, she would have better appreciated just how damn hot he was, gray eyes surrounded by a thick fringe of dark lashes and a sly smile.

Instead, she shook her head. "I'm not ma'am, just Tessa."

"Tessa is a pretty name."

She swallowed. He was flirting. She couldn't handle this right now. "Thank you. I should get back to work."

"My friend is too polite to ask you something," One-Mile butted in.

She frowned. "What's that?"

"Walker..." he growled in warning.

"He thinks you're hot and wants to know if you're down to have drinks tonight. Or sex. He's up for both."

Matt backhanded his buddy in the chest, then sent him a killing glare. "I apologize for my former friend's terrible manners. I'd just like to get to know you."

He seemed like a really nice guy, but now wasn't the time and he wasn't her man. "Sorry. I'm...involved."

"So you and Zy kissed and made up?" One-Mile asked.

Was that how everyone else saw their relationship? As having fallen apart over the past few days? "There was never a fight to start with." Then she turned to Matt. "If you want to get to know a really sweet girl, I know someone I could introduce you to. Madison is—"

"Thanks." Matt looked distinctly embarrassed. "I've spent a Friday night alone before. I'll be fine."

With an apologetic nod, she walked away, then glanced at her phone. She still had ten minutes left on the kidnapper's clock.

Making her way to her desk, Tessa glanced over her shoulder to ensure no one was following or watching, then she opened the device and tapped out an email, attaching the pictures she'd taken and advising them that something would probably be happening soon, but the plan was still forming and she'd know something more later tonight. Then she sent it off and prayed.

A few minutes later, she received a message in return. It contained no words, just a still image of Hallie, looking clean and pink-cheeked. She wore a too-large gray shirt and sat on a shag carpet some soft beige shade, holding a plastic banana, laughing at a cat jumping in the air. It was date- and time-stamped less than five minutes ago.

Her heart soared.

Tessa kept scrolling, hoping there was more, especially instructions on when and how they might release her daughter. Instead she found two additional demands.

`Advise us the minute you know the plan. Email may no longer be secure. Download the Abuzz app and await further instructions.`

She did it immediately. Of course she was going to. But she

couldn't keep living like this. Every day without Hallie was excruciating, but at least she'd had work to occupy her. This weekend, she would have nothing. And if she couldn't tell Zy that she wanted to move in with him, she would have no one. How would she make it until Monday with her sanity intact? She wouldn't. She was going to have to do something else and get creative—now.

The day dragged on for-fucking-ever. The police finally cleared out about midday. Tessa was eating her lunch at her desk, seemingly fixated on her phone when Zy came by to ask her out. Instead, he just kept walking, pushing his way out the door before he hopped on his bike.

God, this sucked, but Trees had put everything into perspective on their last call.

Listen, if she's not guilty, then lying to her about this fake op won't mean anything. You'll just say later that it fizzled due to new intel. She won't question it. And if she's guilty of passing on information...well, you'll find that out—and who she's telling—if some shit goes down that matches your BS. You just gotta hang tough until then.

As much as Zy didn't want to think Tessa could be guilty, he was starting to realize she might be. He'd known for a while that she needed money, but always believed she was the kind of person far too loyal to stab her friends and lovers in the back.

It might be time to rip off his rose-colored glasses.

The second half of the afternoon proved as excruciating as the first. Matt and One-Mile scooted out a little before quitting time to find the cowboy another place to hang his hat while he stayed in Lafayette. Apparently, Matt cramped Walker's style because he couldn't fuck Brea on the kitchen counters whenever he wanted. That was a direct quote.

Leave it to One-Mile to blurt the unvarnished truth.

Once they'd gone, he was alone with Tessa. So he sauntered to the front of the office, stopping beside her desk. If he was going to go all in on this ruse, he was going to do it right and leave no room for error.

"You all done with everything the bosses asked for?"

Tessa jerked her stare from her phone and quickly darkened the screen, setting the device upside down on her desk. If he didn't know her at all, if he'd been evaluating someone he wasn't in love with and trying to decide whether she was up to no good, that kind of furtive shit would move her into his mental guilty column.

"Yes. A while ago. I got Matt everything he needed, too. He's got a log-in and I put him at Cutter's old desk, hooked him up to the printer… He's set."

"It's almost quitting time. Why don't you get Hallie and get out of here?"

Normally, she would have grabbed her things and run to pick up her baby girl and start the weekend early. Now, she blinked, seemingly reluctant. "That's okay. I'll wait the last half hour. Have you heard anything else about the plan to rescue Kimber?"

Her response made him downright suspicious. "Nope. I've got to go visit the bosses after I leave here. So if you'll slide out, I'll head there now and holler when I'm done."

"Oh." She seemed frozen for a minute before she suddenly gathered her things, scooped up her computer, and stood. "I'll wait to hear from you."

"It shouldn't be too long. Afterward, maybe I can take you and Hallie to dinner as an early birthday celebration since I might still be out of town—or out of the country—on her big day Wednesday."

Zy saw instantly she was wholly unprepared for that offer. "Um, well… I can't do that tonight. I just remembered. Cash's father wanted to take us to dinner. For her birthday. It was kind of spur-of-the-moment. But, um…if you'll come by after nine, I'm sure we'll be home."

It wasn't what Tessa said that convinced him she was lying. It was the halting way she said it. Still, he played along.

"Sure. I can swing by then."

"Great." She sent him a stilted smile and tried to make her way past him.

Zy didn't budge, forcing her to wedge herself between him and the corner of her desk to escape. The tactic flustered her. Her hands shook as she sidled free and tucked a blond strand behind her ear.

"I'll see you then, baby."

With a too-quick nod, she shoved out the door and all but dashed across the parking lot.

Oh, yeah. Something was definitely up with her. Granted, that didn't automatically mean she was EM's mole, but it did mean she was hiding something.

He intended to find out what.

Zy gave her about five minutes' head start, then powered down the lights in the office, locked up, and headed out. She should have enough time to pick Hallie up from daycare, but in case she was a little slow or had to make another stop, he took his time, cruising the backstreets on his bike to avoid her catching sight of him as he made his way to her neighborhood.

She was just closing her garage door behind her as he turned onto her street. Perfect timing. Then he parked behind the camper the neighbors were loading up, presumably for their weekend getaway. As the sun set, he strolled across the street to the duplex, settling onto the porch of the unit for sale, in a rocker someone had left so the house would seem homier to prospective buyers. And he waited.

Six o'clock rolled around. No sign of Cash's father, and Tessa didn't leave to meet him. Same with seven. He took a call from Joaquin, but it only lasted a few minutes. Matt was already working the Kimber case, and they hoped to have more information soon. In the meantime, he'd been told to give the cowboy whatever support he needed in the office. Zy assured the man he would and that everything was under control before ending the call. His stare never left Tessa's door.

By eight o'clock, it became clear that she was neither coming nor going tonight. It was possible, of course, that the apple hadn't fallen far from the tree and Cash's dad was as flaky as his son. Or maybe she had decided she couldn't maintain her chipper facade and cancelled. But he played his part and waited, withdrawing his phone to order a hot sub and a bottle of water delivered to his current location. After he devoured that and took a leak around the shadowy side of the vacant house, it was straight-up nine o'clock.

Time to get some answers.

Tessa opened the door, greeting him in a robe and a smile, looking as if she'd just curled her hair and retouched her makeup. She also seemed nervous as hell.

"Hi." She stepped back. "Come in. How was the meeting with the bosses?"

She wanted to get right to the point? Too bad. He was going to make her wait.

Zy shrugged. "Intense. It's a lot of details to work out, especially since we have new information. How was dinner with Cash's dad?"

"Nice," she said with a smile full of forced cheer. "Craig took us to a place that, um…had wonderful burgers and chicken. Yeah, on the south side of town. They sang to her. But Craig is doing well. I'm glad we went."

Liar, liar… But why?

"The whole thing tuckered Hallie out, so I put her to bed. It's just us now."

And he couldn't miss the suddenly seductive note in her voice. She swayed closer.

What the hell? After avoiding him for days, she was suddenly turning on the charm?

Oh, baby. If you're going to play with fire, I'm going to burn you so bad…

"Great." He took her hand. *And if you're willing to seduce me for information, let's see how far you'll go to get it.* "But I'm more tired than I thought, and it looks like I have to leave town soon. I can't say much, but let's catch up next week, when the op is over. And if I'm back on Wednesday for her big day, I'll take you and Hallie to dinner then."

She swallowed. "So the rescue op is definitely on for this weekend?"

"We've got a really solid plan that… Well, sorry. I can't tell you. I'll see you later?"

Tessa squeezed his hand tighter, as if she thought that would stop him from leaving. "Don't go. I-I've been thinking."

"About what?"

"You. Us." She bit her lip—something she only did when she was nervous. "Moving in is a really big step. I know I said earlier that it wasn't a good idea, but…I've reconsidered. I'm open to talking about it."

He wasn't buying it. How fucking long had she been playing him? "That's good to hear, baby."

"And I know you're tired, but I'd love it if you stayed a little longer so we could…talk?" She pretended to adjust the tie of her robe, but she pulled it free. The folds slid apart. And under the thin white terry cloth, what she wore scrambled his brain.

Her blue, lacy baby doll covered less than half her tits. The bow tucked just under gave way to a filmy, transparent fabric that told him she wore nothing underneath except a teeny tiny thong.

Yeah, she was playing him—no question—and it pissed him the fuck off. But holy shit, when he clapped eyes on her, he could barely breathe. And he was more than willing to let her take advantage of him in whatever way she wanted.

"Tessa, baby…"

She shrugged off the robe and tossed it on a nearby chair, then tugged him through the darkened living room and into her candlelit bedroom.

Tessa had definitely ramped up the seduction factor for his visit. Because she wanted something other than sex or love or commitment from him.

Goddamn it.

Later, he'd let himself hurt. He'd wonder why the first fucking time he had truly lost his heart it had to be to a lying viper with big green eyes and gorgeous tits doing her best to play him for reasons he could only guess at. He'd take her engagement ring back and kiss all his dreams of a happily ever after goodbye. He'd wonder how the hell he was going to pick up the pieces of his life to live without her forever.

Now, he was too angry that she'd turned out to be just as self-serving as every other asshole he'd grown up with.

"Zy?" She looked tense. No, worried. "Do you not like this?" She gestured to her lingerie, almost cupping her breasts—and making him lose his ability to speak.

Until something occurred to him. "Who else have you worn that for?"

She relaxed, as if that question didn't stress her. As if she didn't have to lie. "No one. I bought this for you."

When? After she'd decided to screw him figuratively and literally? "You look sexy as fuck."

He could say that with all sincerity. The lace and ribbons framed her cleavage so temptingly, he itched to touch her. The shadow between her thighs was dusky and mysterious and he swore he could almost taste her. His mouth watered.

"Thank you." She stepped closer. "I'd planned to talk to you tonight…but I want to be with you, too. We've only been apart a handful of days, but it's felt like a lifetime."

"It has." Zy couldn't keep the rough note out of his voice.

"Do you want to talk now and get it over with? Or talk…after?"

"Definitely after."

After that, he lost all patience for talk. He flattened her against the wall of her bedroom, gripped her hair in his fist, then slanted his mouth over hers with a groan.

Tessa might have turned out to be a poisonous liar, but she tasted so fucking sweet.

Against him, she arched, then whimpered as he stroked his tongue inside her, loving the way her breath caught. He slid deeper. The kiss turned urgent. He cupped the pert globes of her ass and crushed her lush tits against his chest.

She gasped as she clutched his shirt, hanging on like she couldn't breathe and wouldn't let go.

His lips raced down her neck as he laved at her throat like she was a delicious treat to savor, not a Mata Hari he should unmask.

"I've missed you. I need you. Zy…" With quick fingers, she unbuttoned his shirt. He did nothing to stop her, just let her shove the garment off his shoulders to pool on the carpet. "Take me to bed."

Twenty-four hours ago, he would have believed that whisper. He would have been throwing a party in his head as he carried her across the room and made her his again. He would have gone out of his way to lavish her with pleasure until she was sighing, sated, and smiling.

Not anymore.

"Let's not rush this, baby. I want to take my time with you tonight." *See how desperate I can make you…*

Panting, she shook her head. "No, I can't wait. I ache for you. I've craved you so badly. I've tried not to. I've tried to keep my head and think straight. But when you touch me, you make that impossible. Please…"

She sounded so needy. If he didn't know better, he'd swear her words were sincere. Despite all the evidence of her guilt, Zy still found himself half believing she meant all that.

Then Tessa turned the tables on him, opening her lips against his neck, nipping at his lobe, nuzzling up to his five-o'clock shadow, dragging her tongue down his chest as she plucked at his nipples with pinching fingers and nibbling teeth.

He hissed as pleasure hit him hard. The scent of her arousal drifted between them. Fuck. He needed to keep his head and stay in charge. He couldn't succumb to the desire gnawing at his restraint, but christ, she was undoing him.

Tessa kept kissing her way down his body, breathing hard and clutching him—until she landed on her knees at his feet. And god help him, he fucking loved her there. His body roared in approval with a slam of his heart and a jerk of his cock.

Blinking up at him, she gripped his thigh and tugged at the button at his fly. He yanked the zipper down before helping her shove his boxer briefs past his hips.

She took his cock in her eager hands, and he moaned. Then, with her big green eyes devouring him, she parted her swollen red lips, took him onto her tongue, and sucked him deep.

The hot silk of her mouth seemed to envelop his whole body. Zy closed his eyes with a growl, using a determined fist in her hair to guide and lengthen the stroke of her lips up and down his dick. "Yes, baby. Nice and slow. Watching you wrap your lips around me is…" She swallowed, her throat working the head of his cock into a staggering nirvana. He tugged harder on her hair and fucked her mouth ruthlessly. "Don't stop."

Tessa shook her head, totally unshy about heaping pleasure on him. That turned him on even more.

She didn't give the most practiced blow job he'd ever had, but she sucked him with gusto, eyes sliding shut as if she savored every inch. The little catch of her breath almost convinced him this turned her on as much as it did him, and he wondered how she'd willed her nipples to be so hard under the transparent lace. Hell, maybe she was practiced after all. Maybe he'd underestimated her. Maybe she'd been inserted by the enemy onto this team in the hopes one of the operators would find her his Kryptonite, and he'd been the gullible sap to fall for her.

Then he stopped thinking when her tongue lashed his sensitive crest before swirling around his length. Head spinning, he staggered back to the bed, desperate to fuck her and almost not giving a damn that she was taking him for a ride.

If he didn't need to figure out what game she was playing, he would let her suck him until he came down her throat and do it again just because why not take advantage of the fact she seemed willing to whore her mouth out to serve her cause?

But now, he needed to take control of this wretched drama and arouse her until she turned pliant. Then he'd turn the tables and figure out why she didn't mind selling herself out and for whom she had chosen to fuck him over.

He tugged on her hair, smiling when she gasped as he pulled her off his cock. Using his rough grip to guide her to the bed, he laid her flat on her back, then reached for her tiny blue excuse for underwear.

The wet spot staining the fabric was unmistakable, and when he tugged the silky wisp down, it clung to her pussy.

Impatiently, he tossed the garment away. Her scent steamrolled his senses. His nostrils flared. Hunger roiled in his gut. His restraint snapped. "Spread your legs."

"Zy—"

"Spread them."

Slowly, almost shyly, she did. Once, he would have believed her sweet act. Not now. She wanted to jack up his desire and fuck with his head?

Two can play that game, baby. And I can play it better…

He braced impatient hands on the insides of her knees and shoved them wide, then raked his lips up one thigh before exhaling onto the sticky heat of her cunt.

She trembled and gripped the sheet, wriggling like she needed him now. "Zy..."

He only half listened to the keening that came out of her lying mouth. Instead, he focused on parting her folds with his thumbs and exposing her to his dirty gaze. "I'm going to melt you, Tessa. Whatever you think you wanted out of tonight? I'm going to take you, make you scratch, beg, and scream for me. I'm going to own you, baby. And I'm going to get exactly what I want from you."

The roaring of his heart almost drowned out her answering whimper as he raked his tongue through her naked slit. He plowed her indecently again and again, worshipping her juiciness and sweetness. He couldn't find any fault between her legs. Here, she was everything he wanted, and if the way he devoured her was impolite or obscene? That wasn't going to stop him from dragging his tongue between her swelling folds and tormenting the pouting nub of her clit for as long as he damn well wanted.

"Zy... I can't breathe," she panted, proving that she was a liar again. "Oh, my god."

Her toes curled. Her back arched. She lifted to him in sweet, sweet offering. He gripped her hips and yanked her against his open mouth, covered her with the flat of his tongue, then sucked her without mercy.

Tessa shrieked and twisted. She ripped at her baby doll, tugging at one side of the bow beneath her breasts. The garment parted. Her tits bounced free. She pinched her nipples with greedy fingers and cried out.

Fuck, that turned him on.

He sucked harder on her clit before lashing it with his tongue. She trembled, her heels digging into the mattress. The deliciously frantic sounds falling from her lips cranked him up higher.

"Zy!"

Yeah, she was on the brink. But he'd be damned if he gave her satisfaction now. Maybe not at all tonight. At least not until he got his—climax *and* information.

With a long last taste of her folds, he prowled up her body, pausing to nip and suck at her berry-hard nipples, before he worked his hips between her splayed-wide thighs. Cock in hand, he aligned his crest to her slick opening. "I'm going to shove my way so deep into your pretty little cunt that you'll still feel me tomorrow," he growled in her ear. "Next week, too. Hell, maybe for the rest of your life. No one will ever do you better than me, baby. That's a vow."

"Zy…"

He watched her eyes widen as he sank his shaft into her, barreling past what little resistance her body offered. "Hmm, such a sweet, snug pussy around my cock. That's it. Take every inch of me."

"Yes." Her nails were already in his back and her legs rising to wrap around him. "It feels so—"

"Save your breath. You're going to need it to scream."

Warning delivered, he propelled himself inside her. She cried out, digging her nails in his shoulders and bucking beneath him. Immediately, he slammed his way in again, even deeper this time. She climaxed—moaning, clawing, and pulsing around him.

Zy didn't slow down, just shoved every inch inside her again, scraping her awakened flesh and bottoming out to prod some sweet spot that made her shriek louder and clutch him tighter. He battered her body with pleasure again and again. Her bed frame groaned. Her headboard banged against the wall. Time stood still as he unraveled her without a second thought.

She'd scratched his back to ribbons, and he had lost the hearing in one ear when Tessa's orgasm finally subsided. Not that he gave two shits right now. His first night with her had been great. The following morning, even more amazing. But this? His blood fired. Every hair on his body stood on end. Each nerve ending jolted with her touch.

It wasn't merely because she had a banging bod, was good in the sack, and rocked his world. He couldn't be that lucky. Despite whatever devious shit she was up to, he was still totally in love with her. Sure, her surrender turned him on, but when he was with her, he'd swear they were meant to be forever.

God, he was a stupid bastard.

Finally, her body relaxed. She exhaled a breathy sigh of repletion between her rosy, swollen lips. Fuck no, it wasn't over. Everything inside Zy rebelled against that. Yeah, he shouldn't want to give her another climax. He shouldn't ache to stay inside her half the night. He definitely shouldn't feel this love for her beating in his mutinous heart.

But he did.

Cursing, Zy tore free from her body and lunged to the side of the bed before he gripped her hips, pulled her to the edge of the mattress, and covered her pussy with his tongue again.

If she'd been wet before, now she was dripping. He closed his eyes and savored the sweet-tart taste of her surrender, thrilled as fuck when she keened out his name so loud he was shocked it didn't rattle the windows or wake the baby.

He licked and nipped at her clit mercilessly, feeling his way up her body to pinch her distended nipples. She gasped, her breath catching hard in her throat.

Zy looked at the bounty of her body spread out before him, at her pink cheeks and her eyes glowing with need. God, he'd love to forget all the reasons he couldn't simply lose himself inside her. Who would know if he kept her in bed all weekend, naked and under his cock, so she could never tell his enemies the "plan" and fuck him over?

But then he'd never know who or what she valued more than the man who'd planned to put a ring on her finger and love her for the rest of her life. If he didn't let this play out, he'd never be able to board up his heart.

Under his relentless tongue, the little bud between her legs quickly swelled and hardened again. She screeched out high-pitched pleas and raked her nails across his scalp.

"Zy! Oh, my god… I've never"—she panted—"ever felt anything… Oh! Yes…" she moaned. "Ahhh! So good."

She was about to come again. Not that Zy was patting himself on the back. Sure, he fucking loved that he owned her right now, but he wouldn't congratulate himself on a job well done until he got the information he needed.

His fucking heart had other ideas, shouting at him to stop playing games and talk to her. To assure her that she could tell him anything and that, together, they could fix any issue. But that ship had sailed; he was no Pollyanna. He needed to swallow the bitter pill that Tessa hadn't even tried to talk to him, just chosen to fuck him in every way she could.

He could do the same.

As she surged toward another peak, Zy pulled back, flipped her over, shoved her to her hands and knees, then plunged his cock deep. At his invasion, she cried out, fisting the sheets.

Tessa was tighter in this position. Still, he fucked her like a madman, rattling her bed and her body with the force of each thrust.

It was goddamn January, and sweat dripped from his forehead and rolled down his back. A sheen of it covered her skin, looking so peachy by the candlelight. The narrow nip of her waist, the delicate line of her spine, the graceful curve of her shoulders... She was a work of art. Hips flaring, thighs trembling, ass cushioning his every stroke...yeah. He wanted to possess all of her. He wanted her to be his for the rest of his life. But since that didn't look possible, he was going to make sure she regretted him like hell.

He reached under her and settled his fingers over her clit, rubbing in controlled circles.

"Zy!"

"Like it when I fuck you?"

"Ah...yes!" Her cunt tightened on him. Her clit turned to stone. "Please..."

"I love to hear you beg," he said roughly in her ear. "Get used to that."

He was going to do what it took to hear her desperate, breathy pleas every chance he got before he had to tell the bosses she was a gorgeous, lying sellout.

Then, to make her even more mindless, he slowed his thrusts and lightened his touch on her bud.

Right on cue, she twisted, hips thrusting, seeking more. "Zy, please... Please!"

Tessa might be able to pretend sweetness and loyalty and giving a shit. But she couldn't pretend desire like this. Right here, in this bed, he was forcing her to be fucking honest with him about something, by god.

The problem was that undoing her undid him. His head might

know she was the enemy...but his cock hadn't gotten the memo. Neither had his stubborn heart, which kept insisting he break down the walls between them and talk to her.

Fat fucking chance now.

Her pussy tightened. Her breath stuttered. Zy rolled Tessa to her back, forced her thighs wider, grabbed her ass in both hands, and rammed deep inside her again. "Look at me."

She shuddered as he growled against her mouth, teeth bared, and fucked his way harder into her. But she obeyed, opening her eyes. They glowed as they revealed her soul to him. Of course her pupils dilated and her body raced for the climax he dangled just out of reach. But when he really looked at her, he saw anxiety, need...and love.

Love he wanted to give back to her so fucking badly.

His chest tightened. His heart clenched.

Time to end this show or she would pull him under until he only cared about Tessa, not doing what was right. He was already perilously close to giving up everything he believed in for her.

"I am," she whispered against his lips.

He pressed their foreheads together and plunged into her body as he drilled into her soul. One long, strong thrust led to another, then the next. She twisted under him, cried out, begging him with almost inhuman sounds of need. And still he kept fucking her, doing his best to stave off his rising need for release.

Because once he pulled free from her body, he'd probably never have her again.

Everything inside him fought that notion.

He wasn't braced when she gripped his face in her hands and slanted her lips over his as if she needed to be as close to him as possible.

Zy was done for.

The pleasure he'd been trying to dam spilled over, bursting free. He gripped her even tighter, sank his knees into the mattress, and filled her with merciless strokes. She clung and cried out, her pussy clenching and clutching, holding him as tight as possible.

He let his control go, promising himself this one sublime moment before sanity reigned again. For the moment, he pretended that only pleasure and love—only Tessa—mattered. He'd grill her later. Now he gave himself over to the most combustive orgasm he'd ever experienced. Ecstasy singed his skin and boiled his blood. It strained his back and seized his churning insides as he filled her deep, shaking uncontrollably, his throat grinding his voice as he shouted her name.

His vision began to black out, reducing down to only Tessa. He gave up moving or breathing or being in any way except with her as he unloaded both his seed and his soul inside her.

Yeah, he might have intended to work her over for information, but there was no denying she had fucked him good. He was never going to be the same.

With that terrible realization, he closed his eyes and ripped free from her before he even fucking caught his breath.

Tessa reached for him, her gaze confused and imploring. "Zy?"

He couldn't give in to her now. If he did, he'd stop caring that she was just using him and didn't love him. He'd sacrifice everything for the high of touching her. And he'd fuck his whole life forever.

"I gotta go." He reached for his pants.

A furrow appeared between her brows. Shock. Tears trembled on her bottom lashes. Her lips parted in a soft, sad *O*. She looked a heartbeat from falling apart.

Fuck, did she practice that expression in a mirror? She must. It was so convincing, so seemingly genuine that he almost took her in his arms to reassure her.

"What did I do wrong? I tried to say I was sorry and to please you and—"

"Nothing," he lied, then shook his head. "No, that's not true. It was everything."

Someday, he might be able to forgive her, but he would never forget.

It was fucking hard for a man to admit when a woman had his number so completely he would do or say anything to keep her. He used to think pussy-whipped guys were just losers and suckers who couldn't get laid, so they settled for the first one who did them halfway right. Now he knew he'd been wrong.

And now he knew he'd be forever miserable because no other woman would ever be Tessa.

"I don't underst—"

"I'm pulling out tomorrow night." He tugged on his shirt and rattled off the lies he'd prefabricated. "We know Kimber's location. She's in the state, nearby. It will be a surgical insertion, probably in the early-morning hours. I'll get in. I'll get out—hopefully with Kimber. If no one hears from me by Monday, something went wrong."

"You're going?" She looked horrified. "Alone?"

He nodded. "It's better this way."

Tessa tossed aside the sheet, tears running down her cheeks as she scrambled off the bed, baring herself totally before she threw herself against him. "No. Don't go."

"I have to."

"*You* don't. Please," she begged. "Don't go. These people are dangerous. L-look what they did to One-Mile last fall."

"That's what they'll do to Kimber if I stay here." That was likely the truth. He couldn't get lost in his own fucking feelings and forget that she was someone's wife, sister, daughter, and mother trapped in these people's clutches. And she would probably die if he didn't deceive Tessa now. "She doesn't deserve that."

Tessa went from shedding pretty tears to crying ugly ones as she wrapped her arms so tightly around him he could barely breathe. "Neither do you. Please…"

Zy didn't know why she was begging him not to go. Did she, somewhere deep down, feel bad about deceiving him? Or did she know he'd run into something deadly because she was setting a trap?

It didn't matter. The deed was done. He'd told the lie. Now he had to let the chips fall.

"I don't have a choice." He cupped her face and gave in to his need to cover her mouth with one last lingering kiss. She cried and clung. Then, before his heart fucking bled out, he pulled away. "Goodbye, Tessa."

Resisting her needy eyes and crumbling expression, he turned away, and left—probably for good.

Chapter Eight

As Zy left, Tessa heard the door slam behind him and the click of her deadbolt, followed by the faint rev of his motorcycle out front as he sped away.

Then she heard nothing but the empty echo of terrible, stabbing silence.

What was she going to do?

Her baby was gone, captive of some drug cartel or another. The man she loved had left to destroy those same criminals or ones just like them. Tessa had seduced him for answers to save her baby, and she had the terrible feeling he'd seen right through her. And he'd given her what she wanted to know…but he hated her for it.

Now, she was utterly and completely alone.

Anyone she might have called to talk this through? They were gone, too. Her parents? Dead. Her bosses? Wrapped up in saving their own family. Her co-workers? On Zy's side. The one friend she might have confided in? A captive of criminals herself. Kimber couldn't help her now.

No one could.

She had to help herself.

Around her, the walls of her once-homey duplex pressed in, crushing her along with the inky night's darkness. Tessa stood stock-still, listening to the sounds of her harsh breaths and frantic heartbeat in the hush.

What was she going to do?

She almost scoffed. How many choices did she really have?

Only one. And it would kill her.

On shaking legs, she blew out the candles she'd lit all around the bedroom, then groped her way to her bathroom, flipping on the harsh overhead light. When Tessa looked in the mirror, she blanched.

Her cheeks and chest were still flushed with orgasm. Her lipstick was long gone from her swollen, bruised lips. Mascara ringed her eyes. She looked naked in every sense of the word. And haunted.

It fit. From tonight on, she would never be happy or whole again since Hallie's kidnappers had put her in a terrible predicament: save her daughter or the man she loved.

Protecting one would probably result in the death of the other.

She had to choose tonight. No delays. No excuses.

It was a no-win situation.

What had she done to deserve this karma?

Tessa shoved the useless question aside. Feeling sorry for herself solved nothing.

Fighting tears, she lunged forward and killed the bathroom light before lurching for her bed. It seemed like the natural place to sob over her hopelessness until she gathered the courage to do what she had to.

But as she reached the edge of the mattress, the passion she and Zy had just shared rolled over her senses. The air smelled of sex. The sheets were still warm from his body.

And she couldn't stand the thought that in forty-eight hours he would likely be cold in the ground.

Because her choice to save her daughter would have put him there.

But Hallie was a baby. Her child. What other choice could she make? She couldn't see a way to save them both. If she tried, she might well lose them.

The outcome of her forced betrayal had already been too horrible to contemplate when she'd thought other EM operatives would be assigned to rescue Kimber. It had taken a while to realize that giving the enemy whatever she could scrape together about the planned rescue mission would allow the cartel to ambush and kill whichever of her peers had drawn the short straw. She'd hoped Zy wouldn't be accompanying them. She'd prayed desperately.

She should have known better. Worse, he would be attempting this rescue alone.

Tessa staggered from the bed, against the opposite wall, feeling wretched and hollow. Defeated.

Even her legs stopped supporting her.

She slid down the wall and dragged her knees to her chest, staring out at the darkness, and tried to think of anything. Of any way. Of any possibility. There must be some course of action to preclude the seemingly inevitable.

But what?

If she failed to respond to Hallie's abductors or gave them false information to help Zy, they would show their displeasure by ending her daughter. Poor Hallie would be dead before her first birthday because her mommy had been too naive to see danger coming and too unworldly to save her.

Tessa couldn't live without her precious baby daughter.

But how did she live the rest of her life without the man who completed her heart?

A cry rose from the depths of her soul, wracking her body. Grief poured out. Despair surged in. The sobs stole her breath and splintered her heart.

No, she couldn't give up. She couldn't do nothing.

Struggling to her feet, Tessa made her way to the living room, tossed on her bathrobe, and paced the darkened room. But as she ran through the scenario again, trying desperately to study the situation from another angle to find another solution, she ran into the same brick walls.

She was trapped.

From across the room, her phone rang. Tessa dashed for it, hoping it was Zy. That he wanted to come back. That he wanted to talk. That he'd changed his mind about the mission.

When she lifted the device, it was her private caller instead.

Tessa sucked in a shaky breath to steady herself. "Yes?"

"Time's up, Mama. Do you have information for us or is it a permanent nighty-night for this precious baby of yours?"

She snapped. "How can you threaten an innocent child? What did she ever do to you? What did I ever do?"

"Nothing," he acknowledged with the gravity of someone talking about the weather. "But I can do anything I have to in order to stay alive and one step ahead of the cops."

"You're putting your"—*terrible, scummy, criminal*—"existence ahead of a baby's?"

"If you're trying to appeal to my sense of honor or humanity, I don't have either. It's a kill-or-be-killed world. The sooner you figure that out, the sooner you'll be able to protect yourself and your daughter...provided you make the right decisions and earn her back. Speaking of which, do you have the information we need?"

About Kimber's rescue. About when and where it was going down. About who would be putting themselves in mortal danger to free the bosses' sister.

Tessa clutched her phone tighter. "Yes."

"Did you download the Abuzz app?"

"Yes."

"What's your username?"

Dutifully, she rattled it off. A moment later, she heard a ding.

"That should be the notification that I've requested to be your friend. Accept me, then DM me the information."

"And if I do? If I betray everyone else in my life and I have nothing more to give you, will you finally return my daughter?"

"We'll see. My associates and I aren't convinced this will solve our Edgington-Muñoz problem. If it does, I'll bring her back right away. If not...we'll be in touch, and you'll have to figure out how to tell us what we need to know."

The three beeps in her ear told her the asshole had ended the call. Impotent fury zipped through her. Misery chased it. Was there any end in sight to this fucking nightmare?

With trembling fingers, Tessa opened the app. Her legs felt weak as she stumbled to the sofa, accidentally tripping over the corner of the nearby chair and catching her toe on something soft and squeaky. She flipped on the small lamp of the nearby end table and lifted the object she'd unwittingly kicked out from under the skirt.

Hallie's little stuffed pink elephant. The one she loved to chew on. The one she'd been missing for two days before her disappearance.

Oh, god.

Hot, scalding tears stung her eyes and poured down her cheeks again, agonizing and uncontrollable. They fell onto the toy, staining it with acidic drops and running mascara.

Tessa bit back a cry and swiped at her cheeks, sniffled, and cuddled the little stuffed animal to her chest as if it could bring her closer to her baby. It still smelled like her daughter, fresh and sweet with that hint of baby still clinging.

A million times she'd seen Hallie hold the elephant, kiss it, gnaw on it, or nap with it. She'd give anything to see her little girl happy and smiling and holding this plushie again.

The cost to see her wish come true was reprehensibly high.

It's a kill-or-be-killed world.

Tessa had no choice but to pay the cost.

"Hang on, baby. Mommy will do whatever it takes to bring you back."

Despite knowing she'd made the only choice she could, Tessa wept uncontrollably when she opened the app, typing out everything she knew about Kimber's rescue, and hit ENTER, most likely consigning Zy to death.

After leaving Tessa's house, Zy returned to his apartment and drank—to blunt his anger, to dull his pain. He wished like hell sleep would come, but he sat on the sofa with one hand around the neck of his whiskey bottle while he replayed the night in his head.

So much searing pleasure. So much goddamn agony. Tears he didn't fucking want stung his eyes.

Whoever sang "Love Hurts" hadn't been kidding. It burned and ached like a bitch. There was nowhere to go to escape. He had to endure it like an injury, minute by minute, day by day, until hopefully, maybe, he healed someday.

Right now that didn't feel possible.

How could Tessa hand-deliver him to the enemy for an early death? Sure, she'd cried and begged him not to go on the mission she'd probably known would lead to a grave. But she hadn't been sorry enough to confess her sins.

Maybe he shouldn't be shocked. After all, how many times had he told that woman he loved her? Too many to count. She'd never once said the words back to him.

At least she hadn't lied about that.

Zy lifted the bottle again. His thoughts were too sober. Clearly, he needed to lean harder into the booze to get numb.

But before he could take another swig to drown his sorrows, his phone rang.

Groaning, he reached in his pocket and pulled out the device. Shit. It was Hunter.

"Hey. Is something up? It's the middle of the night."

If one of the bosses was calling at this hour, it wasn't to chitchat. But even expending the energy to talk—and act like his world wasn't imploding—was exhausting him. His voice sounded like it hadn't been used in a decade. Every muscle in his body hurt.

But nothing ached like his dying heart.

"What the hell have you been doing around the office?"

He sat up straighter. "What do you mean? I've done my job."

Zy had taken the position to save his post-military career after blowing up all his goodwill in the Middle East. It was proving to be his undoing since it had only brought him misery. If the bosses were going to pile on him, too, maybe he should fucking quit. Take his savings and buy a camper. Move out to the middle of nowhere. Live alone. Grow a serious beard. Stay the hell away from women.

He only hated that idea because he'd never see Tessa again.

What a sap.

"When we stopped by the office early this morning to talk to the police after those bodies were discovered, Logan was able to swipe one of the victim's phones, along with his dismembered thumb. He took both out to Trees, who unlocked the device and started prowling around. Looks like these assholes are using an app to communicate, which we'll report to their tech support."

"They're using Abuzz, right?"

"How?"

He snorted. "Lucky guess."

But inside, Zy seethed. Only Trees knew he was a part of *that* Garrett family. His parents had always gushed publicly about Ivy-League Theo. Zy, whom they'd refused to refer to as anything but

Chase, was the kid they'd never talked much about to the press. That suited him just fine.

He wasn't about to advertise his connections to his bosses, either. He would rather call his prick of a father again and settle the matter like men. And if dear ol' Dad wasn't in the mood to listen to his son ream him out… Well, Zy knew ways of making him regret it. It was past time that big tech shithole got sorted.

"Well…I don't know what you said or did, but the fucking private board these cocksuckers use to communicate started lighting up an hour ago with information about their kidnap victim. The tidbits they're posting should be helping us, but so far they're not, goddamn it. And there's talk you'll be going in tomorrow night to do their dirty work, whatever that means. They're speculating that you're walking into an ambush that's pure suicide. Where did this BS come from, and why the fuck do they think any of this?"

Zy closed his eyes. So Tessa really had done it. She'd given over his bullshit information to the enemy. Despite all the pleasure they'd shared, not to mention her tears and clinging arms, she'd still sold him out.

He had expected it. Hell, he'd set up the op to entrap her for just this outcome. But her betrayal still hurt way fucking more than he'd thought it would. Than he'd been prepared to bear.

"Zy?" Hunter barked.

An answer. Right. He should already have one canned. He should have anticipated this fucking phone call. But he'd been too focused on Tessa.

"Still here. You told me to run down our mole, that it was either Trees or Tessa." He sighed. "It's not Trees."

"You're telling me that our receptionist has somehow outsmarted me, my brothers, and nearly a half dozen other well-trained operators? Without raising suspicion—or even a brow—until now?"

"It's looking more and more like that, yes."

Hunter paused. "All right. But I'm going to make something really fucking clear. If you two are having a spat or a rough patch, don't you throw her under the bus because you can."

So his boss thought he was a petty, vindictive asshole? Perfect.

Seemed to fit with the rest of his night. "Are you being serious right now?"

"Yeah. I know we listed her as a suspect, but mostly through process of elimination. We've never stopped believing Trees was our man."

"Well, you're fucking wrong. Accept it."

"How do you know? Trees would have the finesse to do this. The connections, the know-how, the—"

"I made up a story about Kimber's rescue mission that will be taking place in the next thirty hours. I told her I'd be going in alone to extract your sister in a surgical strike. That was barely an hour ago, and here you are in my ear. That's not a coincidence."

This time, Hunter was quiet for so long Zy wondered if his boss was still on the other end. Finally, he sighed. "Well, fuck. I feel stupid."

Take a number, pal. "I'm sure she got away with it for this long because she thought everyone would overlook her."

"And we did."

"Yep." Zy knew he was more guilty than most.

He'd somehow equated her being a single mother and the fact she'd needed help with her safety as being some sign that she was too sweet to sell them out. He should have flipped his thinking. Because she was raising a child alone, she needed more money than she made. And for her daughter, she would do whatever it took to make it.

"I want a timeline."

Was he serious? "Sir, I think our time now would be better spent bringing Tessa in and questioning her—"

"I didn't ask what you thought the better move was. If this was strictly my business, I'd probably agree. But I have two other partners, and I think Logan is going to need more convincing than your word, especially since our problems started when Tessa was on maternity leave. Start at the beginning and show me how she could have been our mole for months on end. And if you prove she compromised Valeria's locations or had anything to do with Kimber's abduction, then heaven help her. I might kill her myself."

"You can't touch her," Zy snarled automatically.

"Are you fucking hearing yourself? Buddy, she just sold us all down the river, and you're still willing to go toe-to-toe with me, risk your job and an ass-kicking—"

Zy snorted. "Never gonna happen."

"For a woman who took money to compromise a mission likely to put you in a pine box?" Hunter finished as if Zy had never spoken. "Are you that fucking in love with her?"

"Yes."

"Jesus, clean up your shit. I get that you'd give her your heart; we all do when we fall. But your spine needs to stay yours."

Hunter was right, and that pissed Zy off even more. "Oh, dispense with the friendly advice. Have you ever worried whether Kata would serve you up to the enemy on a platter for a mere buck?"

"No."

"Then you have no idea what I'm going through. So I'd appreciate it if you'd shut the fuck up."

"All right, I'll try—if you build me the timeline. I want to know every time she reached out, every action she took, and every way she flew under our radar. Then I'll zip it. But fair warning: that isn't my strong suit."

Zy wasn't at all surprised. "Fine. It will take a day or two, but—"

"No. You created this fictional mission. The enemy is all abuzz—pun intended—about your superstar solo mission. So you need to produce enough evidence to convince my brothers, so we can confront her and decide what to do next, before your supposed op."

It was the middle of the night, and he didn't really understand the nuts and bolts of how Tessa had betrayed them. Zy knew only that she had. "How the fuck am I going to do that?"

"That's your issue. We hired operators who are problem solvers. Start solving. I'm over here trying like hell to rescue my sister and keep my wife from busting out of her safe house to help."

"Do you have anything new on the Kimber front?"

"Not much." Hunter sighed. "Matt is running down a few things. He's proving to be a master of many trades, and we'll probably hire him if he's game when this is all said and done. But he hasn't been in place long enough to put this puzzle together. We keep hoping."

Zy didn't blame him. It sounded like a shitty situation, and Matt seemed like a decent guy. "I hope it all comes together soon and you get your sister back."

"Thanks. You have six hours to get me a preliminary timeline of Tessa's double cross."

Then the line went dead.

Thirty minutes later, Zy pulled up to Trees's place. The big guy was waiting on the front porch, concern on his face and a shotgun in one hand.

Zy stepped off his bike and gestured to the firearm. "Is that your idea of a warm welcome? I can go if you're that adamant about sleep."

"Ha ha." He relaxed his stance with the rifle. "Just being cautious, keeping out the riffraff, you know. But now that you're here, maybe I should shoot you just for the hell of it."

Go ahead and wound me, pal. You wouldn't be the first one tonight…

"Pass." He sighed. "Sorry. I'm all out of jokes."

"Yeah. You look like someone shit all over your life. I was just trying to lighten your mood."

"I appreciate that, but don't." It grated on his fucking nerves.

Maybe he was a stupid ass for wanting to wallow in his heartbreak. Maybe some stubborn part of him kept holding out hope that when they started putting this timeline together, they'd realize Tessa wasn't guilty at all and find the real culprit. Maybe tonight's information would prove to be nothing more than a crazy coincidence. Hell, maybe someone had even bugged her house and her communications. It was unlikely, but he couldn't rule that out completely.

The only thing he did know right now? Compiling this information would either make the case against her fizzle out…or solidify it for good.

His friend held up a hand. "All right. I'll zip it."

Zy hung his helmet on his handlebars, not bothering to lock anything up. Trees and all his booby traps would kill anyone way before they got their hands on his brain bucket.

His buddy reached behind his back to open the front door. He looked like he was in need of a distraction.

"Thanks," Zy called out.

"Always." Trees's voice sounded subdued, heavy. Then again, he understood the gravity of the situation.

"Where's Laila?"

"In her room, waiting for me to fall asleep before she'll risk getting into bed and closing her eyes."

Zy frowned as he ambled up the steps to the porch. "She still doesn't trust you?"

"She doesn't trust anyone. I'm trying not to take it personally."

One look at Trees's craggy face told Zy he still was. "Even if it's not a knock against you, that's got to be hard. You're the dude most people trust with whatever they value—vehicles, pets, girlfriends."

"Yeah." He rubbed at the back of his neck. "She's not most people."

"Is she making noise about wanting to be with her sister?"

Trees stepped back inside the house and locked the shotgun back in its case. "Some, but Valeria admitted to Laila she's the reason they're apart."

"At least she's not blaming you. Did she ever let you buy her warmer clothes?" *Or anything that covers her tits and ass*?

"Negative." Trees sighed. "No offense, buddy, but could we talk about your misery instead?"

"Why not? Everyone else is."

Zy locked the door after them. Together, they made their way to Trees's kitchen. Subconsciously, he slid into the same chair he had occupied on Christmas Eve. And wasn't the empty chair beside him —the one Tessa had sat in—a brutal metaphor for where he was in life?

"Sorry, man. Tell me what happened?"

He did, leaving out the part where he'd tried to work Tessa's body over to fuck with her mind…only to lose himself in her instead. But Trees knew him well. He could read between the lines.

"This is killing you, and you still love her."

"I try to tell myself I don't. That I'm in love with who I thought she was and I miss what it seemed we had. But I can't lie to myself. She's double-crossed me, and she would only do that for some reason she thinks is necessary. And I can't make myself unlove her."

"I know."

"She's not capable of consciously hurting the people she cares about."

"The Tessa I know? No."

That made Zy feel better…and worse. "Which says she could only do this to me because she doesn't really give a shit about me at all."

"I don't believe that. I've watched her. I've seen the way she looks at you, and I think she loves you. Any chance she doesn't understand the ramifications of what she was doing?"

"No."

"Maybe she—"

"Whatever you're going to say, no. Don't try to make this better. You can't. So let's just get this shit done. The bosses want a timeline of the mole's activities, so…I guess we'll start at the beginning. Go through the backups. See what you can find in the electronic records on the EM servers."

"How long do you have?"

Zy glanced at his phone. "Another five hours, give or take ten minutes."

Trees barked out a laugh. "They don't want the fucking world or anything."

"They never do…"

"I got a spare computer in the office. Would you grab it? I'll start capturing the data sets and pulling them down. Once I've got them, I'll show you what we're looking for, then you can search the records, too. This will go twice as fast if we both look."

"Sure." It's wasn't as if Zy expected to get any sleep tonight anyway, and doing something made him feel better than doing nothing at all. "On it."

When he headed to that corner of the house, he found Laila kneeling at the side of the guest room bed, wearing one of Trees's over-sized T-shirts. A peaceful instrumental tune played softly from her phone. Was she praying?

He'd barely stepped on a creaky floorboard a good twenty feet behind her when she jumped up and whirled around, suddenly crouched in a fighting stance, gripping a shiny, sharp switchblade.

Zy held up his hands to prove he was unarmed. "Sorry to disturb you. Just grabbing a laptop from the office."

When he gestured to the room to the left of hers, she relaxed a little. "Hello, Zy. Go ahead. You are not disturbing me."

Maybe not in the way she meant, but it seemed she found any male presence in her life disturbing. "I'll be quick. You okay? Need anything? Doing all right with Trees?"

"I need nothing except to be with my sister and her son again."

In other words, with family, from whom she took solace. With whom she felt safe. "Hopefully, we can make that happen soon. I know being here is out of your comfort zone—"

"Comfort is not my first concern. Your friend and I should not be alone together." Laila met his gaze straight on, as if she refused to be cowed by him. Or maybe she'd already seen it all in her short life and had nothing left to fear.

"He would never touch you without your consent," Zy assured.

"So you say. But perhaps you are right." She frowned with confusion. "Madison came by. It is clear she would allow him into her bed. It is equally clear that he has not partaken."

"Because Trees isn't looking for an easy lay. He may be big, but he's not a bully. Or a rapist."

"It is my experience that all men eventually reach the limits of their restraint. He will come to the end of his."

Zy shook his head. "No. It's his job and his duty to take care of you. He won't shirk that, especially to touch you against your will."

"I know you genuinely believe that."

And her sad smile said she wasn't convinced.

Suddenly, she glanced above his shoulder.

Zy turned to find Trees standing in the hall. "Be right there."

"You okay, Laila?"

His buddy's usually gruff voice caressed the woman's name with reverence. Yeah, Trees had it bad.

"I am well. Do what you must." Almost reluctantly, she tucked away the switchblade. "I will resume my prayers."

Then she turned and glided to her knees, seeming to tune them both out.

Zy grabbed the laptop and headed toward Trees, not missing the longing in his eyes. It sucked that the first time he'd ever seen Trees truly interested in a woman, she seemingly had zero interest in him—or any man. Zy needed to wrap up his search for the mole quickly so Laila could return to her sister…and leave Trees's place. If not, his buddy's heart would be toast.

"Did she say anything?" he whispered as they headed back to the kitchen.

"Nothing you probably haven't heard. Madison came by?"

He nodded. "To return my house key. She kept up the place while I was gone."

She hadn't done that purely out of the goodness of her heart. "Think she's falling for you?"

"Nah. She's looking for something."

"Love?"

"I thought so for a while. But it's more. She's not happy—with her job, her family, her friends, her hookups. She's searching for something, and I don't think she knows what yet. It's another reason I won't sleep with her." Trees sat at the kitchen table. "She's expecting that someone new in her life will solve her problems, but until she figures herself out, nothing and no one will put a dent in her dissatisfaction."

Leave it to Trees to boil a situation down to a few concise sentences. Granted, Zy only knew Madison from one sweaty night nearly a year ago, but now that he heard his buddy's opinion, it jibed with what he'd observed. "Yep."

"You ready to do this?"

Can I gouge my eyes out with an ice pick instead? It sounds like more fun. "As I'll ever be."

"I got the data sets ready. We need to account for all the breaches in EM Security's information, times where the enemy seemed to know shit when they shouldn't have, and see if we can trace it back to any communication from Tessa, see who it was going to, and how she might have passed the information."

Zy figured they'd be doing something like that. "So what am I looking for?"

"Anything. Emails, website hits, log-ins to online locations that seem fishy. If I have to drill down to the keystroke level, I will. But let's see what we can establish without that since months of that info would take more than five hours to comb through."

"Sure."

"You take January through March. She was on maternity leave most of that time, so the majority of the emails and communications you'll be sifting through will belong to Aspen."

"Oh, god help us all. I'd forgotten about her."

"I'd like to…" Trees grumbled. "I'll take April through August and see what kind of patterns emerge. Oh, and be sure to look at any cookies, plug-ins, or other programs she might have downloaded. I compiled a list of EM-approved software." He set the paper on the table between them. "Anything else is something she would have downloaded without telling the bosses and worth looking at. If you have questions about whatever you find, holler. I'll figure it out."

"Thanks." But Zy wasn't grateful at all. He didn't want Tessa to be guilty. He wanted this to be a big misunderstanding that would just go away.

"You're welcome."

Then they both dived in. Zy wasn't terrible with tech, but he wasn't anywhere near Trees's caliber. Still, he made his way through the first-quarter emails from the previous year associated with her profile pretty quickly. As Trees said, most of them were Aspen's since she'd used Tessa's computer during that timeframe. She had been into some unusual shit, too. Soap carving, competitive cat costuming, and another pastime Zy had never heard of.

"What is toy voyaging? Any idea?"

"No. What the hell?"

Zy looked it up, then gave a dumbfounded shake of his head. "Who sends their toys with strangers so they can be photographed around the world? And why is that a thing?"

"Is it? Really?" Trees looked as confused as Zy felt.

"It is for Aspen. She gave someone this ugly straw hat with flowers to drag all over Europe. The person sent back a bunch of pictures of statues wearing this hat. She seemed really excited. Just before that, she'd been to some resort in Mexico and taken pictures of these weird nesting dolls from Russia and photographed them on the beach, in the jungle, and beside the hot tub." Zy shook his head. "Apparently, they all got a kick out of that."

"Because that's not weird or anything," Trees quipped.

"Not at all."

"I hate to judge, but I'm glad we don't work with her anymore."

"Same. So here's a piece of software either she or Tessa downloaded on January thirty-first, exactly one year ago. The location suggests it was installed onto Tessa's machine. Was she in the office that day?" Zy had no way of knowing since he hadn't begun working for EM Security yet.

"Let me bump that against a calendar I maintained. I told the colonel I wasn't a fan of letting the temp use Tessa's machine because we didn't know her well, but we didn't have a spare at the time. So I kept track of who had control of it when." Trees flipped over to another document on his computer, then frowned. "That was one of Tessa's last days in the office before her maternity leave. She was supposed to have worked with Aspen the following Monday through Wednesday, as I recall. But she went into labor on Tuesday morning and didn't come back until the end of March."

"So Tessa probably downloaded this?"

"Most likely. What is it?"

"Looks like some sort of spyware maybe."

"Let me see."

Zy shoved the computer toward Trees, who craned over to study the screen, his face growing more concerned. "Fuck. This is some hand-coded shit that collects every keystroke, but it also enables stealth remote access from anywhere in the world."

Was he serious? "So whoever installed this could tap into Tessa's computer at will and could see every time she or Aspen hit a key? And they could access our servers without anyone being the wiser?"

"Yep. I begged Aspen to let me scan that computer a couple of times. Every time she said it crashed or she finger-flubbed whatever she'd been typing and ended up somewhere in the computer she shouldn't be, like at a command prompt."

Zy sat up. "Tessa couldn't have had anything to do with this. She's not a computer whiz, and she definitely doesn't know anything about writing code, especially something that involved."

"You think Aspen does?"

Probably not. "Is it possible neither of them did this?"

"Possible? Anything is. Improbable? Yeah. Keep digging. See if you can find any traces of contact in March, around the time we went to Mexico and damn near got ambushed."

"Getting there. After that software is installed, there isn't much in the way of sent emails except to the bosses. It's like...Aspen didn't do that much."

"No, it's not 'like' that. She actually didn't do much. But no fishy communications around the time of our mission?"

"Not that I see."

Trees sighed. "Then again, with remote access and keystroke recording, all anyone had to do was log in to our server themselves and they could mine almost anything."

"Do you think that spyware/remote-access garbage is still on Tessa's computer?" Maybe she had been passing on information without even knowing it.

"No. As soon as Aspen cleared the building, I restored Tessa's computer back to the factory settings, then carefully rebuilt her profile. I didn't trust Aspen not to have unwittingly screwed everything up."

"So the rogue software is gone? And we have no way of knowing who might have been accessing our systems and where the information was going?"

Trees winced. "When you put it that way, I should have looked to see what was on the computer before I wiped it, but I had no idea..."

"You couldn't have." But that didn't help prove that Tessa wasn't their mole...if they could prove that at all. "You finding anything else?"

"Let me finish. Then...we'll talk."

Given Trees's scowl, that was a yes.

His friend worked in silence, seemingly a lot faster now that he knew what to look for. Zy stood and ambled to the coffeepot, flipping it on. He wondered what Tessa was doing right now and if she'd cried when he'd left…or just shrugged and moved on with her life.

He wished to fuck he understood why she'd lied to him, tossed them aside, and sold him to the enemy for a buck. Then again, he'd never understand that behavior.

"Coffee?" he asked Trees.

"Yeah. It's going to be a long night."

Zy glanced down the hall. Laila's light was still on. "Should I encourage her to go to sleep?"

"You can try, but she won't."

With a grim press of his lips, Zy shook his head, made two cups of coffee, and headed back to the table where Trees furiously scribbled notes, peering at the screen, then his list of chicken scratchings growing longer.

Zy was on the last swallow of his java—along with his last nerve—when Trees finally looked up. His friend's grave expression told Zy he wasn't going to like whatever Trees had to say.

Fuck. His heart nose-dived to his belly. His throat tightened. "What?"

"There are footprints of communications from what looks like a Gmail account to an external mail host with its servers in Switzerland."

"Why is that important? Why does the server location matter?"

"Because the Swiss have some of the strictest tech privacy laws in the world. No one is getting their hands on that information. A lot of people use this kind of service. People who don't like their emails being scanned for key words so that online retailers can market to them, for instance. People who don't love government intrusion into their personal life."

"So you have one of these email addresses?"

"Not this particular provider. This one is expensive. But I have one like it. It's also commonly used by people who have something to hide."

"Like criminals?"

"Exactly." Trees shrugged. "Obviously, I'm not saying that anyone who has one of these is up to something nefarious, but I am saying that anyone up to something nefarious probably has one of these email addresses, rather than a simple freebie."

"Let me recap: Someone with Gmail sent messages to a party with a super secure email address who might be a criminal?"

"Yes."

"And?"

"Because the information packet passed through our server, and I have some goodies residing there just in case, I can read the contents of the emails. But I can't prove who the Gmail address belongs to."

Maybe they could figure it out. If they could read the contents of the outgoing messages, they might be able to glean who the Gmail belonged to—and thus, the identity of their mole.

"Are the communications from this Gmail something to worry about?"

Trees scanned, frowned, then sighed. "August eighteenth. The Gmail account owner wrote a summation of the plan Hunter outlined for Walker and me to spy in Mexico. The mission in which he was taken in the parking lot."

Zy's blood ran cold. That breach had definitely been the work of their mole. And the bosses probably would have come to Trees sooner to have him run this down if they hadn't suspected him. "Shit."

"Yep. Shit," Trees confirmed. "There's just one thing about this that's a little weird: the message was sent in the middle of the night."

Zy tried to puzzle that through. "Tessa takes her laptop home with her more often than not. She always said it was in case the bosses needed something during evening and weekends."

"Or maybe she does that in case a certain cartel needs answers day or night."

As much as Zy hated to think it, yeah. "How do we prove whether that message came from Tessa?"

"Without her computer, we don't."

That wasn't what Zy wanted to hear, but maybe there was another way to attack this. "What about Walker's rescue mission in September? That went off without a hitch."

"The one I missed because of truck-stop sushi. Right..." Trees tapped on his keyboard again, waited for a few tense seconds, then started scanning whatever filled his screen. Zy felt as if he waited forever before Trees shook his head. "No. Nothing."

She hadn't sent the enemy any plans about the rescue mission? Hadn't told them when and where and how they were planning to extract One-Mile and hopefully Laila with him? There must be some reason. "Were the bosses keeping the details of that rescue mission better under wraps? Or..." Then Zy remembered. "Wait. Wasn't that when she went to Tennessee because her father died?"

Trees snapped his fingers, clicked onto a calendar, then nodded. "You're right. She wasn't *around* to learn about the plan and pass it on."

Now that he'd gotten over hating to think of Tessa being guilty, anger set in. With every detail they unturned, he was beginning to *see* her step-by-step betrayal. It crushed him. It made him want to nail her for her deception. "But she was back in plenty of time to rat out the location of Valeria's safe house in St. Louis."

His buddy clicked a few more times, then nodded. "I just accessed the server's October backup. Sure enough, here's another communication from the Gmail account to the secure mail host, forwarding the email Walker sent me—via Tessa—with the location's floor plan. And like before, she sent the email in the middle of the night."

"She told the drug lord exactly where to find his estranged wife?"

"Yep. All the way down to the location of her bedroom."

What the absolute fuck? It was one thing for Tessa to sell him out and put his fellow operators at risk. But to take a buck for the location of a woman running for her life from the very man who had threatened her, knowing it would probably mean the end of the woman's life and the murder of a little boy's mommy? That made him fucking furious and sick. Zy would have sworn that Tessa would never stoop that low. But if this Gmail account belonged to her, this was irrefutable proof, in binary form, all stored in backup, that he'd been dead wrong.

The woman he'd fallen in love with? There was a good chance she was a myth, and he'd never known her at all. The single mom scraping by to do her best by her daughter and taking care of those around her with a warm smile? A facade coated in a whole bunch of bullshit. For weeks, he'd stubbornly refused to believe that Tessa could be guilty of anything more than an inadvertent parking violation. Now that he'd seemingly exposed the schemer who could betray anyone if it suited her purposes? He would happily serve as her judge, jury, and executioner.

"Anything else? Did she divulge the location of Valeria's safe house in Orlando, too? And who would she be talking to now that Emilo is dead?"

"I can't tell." Trees clicked a few more times, then scowled. "I don't see specific communications this month, but she might have realized someone was on to her and switched up her mode of talk. I won't know until I get my hands on her computer. You gotta get it for me, man. Now."

Yeah, he did. Whatever it took.

That meant he had to go back to Tessa's place. And after their ugly parting, what excuse could he possibly give her to let him back in? If she acquiesced, if she welcomed him in any way, how would he keep his hands off of her? His lips from her lush mouth? His body from invading hers?

"I know this is going to fuck you up for a while," Trees said. "I hate that like hell for you, but without her computer, I can't prove what Tessa is up to or how she's doing it. And if I can't do that, more people may die." Trees looked down the hall, at the light from Laila's room shining this way. "People who deserve to finally live."

Zy stood. Trees was right, and he had to stop thinking like a sap with a broken heart and start thinking like a fucking operator, trained to do whatever he must. "I'm on it."

Chapter Nine

Zy felt the wintery wind zip through him as he headed down Trees's country road back to town. It was late. So late almost no one was out. He encountered a total of two cars in thirty minutes and didn't hit a single red light. Part of him wished he had. It would take longer to reach Tessa's place that way.

Fuck, what was he going to do if the mysterious Gmail account belonged to her? If he could prove that she was guilty of both not caring whether he lived or died *and* selling out the bosses, too?

He tried not to dwell on that. He had objectives: Get into Tessa's house. Locate her computer, usually in her bedroom. Find a hidden corner to pry it open. Depending on what he found, he'd plan accordingly. If the Gmail didn't belong to her, he'd still have to deal with her other lies. But if it did…

Heaven help her because all kinds of hell would rain down.

His phone rang as he pulled to the curb. A normal person would wonder if Trees had a sixth sense, but Zy knew his buddy had calculated exactly how long the trip should take this time of night and had set himself a reminder.

"Right on time, you uncanny bastard."

"You made it?"

"Yeah. Heading up her walk now."

"On standby here."

"Hooking up my earbuds…" Zy pushed the attachment into the port, then fitted the piece in his ear. "Ready. Going in with the key now."

"Roger that," Trees said, then fell silent. "Tell me when you find her machine."

With his heart hammering, Zy focused on using the light from his phone in one hand to illuminate the lock so he could slip the key into it with the other. It snicked inside on the first try and turned with almost no discernible sound. He knew the door didn't creak and Tessa didn't have an alarm system. So once he was inside, the only thing he had to worry about was either waking her up or somehow fucking up.

Zy knew the layout of her unit well, but he was surprised when he didn't walk into a darkened living room. Instead, the little light over her stove a dozen feet away glowed softly. A glance around—which he hadn't taken earlier tonight—told him that Tessa hadn't picked up much lately. Her shoes looked as if they lay exactly where she'd kicked them off when she got home from the office. She'd doffed her work clothes and draped them over the arm of the sofa, forgotten. Her keys sat on the end table, half hanging out of her purse. A collection of empty water bottles and soda cans littered the coffee table.

Zy frowned. Months ago when he'd stayed here with her and Hallie, when she had been at her most frayed and exhausted, she'd picked up the house meticulously every night. Now it looked as if she hadn't bothered in a while, as if she no longer gave a shit. Why?

It was also unlike her not to be in her bedroom, door closed, at three a.m. But Tessa reclined on the sofa, curled into a ball, head lolling onto the back as she slept under one of Hallie's baby blankets. What the hell? She must be uncomfortable, not to mention freezing. Why was she here instead of on her cozy, queen-size marshmallow of a mattress? And why, even in the shadows, did her eyes look puffy and red?

Was something bothering her? Guilt maybe?

He shouldn't worry about her housecleaning habits any more than he should worry about her feelings now. But even as he told himself that, he lifted the quilt lying on the back of an armchair and spread it open, softly draping it over her body. For a moment, she stiffened. Stifling a curse, Zy retreated to a dark corner of the room, but she settled again moments later, sighing as she melted back into sleep.

Bent and stupid; those were the best words to describe him now. He was too focused on Tessa and her comfort when he should be figuring out just how corrupt she was. He had a fucking traitor to catch before she could endanger any other team members' lives.

On the heels of that came another terrible thought, but he'd shelve it until he had her computer wide open for him to examine. He didn't have a choice.

Antsy now, Zy zoomed from the living room to her bedroom, looking for the laptop. Sure enough, it sat on the corner of her dresser, where she usually stashed the device at night.

"Got it," he whispered into the earbud's microphone.

"Good. Find a quiet place to set up."

Zy needed to think. When they'd planned this, he and Trees had both agreed it made sense for Zy to scan the machine at Tessa's with Trees's remote help, rather than schlepping it back and forth. He'd only bring it to the ranch—and potentially tip their hand—if necessary. After all, if Tessa woke up while he was gone and realized her computer was missing, the jig was up. But all along, he'd been sure Tessa would be in her bed, so he'd intended to tuck himself in the little dining alcove or even hang out on the sofa she currently occupied.

Time to improvise.

He didn't dare go into her bedroom or bathroom in case she woke up and headed that way. Ditto with anywhere in the open area of the living room, dining room, or kitchen. That left Hallie's bedroom and the guest bath. Well, he supposed he could try her laundry, but it was more of a closet than a room. And the tight space of her garage wouldn't give him anywhere to work unless he sat in her car…which would beep as soon as he opened the door.

Fuck.

He crept out of the master bedroom, past Tessa, bypassing her damn shoes, which would have been easy to trip on, then straight through the kitchen. He stopped in the little hallway then. Hallie's bedroom—the chances of waking the little girl with a computer light seemed slim—with the glider? Or the postage-stamp guest bath?

Staring back and forth between the side-by-side doors, Zy deliberated, then reached for the knob on the left and pushed into the little bathroom. He might not wake Hallie with the computer light, but if Tessa had the baby monitor tucked under her blanket and he woke her by being here in her daughter's room…there would be no logical explanation.

Slowly, he shut the bathroom door, quietly closed the lid on the commode, then flipped on the light. "All right. Let's go."

"Got the USB drive?"

"Yep." Trees had given him the device before he'd left his buddy's place. "Inserting it now."

"Since this allows me to bypass her log-in and password requirements, once I remote connect, I can take down any other security she might have and get into any program she's loaded."

Zy had figured as much.

The light on the USB drive lit up. Her computer zipped past the log-in screen and quickly loaded her desktop. Damn, Trees was good.

"You're a go."

"Perfect. Give me a minute with it. You don't have to babysit. If you need to check on something out there—"

"I don't." If he looked at Tessa again, he'd only feel sympathy she didn't deserve. Even now, he could all but feel her across the house, soft and warm and upset about something she wouldn't explain. And it was killing him.

In the next five minutes, he would probably know just how duplicitous she was...and suddenly, he didn't want to. Instead, he wanted to grab her, throttle her, understand her, fuck her within an inch of her life, pleasure her until she didn't have the strength to lie to him anymore, then love her so much she could never hurt him again.

It was official; he was a sucker.

"All right. Hang tight."

Through the earpiece, Zy heard Trees clacking on the keys of his own computer. The screen of Tessa's laptop flashed as he started a scan, minimized it, then flipped from one program to the next. Finally, he pulled up the prompt for Gmail. Trees typed in the log-in name they'd captured earlier from their deep dive into the server and his device grabbed the password from cache.

Instantly, the screen filled with a neat row of emails.

The Gmail account was Tessa's.

Fuck.

Betrayal flashed through him. His blood froze. His heart stuttered and stopped.

Zy didn't think then, just reacted, slamming the lid shut and yanking the USB drive from the slot.

"The display went dead. What the hell happened?" Trees barked in his ear.

"I severed the fucking connection. I need a minute."

"To process the fact she's guilty?"

Yeah. And that she'd been lying to and deceiving every single one of them, especially the chump who had given her his heart and wanted to put a fucking ring on her finger. And now he had to face what he'd been avoiding earlier.

What if she'd had something to do with Kimber's kidnapping?

Until now, Zy had never known he could both love and hate someone so much at once.

Trees sighed. "It's okay, buddy. I didn't get to see all her emails, but I saw enough to know I'm going to need more than a five-minute dive into them. Bring the laptop here."

Zy closed his eyes. He didn't fucking want to, but what he wanted meant nothing now. "Yeah."

And the woman, too. He'd drag her along. It was definitely time to make her answer a slew of questions. And he wasn't letting her go until she finally gave him the fucking truth.

Once Zy had Tessa's computer shoved into a pocket on the door of the driver's side in her sedan, he opened the garage, pulled his bike into the tight space beside her vehicle, grabbed a little something Trees had shoved in his hands before he'd taken off—just in case—and stealthed his way back into the house.

He was almost done with prep for Tessa's transport, but now he had to think of Hallie. He didn't want to risk waking the baby in the middle of the night, and an interrogation was no place for a little girl. He couldn't leave her here alone, but they had no way to care for her out at Trees's place. No diapers, no playpen, no baby food… And he didn't have time to pack half the fucking house. If Tessa knew anything about Kimber's disappearance, he needed to pry it out of her ASAP.

"I need help," he murmured into his microphone as he stood in the middle of the kitchen.

"Anything."

"Call Madison for me?"

"Right now? Look, I know you're pissed at Tessa, but this isn't the time for a revenge fuck. And it's disrespectful to think you can use Madison—"

"I need a babysitter," he growled as quietly as possible.

Zy intended to wake Tessa up, but in his time. In his way. Once he was sure she had absolutely no means of escape.

"Oh. Good call. Laila could watch her, but the fewer distractions the better."

He didn't know how ugly this would get. "Agreed."

"Gimme two."

Zy agreed, then looked around to see if he needed to bring along anything else of Tessa's in case it took him a while to break her. He had no idea what she wore under Hallie's blanket and he didn't really care. He'd already seen it all.

Yeah, but how good are you at resisting it?

Trees popped back on, thankfully killing Zy's mental train of thought. "She's on her way. She only lives about half a mile from Tessa, so expect a knock at the door shortly."

"Thanks."

"You're welcome. Text me when you're on your way here. I'll be ready."

"Prep a place to put her just in case she gets any notions about being a runner."

Trees scoffed. "In the middle of the night? In the middle of nowhere? In January? Then again, if she's as guilty as we think…"

"Yep. See you shortly."

They disconnected the call. Zy turned on Tessa's front porch light, then slipped out to wait for Madison. Not three minutes later, she drove up, parked at the curb, then hopped out, wearing a pair of tight yoga pants, a happy pink sweatshirt, and her long hair in some knot on her head that made her neck look long and graceful.

She approached him cautiously. "What's going on? Are you okay?"

No, he was fucking falling apart, and he felt like shit for the way he'd treated Madison in the past when she'd been nothing but nice and welcoming. "Thanks for coming, especially in the middle of the night. I need to interrogate a baby's mother."

"I'm confused. Trees asked me to watch Hallie. I thought maybe there was a medical emergency. But you're going to *interrogate* Tessa?" She looked horrified—and worried for him. "You love her."

God, could everyone tell his heart was breaking?

"The baby is asleep. Don't expect her to wake for a few hours. Make yourself at home and wait to hear her. Call Trees if you need anything. Otherwise…we'll stay in touch."

"Yeah, okay. I don't have a problem with that, but maybe someone else should do this. You're upset."

Fuck, why couldn't he have fallen in love with Madison? She didn't excite him…but she would never have betrayed him. Maybe the trade-off would have been worth it.

Then again, he'd always been a rebel. It stood to reason that his heart—like the rest of him—would do exactly what it wanted. And it only wanted Tessa.

"This is my job. I need to do it. Will you be okay here?"

"Yeah. Of course. If anything happens, my dad is just down the road." She reached out hesitantly, cupping his arm so gently he almost didn't feel it. "And whatever happened in the past, I'm your friend, too. If you ever want to talk…"

She meant well, but his insides curdled at her pity. "I appreciate that. It's months too late, but I want you to know I'm sorry for the way I acted when we first met. I shouldn't have used you."

"Zy, I knew how it would end before it even began. And I was okay with that because I knew you would make me feel good. The pleasure was worth the pain."

But she shouldn't have to settle for that. She deserved someone who appreciated all of her, especially her heart. "I hope you find what you're looking for."

"I will. Someday. And before you warn me, I know Trees won't give me what I want, either. But he seems like someone who needs friendship and comfort. I just want to help."

Even at her own expense? Madison was more selfless than he'd ever been, and some lucky man smarter than him would scoop her up someday…

He brushed a kiss across her cheek. "Find someone who treats you like a queen and knows you deserve the world."

She pulled away with a smile. "I'm looking for him all the time. He's around…somewhere. In the meantime, do what you need to. I've got things here."

"Stay on the porch until I pull away with Tessa." If she fought, Madison might not be prepared to see him forcibly drag the woman from her house. "Then head in, lock the door behind you, and holler if anything comes up."

"Sure."

"Thanks."

He slipped back into the house. Tessa still slept, unmoving, on the sofa. He debated how to proceed. Best-case scenario? She wouldn't wake up until he had her all locked up and tied down at Trees's place. There would be no escape then. Worst case, she would scream like a banshee the instant he reached for her.

He'd do himself a favor and prepare for that.

Zy plucked her car keys off the end table and pocketed them, swiped her phone from her purse, and opened every door between the living room and the passenger's door of the sedan. Then, mood grim, he headed straight for Tessa.

When he fitted his arms under her, she barely stirred. He scooped her up against his chest, and her breathing barely changed. Her head rolled to his shoulder and she settled against him with a sigh, as if, when she was most vulnerable, she trusted him.

The thought skewered his heart.

Finally, he settled her in the passenger's seat, tucking the blanket securely around her before cuffing her wrist to the door and gently shutting it. Still, she didn't flinch, blink, or wake.

Zy scowled. It was unlike her to sleep like the dead, but he couldn't afford the time or mental energy to care why except that the extraction had gone off without a hitch…

Finally, he nudged the door between the kitchen and the garage shut, then hopped into the car. Tessa didn't stir at the beeping of the open door, nor when he started the car. She really must be exhausted…

He backed out of the driveway, shutting the garage door with the remote, then waved at Madison as he took off down the street. He craned his head until he watched her walk inside Tessa's duplex. Hallie would be fine now. She'd be in good hands.

But that left him alone with Tessa.

He hooked his phone back up to his earbuds and dialed Trees, who picked up on the first ring. "You out?"

"Yeah."

"And you got her, no problem?"

"Yeah." Zy looked over at Tessa, still peacefully sleeping. "You'll see when I get there."

"Sounds good. Laila finally gave out and fell asleep a half hour ago, when I left to prep the bunker."

"She needs it." And wasn't it horrible that the poor woman felt safer alone than anywhere near a man?

"She does, and I don't want to risk waking her. Bring Tessa straight back."

"Yep. Just be waiting in case I need help."

"Sure." Trees hesitated. "You okay, man?"

"Enough to do what I have to. The rest…I can't talk about it now." He'd have to unpack that later.

"All right. How much time before you have to report to the bosses?"

"Ninety minutes."

"We'll need to work fast, then. You brought the computer, right?"

"Yep. Phone, too. Just in case."

"Good thinking. I'll disable the security so you can drive through."

Then they disconnected the call. Zy sat in the silence, casting an occasional glance at Tessa, who still slept as he drove through the inky night.

Along the way, he encountered more cars than when he'd headed into town, but civilization soon gave way to the occasional house or farm. Paved roads turned to dirt. People disappeared. It gave him time to think.

Would this be one of the last times they'd ever be alone together? That he would ever see her? She was getting fired, no question. Nothing he said or did could stop that. But if she'd had anything to do with Kimber's abduction, she might be going to prison, too. He hated to think of what would become of Hallie. And why the fuck would she have betrayed everyone who cared about her? Was she really that hard-up for an almighty dollar? Had he ever meant anything to her? Or had he merely been a part of her smokescreen? Had she pretended feelings for him, even let him into her bed, to keep suspicion from casting its long shadow over her?

Zy hated to think she was that premeditated…but the evidence looked damning. She'd gotten away with her scheme for so long because he'd refused to believe she could be guilty. He wouldn't make the same mistake again. As far as he was concerned, no matter how much he wished or wanted otherwise, she was guilty as fuck unless she could prove him wrong.

When he made the sharp turn onto Trees's bumpy drive, the cuff around Tessa's wrist attached to the hard plastic of her door handle jangled and rattled. Between that and the hard bouncing of the car, she began to stir.

"Wha…?" Her lashes fluttered open and she peered out at the blackness through the windshield, then whipped her gaze to him. "Zy? What's going on?"

He said nothing.

"Where are we?"

"Somewhere I can make sure you answer questions."

"About what? I don't understand." She jerked her arm toward him —only to be stopped by the metal cuff. "What the hell?"

He turned and pinned her with a glare full of the twisting, wretched fury boiling his blood. "I'm asking the questions tonight, *baby*."

At his sneer, she flinched. "I can explain."

A de facto admission of guilt. He should have expected it, even applauded the fact they were making progress. Right now, he was too fucking full of rage to be happy about anything.

"Oh, you're going to. And I'd better not get anything but the goddamn truth this time or so help me—" He broke off before he did something stupid, like warn her. If he needed to do more than threaten, he wasn't going to waste words. He was just going to start applying pressure. Fuck the gloves; they were coming off.

"Zy..." Her voice trembled, and he turned to see tears filling her eyes and spilling down her cheeks. "I never wanted to hurt anyone—"

"But you did." He slammed on the brakes suddenly at the end of Trees's driveway, sending her lurching forward in her seat. Then he shoved the gear shift in park, threw off his seat belt, and turned to glare at her. "Not another fucking word until I say so. You've played me for the last time, so save your quivering lips and pretty tears. They won't work on me anymore."

Trees emerged then and eased the passenger door open. He unlocked Tessa's wrist with his cuff key, pocketed his gear, then tugged her out of the car. "Let's go."

She clutched the blanket against her, trying frantically to wrap it around herself with her free hand as she sent his buddy imploring eyes. "Trees... Talk to him. Please. It's not what you think—"

"Shut up." It fucking infuriated him that she tried to use his best friend's sympathies against him. "God, how fucking low are you willing to stoop? It's done. You're caught. We're over."

"But it's not—"

"I don't care! I don't..." Zy fought to dam the hot lava of outrage as he grabbed her arm from Trees's grip. After a glance back to see that his buddy had scooped up her laptop, phone, and keys, he dragged her straight for the bunker. When he reached the opening, he lifted the heavy metal lid and gave her a shove. "Get in."

She shook her head, panicked and digging in her heels. "What are you going to do to me? What's—"

"A lot less than you deserve." He lifted her—blanket and all—ignoring her screeches, and hauled her against him, trying like fuck not to notice her curves, her warmth, her familiar scent. The quilt slipped to reveal her bare shoulder. He tried not to wonder what she wore as he stepped onto the metal ladder and headed down with his prize.

"No! Don't. Stop, Zy! Please..."

At the bottom, he set her on her bare feet and nudged her toward an empty metal chair under a single light bulb. "Pleading won't work with me anymore. I'm going to interrogate you, Tessa. I'm going to let you sit here alone for fifteen minutes. When I come back, I'm going to have a metric shit ton of questions for you about who you betrayed, when, and why. And I better get answers that jibe with the evidence we've got or I swear to god being in this hole will seem like paradise when you're done dealing with me. The worst part? I convinced myself I was so fucking in love with you. And all you did was stab me in the back and rip my heart out through the hole you left. I won't give you that chance again."

She gaped in incredulity—or was that horror?—before she curled up in the chair and gathered the blanket around her protectively. Zy steeled himself against the fear in her eyes and the tears falling down her face. He tried not to be moved by the fact she was crumbling before his eyes. He did his fucking best not to care that she curled her knees against her chest, lowered her face, and sobbed.

It took everything inside him not to cross the handful of feet between them and wrap her in his arms. The fact he still wanted to, despite everything, told him he needed to get distance between them now. Or he would do something stupid, like believe her, again.

With a curse, he forced himself to block out the sounds of her sobs and ascend the ladder, slam the lid on the bunker, and lock it.

Then Zy closed his eyes, sucked in cleansing breaths, and told himself he'd done the right thing—the only thing—he could do. Fuck, he wanted to fall to his knees, and it was taking every ounce of his strength to stay upright. He couldn't let her take him down.

"She's destroying you," Trees said quietly.

Zy tore his eyes open, shocked to find them wet with acid tears. "I don't know how to fucking stop it."

His best friend through thick and thin stood beside him, hand on his shoulder. "If you were able to do the forensic dive on her computer, I would interrogate her for you…"

But he couldn't. Zy barely knew enough about Trees's specialty to be dangerous. And the big guy didn't have experience in forms of interrogation, especially the dirty ones. Zy had never had a problem finding his spine and doing what needed to be done…but he'd never fallen for the enemy, either.

"I know."

"You're not up for this." Trees shook his head. "We need to call someone else."

"There is no one, man. The bosses are wrapped up in saving Kimber. Kane has Valeria. One-Mile…"

"You going to let that crazy son of a bitch near her?"

"Fuck no." Even when he was furious with Tessa, even when he suspected her of the worst, here he was…still trying to protect her like a fidiot. "I have to report something to the bosses in an hour. And if she's at all involved in Kimber's kidnapping—"

"They're going to call the police."

Zy nodded grimly. He might be the one to help separate her from her daughter, put her in prison, and end her life as she knew it. No, he wasn't taking the blame, goddamn it. *She* had done that. He had simply caught her. "I can't stop it."

"You can't."

In the back of his head, some voice not wrapped up in bubbling rage warned him against being rash. It begged him to at least listen to Tessa. But that had to be his shattering heart. What fucking reason could she have that would make it okay to sell everyone out to dangerous criminals?

"Motherfucker."

"The universe owes you for this, man."

No, it didn't owe him a damn thing. No one did. Sometimes life was rough, and all he could do was suck it up, try to get through, and hope that someday he found someone who made his heart rev and fall like Tessa.

He had to get through today first, and that wouldn't be easy. His lack of sleep collided face-first into his heartbreak. When had he ever felt this fucking wretched? Never, but he had to stop boo-hooing. That wouldn't get the job done.

"I need a drink."

It said a lot that Trees didn't refute him, just nodded and led the way inside, straight to the whiskey. Zy knocked back three fingers with a sigh.

He could do this. He could find the will and the strength. He would get through this.

"Have you started going through her things yet?"

"No. I know I'm going to find more, and I hate to pile on right now."

Zy snorted. "This is probably like ripping off a Band-Aid—better to do it all at once so the sting goes away faster."

"Maybe. I think what's killing you now—besides the fact she ripped out your heart—is the not knowing. Exactly what she did. Why she did it. Why she dragged you into it."

Trees wasn't wrong. "There's a part of me that keeps insisting this isn't like her, that she would never hurt anyone—much less everyone—without a damn good reason."

"You mean other than money?" Trees raised a cynical brow.

"I know that's enough reason for most people, but..." Zy shook his head. "Or maybe she snowed me so fucking bad I was willing to believe everything, even her goodness."

"You have an instinct about her, and they aren't usually wrong. One of the things I've always admired about you is your people skills."

Zy had to laugh. "You only think mine are good because yours suck ass."

"Mine do. But yours are a cut above."

"You saying you think my instincts are right and that she's somehow innocent?"

"No. The black-and-white I see tells me otherwise. But straight up? You might know how to get to the bottom of her faster than anyone. I said before that I think she loves you. And I still think that's true...at least in her way. Go use her own tools against her."

"What do you mean?"

"Emotion. Appeal to her good side. Get under her skin. Hell, peel off her clothes and fuck her brains out if that works."

That mere suggestion should not excite him, but Zy already knew he was a shameless, twisted chump when it came to Tessa. If fucking her one last time was even remotely on the table? It was twisted and wrong, but hell yes.

"You have to do whatever you can to worm the truth from her. I can give you hard evidence, but only she can fill in the gaps and explain *why*."

Zy snorted. "If what we suspect is true, Tessa only has a passing relationship with the truth. Why should now be different?"

Trees was silent for a long moment. Finally, he grinned. "Did you ever stop to ask why I had handcuffs handy? You already asked once why I had rope in my nightstand drawer. You know I'm a control freak. Do the math."

The obvious smacked him in the face, and Zy was almost embarrassed he'd been so stupid. "You're a Dominant. Like the bosses."

"See, I knew you'd eventually get smart." Trees leaned closer. "Keeping it real, man. I think that's your instinct, too. But if you've never partaken, it's cool. Just…um, word of advice? When you want the truth from a sweet little thing like Tessa—"

"I think we've determined she's not sweet."

Trees shook his head. "Don't confuse her acts with the woman herself. She's gotten herself tangled up in this shit for reasons you and I may never fully understand. But your instincts are right. She's naturally sweet. A pleaser."

"Submissive?" Was that what Trees meant to infer?

His friend shrugged. "Maybe. Probably. But you don't know if you don't try. So here's my advice: if you spank her and she comes up biting your head off, then probably not and you should stop immediately. But…if you try and she doesn't? If she melts? It just might make her pliable enough to be honest. Worth a shot, anyway."

If it broke her down and he got some real fucking answers? "Hell, at this point, I'm willing to try anything."

Trees clapped him on the back. "You might just be surprised. And if I'm right, a bunch of my equipment is down there. You can thank me later."

Zy should have figured out his buddy's predilections sooner, but he'd never given much thought to Trees's sex life. On the other hand, the big guy made some good points…

Admittedly, if he had ever been tempted to tie a woman down and have her submit to him, it was now. It was Tessa.

He didn't have the strength to fight both her and his own needs.

Zy yanked his phone from his back pocket and settled it on the counter. "I know I'm running out of time. If the bosses call, stall them. But I don't want to be disturbed. I'm not coming out of that fucking bunker until I have answers."

Chapter Ten

Shivering from more than the cold, Tessa wrapped the blanket around herself tighter and paced the underground shelter, trying to process her horrifying new reality. But one thing was clear: somehow, Zy knew she'd betrayed EM Security Management.

Did he know why? He must by now. Could he simply not forgive her?

God, she had to get out of this mess, but how? He'd locked her underground without a way to contact anyone. Cold fear filled her. How long would he keep her here? And what if Hallie's kidnappers called? What if they had new demands she wasn't around to placate? What would happen to her baby?

Hot tears fell. She wiped them away. They were useless, but they wouldn't stop, damn it. Nothing ripping her apart would.

If she hadn't been already, she would soon be fired from her job. Not that it mattered, because kidnappers weren't good people, and as much as Tessa hated to even think this, the reality was she might not need to provide for her daughter anymore.

Then there was Zy. The man who had dragged her underground wasn't the man she'd fallen for. This version of him was harsh and unforgiving. Pure warrior. There would be no reasoning with him. He'd become an enemy combatant with no compunction about doing whatever necessary to compel her surrender.

As the minutes dragged on, worry warred with regret. Neither did her any good. She had to live with the reason she'd never told Zy about Hallie's abduction. It was the same terror for her child that had prevented her from sleeping for days—until tonight.

Earlier, after Zy had fucked her with such desperation and anger, she'd showered and fallen onto the sofa, curled up and sobbing with Hallie's blanket for all she'd lost. Then she'd fallen into an exhausted slumber. That was the only reason Tessa had to explain how Zy had transported her without waking her to wherever he'd stashed her.

Despite a few hours' sleep, she still felt as if she'd been run over by a train. She was definitely too tired to hold up her shield anymore, especially to ward off Zy. She just wanted him to come back.

She would talk now—she didn't have much choice—and pray her confession wouldn't mean the end of her sweet little girl. Hopefully, Zy would understand why she hadn't been honest with him, why she'd chosen to betray the bosses, and he would forgive her someday. But she didn't expect him to.

He would probably hate her for the rest of his life.

Despite that, she would raise the white flag and offer up whatever surrender he wanted if he'd save Hallie. Afterward, she would leave and never darken his path again, even though it would break her heart into a million pieces.

She had no idea how much time had passed when she heard the scrape of metal and the squeaking of hinges. A chill swept in as the door to the bunker opened. Zy started down the ladder and slammed it behind him, locking it and pocketing the keys before jumping to the ground. Then he turned to face her like a demon with vengeance in his eyes.

Tessa's heart rattled in her chest. She took an involuntary step back. "Zy."

His smile turned nasty. "Imploring me won't do you any good, Tessa. Neither will backing away. There's nowhere to go. So let me tell you what's going to happen."

"I'll do my best to explain."

"No. I'm going to ask questions," he insisted. "You're going to answer directly and concisely. The minute you lie to me…" He shook his head. "Don't. Sorry won't even begin to describe how I'll make you feel. That's a vow."

Now he was scaring her. "But—"

"Stop. Until I start asking questions, I'm the only one talking. Sit in the chair." He pointed. "Now."

Why? So he could stand over her and berate her without really hearing a word? That wouldn't help her explain and it wouldn't clear the air between them. "No."

He prowled closer. "Sit. In. The. Chair."

She side-stepped him—and found herself in a corner. "Don't do this. Don't keep me locked in here."

Brow raised, he pursued her with a handful of slow, deliberate steps. "I told you to fucking sit."

Even as she wondered where she was going, Tessa scrambled and tried to dodge past him—the flight instinct of prey looking for escape.

Zy made sure she had none.

He grabbed her arm and tugged her back to the corner. She stumbled on the blanket pooling around her feet. Zy caught her and lifted her free from the heavy quilt before she tumbled to the floor.

She was stark naked.

The moment he laid eyes on her, he froze and stared his way down her body. His gaze burned hot. His eyes raked her unrelentingly.

Tessa's heart skidded to a stop before it began to thunder in her chest. She looked up at him. Their stares locked.

The hunger in his eyes stole her breath.

"Goddamn you," he breathed.

Before Tessa could question why he'd cursed her, he yanked her flush against his body, arms banding around her like a vise, then he seized her lips with his own.

His punishing kiss was the last thing she should want, but now that they were pressed together, her body against his strong, solid form? She needed him. Craved him. Couldn't stand a moment of not being with him. His nearness gave her strength. His closeness promised that all wasn't lost. The passion of his lips shoving hers apart and his tongue forcing his way into her mouth said he was still invested in her. Whether he wanted to or not, he still cared.

God, she needed that—and him—as much as she needed air.

Tessa threw her arms around his neck, plastering her body to his, and kissed him back. She gave him her fears and worries. Zy took them all, sweeping them up and aside with every dominating lash of his tongue as she melted into him, wrapped her legs around him, and rubbed against him in an unabashed, silent plea.

He tore his lips free, panting harshly in the otherwise silent space. "Fuck, I need you."

"I need you, too."

"Don't fucking lie to me."

She shook her head, begging him with her eyes. "I swear."

With a growled curse, he took the last handful of steps to the metal chair, threw himself into it, and dragged her onto his lap, forcing her to straddle his hips. "Prove it."

The situation was grave, but being this close to him made Tessa tremble with head-to-toe desire. "Yes."

Then Zy lurched forward. Without an ounce of gentleness, he grabbed a fistful of her hair and tugged until his lips hovered a mere breath from hers. She surged closer, clutched his face in her hands, and closed the remaining distance.

She kissed him feverishly. Her body leapt to life. Her heart roared. Her skin sang. Her nipples tightened. Her pussy wept. For him. Always for him. Only for him.

Tessa pressed her body to his everywhere she could—lips, chests, abdomen—and rocked against him. Beneath his denim, his cock was like an iron bar, riding the most sensitive spot between her legs and arousing her so head-spinningly fast she whimpered.

He tore his lips from hers, his breaths hard and harsh. "More. Don't you dare hold back."

"I can't, not from you."

"Then make the most of now; it's the last fucking time I'm going to touch you."

Her heart contracted, threatening to crumble, but she refused to waste this moment on regret and tears. He'd given her one last chance to meld with the man she loved and drink in his strength. She needed it. She was taking it.

Tessa nodded and clutched his shoulders before she bent to nuzzle his salty-musky neck. His skin was soft, velvet over steel. She dug her fingers into the shorn hair at his nape and dragged her lips up to his lobe with a nip. He shuddered. His breathing quickened. She couldn't resist more.

She planted her mouth along his jaw and kissed her way down, shoving his T-shirt aside to bite into the firm bulge of muscle between his shoulder and his neck. When he hissed, she laved the sting with a long lick, loving the slightly salty flavor of him on her taste buds. Then she dragged her tongue from the hollow between his collarbones upward, flattening over his Adam's apple and nipping at his chin before he lost patience, cursed, and fused their mouths together for another violent kiss of rough breaths and desperate grips.

Finally, he pulled back. They stared at one another for a long, panting moment. He swallowed hard. She nearly lost herself in the demanding blue of his dilated eyes.

Then he dropped his gaze to her breasts. She felt his visual touch like a caress, her nipples tightening painfully, even before he took them in his hands and lifted one to his mouth with a groan. He sucked hard. The contact was electric, his very touch pumping her with enough wattage to jolt her heart back to life. Her womb clenched in empty pleading.

Tessa arched toward him, tossing her head back and gasping out his name. His tongue swirled around one sensitive crest, then the other, before he sucked, laved, and pinched them in turn. Pleasure rose inside her, hot, hard, and fast, as he ate at her nipples with a merciless grip and a growl. She pressed restless, frenzied kisses to his temple, his forehead, clutching him against her body as if that could keep him with her forever.

He pulled free and tugged on her hair again. "Are you wet for me?"

"Yes."

"I'm going to fuck you."

"Please."

Zy broke away just enough to work at his fly. She attacked his T-shirt, jerking it up his torso and tearing it from his body, interrupting him only long enough to free his arms. As she tossed the black cotton across the room, he shoved his pants to his hips. She took his cock in hand, stroking his imposing length, worshipping his iron girth, and reveling when he hissed her name in agonized pleasure.

As if he couldn't wait another second, Zy lifted her and aligned her over his cock. The moment his crest settled against her slick opening, he gripped her hips and shoved her down to submerge every last inch of his shaft inside her while thrusting up with a snarling moan.

Tessa cried out. Her flesh stretched and stung and burned. It hurt, just like their love. But she absorbed it all, thrilled to be taken by him. To be one with him again.

"Fuck, baby…"

His growl tightened the need between her legs. But that was nothing compared to the jolt of sensation that coiled inside her when his palms crushed her hips and his fingers dug into her fleshy ass and he began plowing into her, one long, urgent stroke after another.

Tessa felt invaded and adored at once.

Zy sucked her nipple between his teeth and suctioned it against the roof of his mouth. She tugged on his hair and pressed his face against her chest, chanting his name, as arousal soared, churning between her legs.

"More. Zy… Please." Tessa closed her eyes and pulled him into her, straining to get as close as possible as she gave herself over to his fevered rhythm.

"Can't stop. Want you. So. Fucking. Bad."

"I want you, too. I never stopped."

He scoffed. "I never mattered to you."

The fact he thought that horrified Tessa. She grabbed his face. "You were everything to me."

She ached to tell him that she loved him and had for months, that she hadn't said the words before out of an abundance of caution. But he wouldn't believe her now. And if this was the last time he would ever touch her, it didn't matter. He'd already resolved to hate her, and she should let him go before his feelings for her turned toxic.

"You were my world. I bought you a ring." He tugged on her hair and forced her to look into his eyes. The anguish there nearly undid her. "I wanted to marry you."

Bittersweet joy made her eyes sting even as grief broke her heart. "I would have said yes."

He scowled. "Shut up and fuck. That's all we have left."

Then he said nothing, just worked like a maniac to fill her harder and faster. His muscled thighs spread and braced on the concrete floor as he forced his way deeper, to the limits of her body. His arms trembling and jaw clenched, he used every ounce of his strength to merge them together as if, even if he hated to admit it, he wanted to fuse their bodies together into one. Since protesting was pointless, she gave in, gripped him in every way possible, and bobbed on his cock until she was breathless.

A sheen spread across her back, cooling her skin in the damp subterranean air. It matched the humid slick now on Zy's muscled chest. Beads began to run down his temples. He ground his teeth, his neck straining, his tendons standing out, with every insistent shove inside her.

None of that slowed him down.

Bliss surged. Her breaths caught. Love she couldn't stop feeling spilled from her heart to the kisses she dropped onto his face and lips, onto her tongue as she delved into his mouth and tried without words to confess her feelings.

His breathing picked up pace. He groaned into her mouth as the head of his cock bulldozed over nerves deep inside her that had awakened again the moment he touched her. Tingles became a coiled ache as he worked her over with a ferocity that stole her breath. His lungs labored like a bellows when he lifted her writhing form as if she weighed nothing, then slammed her down again, his joyless smile all teeth as she dug her nails into his shoulders and cried out.

An unbearable pressure built behind her clit. Her breathing quickened. Her heartbeat roared in her ears.

The end was near.

He tugged on her hair again until she opened her eyes to him. "You're going to come for me."

Zy knew her so well he didn't have to ask. It was as if he owned her body, as if he commanded her heart, as if all he had to do to unravel her was touch her.

"Yes."

"I want to drag this out and make you suffer." He gritted his teeth. "But fuck..."

Tessa wouldn't have thought it possible, but Zy pounded into her with more fervor. His entire body tightened. His cock hardened. He closed his eyes, shutting himself off from her.

The severed connection panicked her. "Look at me."

His eyes zipped open. Their gazes joined. The connection yanked on her heart and sent her pleasure soaring even as she wanted to sob that the end had come.

"Zy!" she screamed as her ecstasy crested, her womb clenched hard. She splintered into so many pieces she knew no one but him would ever be able to put her back together.

I love you. I love you. I love you.

"Tessa...baby." The deep furrow between his brows bespoke the unrivaled pleasure and the horrible pain. "Fuck. *Fuck! Yessss!*"

As he filled her with everything he had in a hot jet of need, he crashed into her body over and over with a growl that drilled her ears and filled her head. Then they were panting together, Tessa limp against his chest. She fought to drag in enough air even as she tried to stave off inevitable tears. But it was useless. Drops were already rolling down her cheeks when he cried out one last time, then looked at her with wet, accusing eyes.

That one look told her she'd crushed him.

"Zy... I'm sorry. So sorry," she sobbed. "I never wanted to hurt you. I—"

"You destroyed us both, and now you have to live with it."

Of course he thought that. And with all the anger, betrayal, and lies between them, he would never trust her again.

Tessa didn't know what would happen next. All she knew was that she loved Zy more than she thought possible, that fate and criminals had put them on opposite sides of this mess...and there was no way out.

"I can't do this anymore," he said abruptly as he lifted her off his still-hard cock, then set her in a heap at his feet and stood.

She scrambled up from the concrete. "I didn't do it to hurt you. If you believe anything at all, believe that."

"You still betrayed me. You lied to me. You played me," he muttered as he buttoned his fly with shaking hands.

"I didn't. I never played you. I never would," she hurled, hot tears clawing at her eyes. "Everything I felt for you was real."

"Bullshit. Every time I fucked you, you were really fucking me."

"No." She shook her head. "You don't know what happened, what they did..."

"I do, and you're going to explain everything because everyone we work with deserves to know the truth. But your words don't mean anything to me anymore."

His harshness took her apart. She didn't want to cry in front of him, but she couldn't help herself. The pain of losing him—on top of everything else—was more than she could bear. It was all she could do not to fall to her knees.

But she refused. She didn't want to regret everything. All she could control was the way she reacted.

"Stop crying." His voice sounded strained, as if her pain caused his.

"I'm trying," she sobbed out.

"I can't take it. Jesus..." He grabbed her shoulders and tried to keep her at arm's length, but a handful of seconds later, he shook his head. "Fuck."

Then he pulled her closer, giving her his comfort. Tessa clung to him, grateful for his warmth. Until she realized it was nothing more than pity.

Gathering all her strength, she sniffled and wrenched free. "I'll be fine. What do you want to know?"

He swallowed, not quite meeting her gaze. "Did you have anything to do with Kimber's kidnapping? You better tell me the fucking truth. I will find out and—"

"No. Absolutely nothing. I swear." Even the idea horrified her. "I was as shocked as you were. I would never... She's my friend."

Zy just raised a brow at her.

"Whatever you believe, if you ever loved me at all, the *me* you know"—she slapped an earnest palm to her bare chest—"then believe I would never have hurt her. Ever."

"Right. You'd just hurt me. Got it."

Did he not understand? "What the fuck did you expect me to do?"

"Honestly? I expected you to love me someday. I expected you to be my goddamn wife, let me be a father to Hallie, and to let me give you more children so we could spend fifty fucking years together. But I never expected you to look me in the face and smile while you stabbed me in the back."

"If you think I gave the enemy secrets just to hurt you, then you don't understand me at all. You never loved me. And you're right; we don't have anything to say. Get Trees in here. I'll explain everything I've done. Maybe he won't throw my mistakes in my face."

Then, because it hurt too much to look at him, she scampered to her blanket, wrapped it around herself, and held back the tears tightening her throat.

She'd cried for the last time for Chase Garrett.

Zy raked a hand through his hair as he stared at Tessa's stiff back, wrapped protectively in the quilt again. She'd shut him out. No surprise. He'd said things designed to cut her as much as her lies had shredded him. Now, seeing that he'd hurt her, he wished he'd kept his fucking mouth shut.

Was it even possible he'd misread everything and fucked up? Or was that his stupid, hopeful heart trying to absolve her of guilt for his own sanity?

Probably. She'd sold him out; they both knew it. Still, she wasn't the sort to act as if she'd been wronged without a damn good reason, and now he had a nagging feeling he didn't know the whole story.

Zy wasn't sure what to believe anymore except that Tessa wasn't the only one he couldn't trust. He'd come to interrogate her…and ended up violating her instead. He shouldn't have, but he hadn't been able to control himself for even ten fucking minutes. Now, he seethed with anger. He didn't know what to do next, how to handle her, or how to make the goddamn pain ravaging his chest stop. He wanted to trust her…but didn't. He tried to hate her…but he couldn't.

He loved her too damn much.

And tonight had only underscored one indisputable fact: he was totally compromised. And no matter what she'd done, he belonged to Tessa.

Fuck, he needed to make some decisions.

As soon as he got some answers.

With a ragged breath, he stepped toward her. "You swear to God you had nothing to do with Kimber's abduction?"

She turned even more tense. "Nothing. I promise."

"Is that your final answer? Think carefully. Trees has your computer and your phone upstairs. He's taking both apart now. He'll know the truth in the next few minutes."

"I only passed on information after the fact. I didn't—" Her shaky voice stopped, and she still wouldn't face him. "Explanations don't matter to you, so yes, that's my final answer."

Maybe he wasn't the best barometer of her sincerity, but everything in his gut—the killer instincts Trees swore he possessed—told him to believe her.

"Okay. That's good." If she'd been honest, there would be no reason to call the police. No trouble with the law. No possibility she was going to prison.

But that left her in trouble with the Edgington-Muñoz brothers. She would be out of a job by sunrise. She would need money for herself, for her daughter. From somewhere. From someone.

He could be that person. He could marry her, keep her safe and in comfort. In exchange, she could spend the rest of her life owing him—and paying him back however his cock wanted. Zy would be a lying motherfucker if he said imagining all the ways he could extract repayment from her didn't make him both happy and hard.

But that wasn't why he refused to let her go now. He fucking loved her and that was never going to change.

"Let's go back a year, before you went on maternity leave. Who gave you the code for the spyware and remote access software you installed on your computer?"

That finally had her turning to him, her face so full of confusion he didn't think she could fake it. "I have no idea what you're talking about."

Maybe the enemy hadn't told her what the code did. "Before you left, did someone give you a USB drive or email you a program and tell you to install it? Did you double-click something from whoever you're sending information to?"

She gaped as if she couldn't find the right response, almost as if he was having a conversation she couldn't comprehend. "I wasn't passing information back then. No one gave me anything, and I certainly had no reason to betray the colonel."

Was she saying her enmity had something to do with Hunter, Logan, and Joaquin? If she didn't like their hardball management style, she wouldn't be the only one. But if she hadn't installed the code onto her computer, who had? Aspen didn't seem that smart, so it had to have been Tessa. Unwittingly, perhaps. Or maybe she didn't remember now. It had been over a year ago.

"What about last March, before we met?"

"What about it? I was still out."

He nodded. "Yeah, but were you contacted by someone who wanted information about our mission to Mexico?"

"No. I didn't speak to anyone about anything work related until I came back from maternity leave. And no one has ever asked me about our missions to take down Tierra Caliente."

"C'mon, Tessa. We found communications from your Gmail account to a secure email service we're pretty sure belongs to someone in the organization, communicating our mission plans to them."

Her eyes went wide with something between abject horror and shock. "I didn't do that. I didn't! I swear."

"Then how do you explain the emails?"

"I don't know. I can't, and I know that makes me sound guilty as hell, but I didn't do it."

She seemed so fucking earnest. Was it even possible she was telling the truth? Had someone maybe gotten ahold of her computer? Or was she tossing up another smoke screen?

Her frown deepened. "Zy, you've asked me about Kimber and the cartel. What is it you think I've done?"

"For nearly a year, EM Security Management has had a mole. The bosses have talked to me about it off and on for months. Process of elimination has led them to believe it's either Trees or you. On Monday, they gave me two weeks to figure it out or we're all fired."

She shook her head, eyes going wider with even more distress. "Oh, god. No. No! I didn't— I had no idea... Is that how Walker was taken and held prisoner?"

"Yeah. The cartel knew we were coming because someone inside our four walls told them."

Tessa shook her head. "I swear it wasn't me."

He cocked his head, wanting to believe her so badly…but logically, he didn't see how. "The only successful mission we had in Mexico was when we rescued Walker. You'd left town for your father's funeral."

She shrugged like she was at a loss. "It must be a coincidence."

That would make it an awfully big one. "Your Gmail account was also used to forward the floor plan of Valeria Montilla's St. Louis safe house, the one Walker sent to you with instructions to pass on to Trees, over to the cartel."

"I don't know how. But that wasn't me. Maybe someone who wants me to look guilty hacked my account? But I did nothing with that message except forward it to Trees via my company email, just like Walker asked."

Tessa had a point he hadn't considered sooner. If someone wanted to frame her, how hard would it be to hack a freebie email account and do their dirty work, leaving behind an easy-to-follow trail? As scenarios went, it wasn't impossible. But why would someone choose her to target?

He didn't know, but was that really the important question? He was grilling her about things the bosses would want to know. Fuck that. He had questions of his own.

Before he told her what he intended for their future, he was going to figure out exactly how much she had betrayed him…and how much he didn't dare trust her.

"Let's talk about something I *know* you did, and don't you dare tell me otherwise." He growled in her face. "You told someone else the 'plan' to rescue Kimber. The one I told you about less than eight fucking hours ago. You going to try to deny that?"

She flinched. "I didn't have a choice."

"Bullshit. You always have a goddamn choice." He couldn't stop his anger any more than he could resist the urge to touch her again, so he gripped her arm and yanked her closer. "Did you understand that, by passing the information on, you could be sending me to my death?"

"Yes." Tessa closed her eyes. Anguish twisted her face. "And it was killing me."

Zy didn't want to be moved by her tears. "But you still did it."

"Not because I wanted to, and only because you had a chance at surviving. And my choices were so unthinkable that—"

"What the hell are you talking about?"

"You don't… I thought you said you'd figured this out."

Now he was confused. "Are you saying someone's holding something over your head?"

Tears pooled in her red-rimmed eyes again and spilled onto cheeks already stained with silvery paths. He, with all his alpha-hole bravado, couldn't bring her to her knees when he'd tried to make her hurt like he was. But whatever upset her now had her sinking to the concrete with a thud, her face buried in her palms as sobs wracked her.

Oh, fuck. "Baby?"

A sudden pounding on the bunker's lid sent Zy whipping around. Talk about shitty timing…

"Zy!" Trees shouted, banging on the metal lid again.

"Damn it," he growled, then ascended the ladder enough to unlock the portal.

Trees ripped it open and clambered onto the rungs, then jumped into the bunker. He turned, looking somewhere between stunned and annoyed as he glanced between Tessa, barely clad in the quilt, and him, still sweating and half-dressed.

"I guess you didn't spend your time with Tessa finding out what the fuck has been going on." And Trees sounded more than a little pissed.

"Can it," Zy barked as he bent to cup her shoulders and help her to her feet.

Trees slanted an incredulous stare at Tessa. "Why haven't you told him? Why haven't you told anyone?"

She reared back. "You know?"

"Yeah, I do. And—"

"Know what?" Zy roared, looking back and forth between them. "Stop fucking talking circles around me and spill."

Neither spoke for a long moment.

Tessa bit her lip, like she was terrified to say a word, then she blinked away her tears, stifling another sob. "The man who accosted me in the parking lot on Tuesday?"

"Yeah, I remember. I'm still trying to identify him."

"That night, he abducted Hallie. When I woke up Wednesday morning, she was…g-gone."

Zy felt his stomach drop to his feet. He scrubbed a hand down his face as the implications of her words rammed him in the solar plexus. "Oh, god. Tessa…baby. You've been passing on information to save Hallie's life?"

"Exactly," Trees confirmed when Tessa was too broken to answer.

Fuck. She'd done what she thought necessary to keep her daughter alive. He'd had no idea…

But he still had a thousand questions.

If Tierra Caliente had Kimber, why did they need Hallie, too? And why hadn't Tessa come to him the minute she'd realized her baby was gone? Last but not least, if the girl had only been gone a handful of days, who had engaged in the espionage that had fucked EM Security for nearly a year?

Zy turned to Trees. "Tell me what you know."

"Not much since I didn't get to finish the forensic deep dive on her devices. Madison started texting me about ten minutes ago. She went to peek in on Hallie and found an empty crib. She panicked and—"

"You tried to make sure my baby would be looked after?" Tessa blinked up at him in shock.

"Of course. I wouldn't let anything happen to her." But he had. And he'd been so fucking absorbed in his own pain and betrayal that he hadn't even stopped to think her daughter might be in danger. Then he'd heaped blame, shame, and fury on top because why not win asshole-of-the-year honors?

Suddenly, so many things made sense. Why Tessa had refused to let him in the house when he'd come by Wednesday night. Why she'd lied Friday about her dinner with Cash's dad. Why she'd seemed suddenly lukewarm about moving in with him. Why she'd betrayed him.

"Tessa, I'm so fucking sorry." He lifted her face to his, crushed to see her red-rimmed eyes haunted with fear and grief. "Why didn't you tell me?"

"Because they threatened to kill Hallie if Tessa said a word to anyone," Trees supplied. "As soon as I talked Madison off a ledge, I started reading Tessa's Gmail account."

When he whipped Tessa's phone from his back pocket, opened it to the first video the abductor had sent of her baby girl, and pressed play, Zy watched in horror. "You've been dealing with this, completely on your own, since Wednesday?"

"I couldn't risk her by telling anyone." Her broken voice hurt like a stab in the chest.

"Oh, baby. If I'd known, I would have moved mountains to help you."

"They're watching me. They threatened… I didn't know the bosses think we have a mole, but I knew some things hadn't gone right. I'd overheard conversations that suggested information that shouldn't get out somehow was. I was too afraid of what would happen to my baby if I opened my mouth."

He drew her stiff body against him. He hated her choices…but he completely understood them. And now wasn't the time to assure her that, no matter what, he would always be there to help her, hold her, pick up the pieces, and love her. After the way he'd treated her tonight, why would she believe him?

Trees nudged the phone in Tessa's direction. "I know this is tough…but you've got a new message." Then the big guy turned to him with a grim expression, and Zy dreaded whatever his buddy planned to say next. "And I don't have to tell you what app they're using."

"Abuzz? Fuck." He sighed. "That cocksucker. I reamed him out once. He just never fucking listens."

"Who?" Tessa's hand shook as she took the phone and opened the app, looking terrified.

"Phillip Garrett," Trees helpfully supplied.

Usually Zy hated to mention this relationship, but if he'd berated Tessa for keeping secrets, he couldn't very well keep his own without being a fucking hypocrite.

"The billionaire who owns Abuzz?" She didn't seem to grasp why they were talking about him.

"Yeah." He sighed. "My dad."

Her eyes widened, then hope lit them. "Really? He could help us track down or pinpoint the location of the kidnapper keeping Hallie."

"The whole Tierra Caliente cartel has been using the app to communicate for months. I warned him once, and if it's still going on, they're paying him to look the other way. He won't help. Dear ol' Dad is more interested in making a buck than doing what's right."

Trees nodded. "It's one reason they don't get along."

"One of many."

Tessa looked at him as if she barely knew him anymore. "You grew up with a billionaire?"

He smiled tightly. "And the billion problems that go with that."

"And you never told me?"

It wasn't exactly the same thing…but she might have a point.

He cleared his throat and stepped into problem-solving mode. Nothing mattered until they had Hallie back. "The kidnapper sent a new message? What does he want now?"

She was almost afraid to find out.

Her fingers trembled as she opened the DM. The account was a shell with a generic screen name, no picture, and no personal location. Nothing to help him identify who it might belong to. But given the slew of messages this person had sent over the last few days, whoever had set up this account was by no means inactive.

Tessa scanned the screen, brows furrowing. "Something I don't know how to give them."

What? Zy wrapped an arm around her again, mentally cursing when she stiffened at his touch. "Let me see. Let me help you. You've been dealing with this by yourself for too long, and I can—"

"You can't," she screeched almost hysterically. "See for yourself."

When she shoved the phone into his hands, he scanned the demand —then wanted to throw the fucking phone across the room.

`Who is the mole leaking EM Security's information to outsiders? You have twenty-four hours to provide information and proof or Hallie will pay with her life.`

CHAPTER *Eleven*

Minutes later, Tessa wordlessly took Zy's hand as he helped her from the bunker, then wrapped the blanket around herself tighter as she entered Trees's place. She was relieved to finally have her oppressive secret out in the open. She was even more hopeful to have allies in saving her daughter. Incredibly grateful, too.

But in every other way, she felt crushed by the ruthless side of Zy he'd shown her tonight.

Would he ever forgive her?

As soon as they entered the house, the men went into crisis-management mode. Huddled in one of the kitchen chairs, she shivered in the morning chill until Zy pulled her onto his lap and against his big, furnace-warm body. In the past, she would have taken his comfort happily. She would have basked in his affection, feeling so safe in his arms.

Not anymore. The rage he'd directed at Tessa chilled her to the bone. She felt chastened and ashamed of what she'd done. She'd made every decision by following her motherly instinct to put her baby first. She'd hated that that meant sacrificing Zy. Obviously, he did, too. She didn't want him warming her now out of pity.

Tessa wriggled away from him. "Mind if I take a hot shower, Trees?"

"Feel free. Down the hall, first door on the left. Towels are in the cabinet."

"Thanks."

Zy stood. "Do you need—"

"Don't worry about me. I'll be fine." She didn't want him feeling obligated to do anything except help rescue Hallie.

Tessa escaped to the bathroom, closing the door with a shaky sigh as she fought tears. It was warm and quiet here. She could get herself together. If they were going to save Hallie, she needed to gather her fortitude. She might need it as a shield against Zy's wrath.

A few minutes later, she was still seeking calm in the shower when he knocked. "Baby? I asked Trees to meet Madison somewhere between here and town so you'll have a change of clothes. Anything in particular you want?"

She was grateful he'd thought of that. "Just something warm. Thank you."

"Sure."

Tessa heard his footsteps retreat, then the two men exchanged a few unintelligible words. A door shut. Quiet descended.

The rhythmic pelting of the shower spray on her back should have soothed Tessa. But reality kept its stranglehold on her. Another day had dawned without her baby. The man she'd given her heart to now thought of her as the enemy. The fact she'd only given away company secrets under the worst sort of duress didn't matter. Until now, Zy hadn't known why she'd done it, and when he'd discovered her deceit, he must have been shocked, baffled, and hurt. Horrified and angry, even. He obviously felt betrayed.

His viciousness when he'd lashed back had cut her to the quick.

Maybe she'd made a mistake in not telling him about Hallie's abduction sooner, but her misstep had been borne out of fear. He'd responded by funneling his anger into contempt and done his absolute best to punish her with his words and his body.

It's the last fucking time I'm going to touch you.

Shut up and fuck. That's all we have left.

I never expected you to look me in the face and smile while you stabbed me in the back.

You destroyed us both, and now you have to live with it.

Yes, he'd been less combative once he'd learned about Hallie's plight. But she got the message loud and clear.

They were done.

I expected you to love me someday. I expected you to be my goddamn wife, let me be a father to Hallie, and to let me give you more children so we could spend fifty fucking years together.

Tessa closed her eyes against more tears. She had been hoping for that, too. But she didn't see how he could ever forgive her. And they would probably never come back from all the damage they'd sustained tonight.

She turned off the hot spray and stepped out of the shower. Her body felt closer to human. The rest of her? A terrible jumble of anxiety, hurt, guilt, regret, and despair.

God, she'd give anything to hold her daughter again, kiss Hallie's downy head and hear her baby laugh. It nearly killed her to think she'd probably never do that again. After all, how could she possibly locate EM Security's mole in less than a day when he and the bosses—professionals—had already been searching for months without an answer? The obvious response terrified her.

She couldn't.

Tessa nearly broke down again.

Through sheer will, she forced herself to towel off as Zy knocked. "I have a clean blanket if you want to wrap up in something before Trees returns with your clothes."

Not her first choice, but if she didn't cover herself… Well, she'd experienced the outcome of that scenario less than an hour ago. Her battered heart might need a break from Zy, but her traitorous body craved the man. As good as she felt when he was inside her, he didn't want her anymore except sexually. She couldn't settle for just part of him, and it wasn't smart to fall more in love with him just as he was falling out.

With her towel wrapped securely in place, she opened the door a crack and took the blanket. "Thanks."

"Baby, we need to talk."

She draped the fresh quilt around her body, folded the towel, then stepped out of the bathroom, brushing past Zy and out of the too-narrow hallway, before she turned to him. "I don't want to argue again. Not that I can keep up with you…"

"I'm sorry."

For what, exactly? Setting a trap? Fucking her despite suspecting her of the worst? Tearing out her heart? She'd given him just cause to do all of that.

She turned her back on him. "No, I'm sorry for giving you a reason to hate me. How long before Trees returns?"

Because without clothes, when she stood this close to Zy, she felt entirely naked.

"Tessa, I can't hate you, baby. I know you're worried as hell and scared. I know you feel alone in this, but—"

"I *am* alone." She faced him. "That bastard took my baby, the only person who loves me unconditionally."

"Tessa, I love—"

"Stop. Just…don't." Why was he trying to make her feel better with lies? "You know, Cash is a lot of things. He's flaky and insincere. He's unreliable and selfish. He's lazy, he's dismissive, and he's got a regrettable amount of charm, which I fell for in a stupid, weak moment. But I was never under any illusions about who he really was. But you had me dazzled from the beginning. So helpful, caring, polite, and kind. Protective and concerned. You even weren't too macho to wear your heart on your sleeve. You've got a face made for seduction and a cock made for sin. The perfect man." She sighed, fighting more useless tears. "But you didn't even try to forgive me. You ended us without hesitation. Without even asking me why."

"Tessa, I…" Zy frowned like he wasn't sure how to respond. No, like he didn't know what to say to soothe her hurt. "It was my job to find out who was betraying EM. I assumed you were selling information for money. I was angry."

"And I hate that I let that bastard maneuver me into such a terrible position. I died a little inside every time I had to double-cross you. But what else could I do?"

"I didn't know what you had going on. You didn't trust me with your problem. Baby, I could have—"

"What? Mounted a rescue the enemy might have learned about before it went down? Then what? I'd be burying my baby. Zy, I'd never recover from that, and she deserves a life. Maybe someday you'll understand and forgive me for not handling things the way you would have. Maybe not." She shrugged. "But every time we spoke after Hallie was gone, I tried so hard not to hurt your feelings. And what did you do tonight the first chance you got?"

"Everything I could to hurt you." He dropped his head with a long sigh of regret, then slowly lifted his stare. "I fucked up. And I don't have anything to offer you except my apology, my help, and my love."

He didn't mean half of that, and she didn't want to latch on to false hope. "Right now, I only need your help."

He swallowed like her words were a bitter pill. "You have that, no questions asked. We'll talk about the rest once Hallie is safe."

That was for the best. They had less than twenty-four hours to solve a mystery no one had cracked in months. Somehow, they had to figure this out now. The yawning chasm of pain between them would have to wait.

"If the mole isn't Trees or me, who else can we look at?"

"Inside EM? No one. Why don't you sit at the table, baby? I don't know if Trees has any tea, but I can make you coffee and breakfast."

Tessa didn't think she could eat much now, and his offer felt too much like pity. "No, thanks."

"You've barely slept and you're burning your candle. I know from experience that if you don't fuel up, you'll crash."

She couldn't worry about herself now. She had a baby out there, in the clutches of strangers, who might as well have put a ticking time bomb in her innocent hands. But for some reason, he also had that stubborn, not-moving-an-inch look on his face. "Fine. Coffee and something small that takes less than two minutes to make."

He nodded as he settled a palm on the small of her back to usher her to the table. She drank in his touch. Ridiculous because it was merely a polite gesture, but she still savored it since this might be one of the last times he ever touched her.

"Cream? Sugar?" Zy asked.

"Lots of both. There's a reason I don't drink coffee."

Less than two minutes later, he brought her a steaming mug full of liquid that looked more creamy beige than black, along with a nutty, chewy protein bar that didn't change her less-than-favorable opinion of prepackaged cardboard meals. But the coffee warmed her insides, and the bar perked her up.

Zy brought his own to the table, his coffee steaming and black, and sat beside her with a sigh before he dug in. "Let's start at the top.

When Trees returns, he can help fill in any holes we may have missed. Maybe we'll have a working theory by then."

She nodded, reaching for her phone, too terrified to let her only link with her child go. "It started last January, you said?"

"The Friday before you left on maternity leave. What were you doing?"

It had been a year ago. She didn't remember exact details, but she recalled highlights. "The colonel and the guys got me a cake and tried to throw me a shower. Carlotta probably had a hand in it. Maybe Kimber, too. But neither was there. Um…Aspen was with us again that day. She'd been there off and on for almost a week. She wasn't very good at anything she did, but she tried."

"We noticed that, too." Zy frowned. "Who chose her to temporarily replace you and why?"

"The local temp agency didn't have anyone who fit the colonel's checklist and wasn't looking for a temp-to-perm arrangement. And he didn't want to mislead anyone. I was talking to Cash about it one night after work, not long before he walked out. He suggested Aspen. He said he'd met her at his last job, waiting tables at some steakhouse along Highway Ninety. She was their bookkeeper. But the steakhouse was closing down, and he said Aspen only needed temporary work because she had another job lined up come April. It seemed perfect."

"My initial impression of Aspen had me thinking she wasn't smart enough to plant any sort of spyware or remote-connect software on your computer, but maybe that was an act? Anyway, let's say she installed it. That was exactly a year ago. It remained there until she left. Trees removed it just before your return. That would explain how the details of the March mission—"

"The one where you were injured?"

"Yeah. That may be how that info leaked and the op went south."

"But how would Aspen know anyone from a cartel?"

Zy shrugged. "I don't know. Let's keep following this path and see if it leads us anywhere. She might be a mastermind, but she might also be just another pawn."

Tessa studied him, trying to focus purely on their discussion and the evidence, not the warmth of his body so close, not the way his stare lingered, not the memories of his hands on her…

As heat climbed her face, she looked away. "What happened next?"

"You came back, and every mission we undertook that wasn't related to Tierra Caliente went off perfectly—until August twentieth. By then, Aspen was long gone. So was the tracking software. No one new had joined the crew. There should have been no way for that information to leak out." Zy frowned and reached for her computer, the Gmail popping up immediately. "Who else had access to your laptop then, when Walker was first captured?"

Tessa tried to think it through. "Everyone in the office, like usual."

He scanned the emails. "At three forty-six a.m.? You take your computer home most of the time…"

Suddenly, the awful truth snapped into place. "Cash."

Zy sat up straighter. "He was living with you."

Tessa nodded. "And he had some weird job supposedly testing video games, of all things. He'd be up all night with his team or squad or whatever he called them. If he forgot to put his headphones on, I'd hear the gunfire whenever they stormed the bunker or took back the headquarters."

He frowned. "Testing video games?"

"That's what he said. It's the perfect job for him. He likes to keep vampire hours. He likes to pretend to be all big and bad. He likes to expend as little effort as possible for his paycheck. But I couldn't complain. He apparently got paid well and on time because he never missed making a payment to me."

"Tell me more about the video games."

"War-type games. Battlefields and soldiers and missions…"

"No, I mean, did you ever see the names of these games? Did he talk about when they'd be released?"

Why did it matter? "No. They all seemed the same to me, but they weren't new games from what he said. And I never understood why any game manufacturer would pay someone like Cash to test a product they had already released to the public."

"They wouldn't."

Of course not. It had been a lie. And now Tessa wished she'd questioned Cash more. "He was taking money from the cartel—to spy on EM with my computer?—and using his games to confuse me."

"That's my theory. And if he and Aspen knew each other…"

"Then…you're thinking it was a coordinated effort?"

"It's logical."

It was. It was also conjecture—not the proof Hallie's abductor wanted—but this was more theory than Zy'd had previously. They were getting somewhere. That gave her hope.

"And the September mission to Mexico went off perfectly because—"

"I left my computer locked up at the office. When I got the call about my dad from Kathleen, I ran out too quickly to even think of bringing it home, so it sat on my desk."

"I remember. Fast-forward over a month later, to the end of October. Cash was still with you. He could have forwarded the plans to Valeria's St. Louis house to the cartel via your Gmail. That was done in the middle of the night, too."

Tessa nodded. "He was on my sofa, playing video games, until you helped me kick him to the curb in mid-November."

"I remember. Prick."

She wasn't going to argue with Zy's assessment, but that didn't make him any better in her book. "What happened next?"

He paused, seeming to sort through his mental timeline. "The location of Valeria's Orlando safe house was discovered and ransacked five days ago."

"That was before…" Tessa forced herself to finish that sentence. Getting to the bottom of this would only help her baby. "Before Hallie was taken. I didn't tell anyone anything about Valeria's safe house. I didn't even know where Walker had moved her."

"Then that's a hole in our theory because Aspen wasn't in the office and Cash wasn't at your place. The tracking software was gone, and there should have been no way for Tierra Caliente to ambush Valeria's new location."

That worried Tessa. "We've got to be missing something. I can't just give Hallie's abductor a theory. He wants proof. If he doesn't get it, you know what will happen."

"Yeah," Zy said grimly as he reached for her hand to squeeze it. "Try not to panic. We'll figure this out. And maybe we're going about this wrong. I have an idea..." He whipped out his phone, tapped on the screen furiously, clearly sending someone a text.

"What? Are you thinking someone else can help us?"

Just then, Trees opened the front door, reading his cell. "No, buddy. I won't be much longer at all." Then he turned to her, holding out a familiar overnight bag. "Madison said this should get you by for a day or so."

Tessa rose, gripping the blanket and taking the sack by the handles. "Thank you. And please thank her for me."

As much as she'd wanted to dislike the woman Zy had once nailed, Tessa couldn't be petty. Madison was actually sweet.

"She said she was happy to do it."

"I'll go change." She headed to the bathroom.

"I'll catch Trees up on our theory," Zy called to her retreating back.

With a bob of her head, she shut the door behind her, then tore into the bag. A bra and a pair of underwear. Jeans, a sweatshirt, socks, tennis shoes, and pajamas—all the basics. Plus her hairbrush, a lip gloss, her favorite mascara, her moisturizer, and her birth control pills. Tessa didn't give a whit that Madison had obviously prowled through her vanity and closet. She had some much-needed items, which she put to good use.

Afterward, she emerged to find Zy and Trees sitting together, heads bent in low conversation. Zy talked. Trees nodded, then offered something seemingly contrarian, judging from Zy's scowl. After some more back-and-forth, they reached a decision that suited them both.

"What do you think, Trees?"

He glanced her way. "Um...you look fine."

She rolled her eyes. "That's nice, but no. Of our theory."

"I think you're right. And we came up with a plan that should work. You two will execute it perfectly."

"For the record, I object." Zy looked distinctly displeased. "Tessa shouldn't be mixed up in this."

"If this plan gets me any closer to Hallie, that's exactly where I need to be." Tessa hadn't imagined Zy would allow someone without his kind of experience near the danger, but she'd do her best to help the operation. "I'm glad you relented."

"Only because I've got to stay here." Trees pulled at the back of his neck. "I'm going to grab some shut-eye. It's damn near five a.m. You two should do the same. 'Night."

Trees disappeared into the master bedroom, leaving her alone with Zy. "Tell me the plan. I'd like some input. She's my daughter, and I don't want to risk her—"

"I would never risk Hallie, but we need more information. Let's start with Cash."

Her eyes widened. "But if he's in on this—"

"I have ways of making him talk…and making sure he can't talk to anyone else before we rescue Hallie." He grabbed her shoulders. "Whatever you think about me, at least believe I'm capable of that."

Tessa didn't argue. "I don't doubt you. What's next?"

"Sleep."

When she opened her mouth to protest that they didn't have time, Zy countered her softly. "Just a couple of hours, baby. I doubt Cash is awake at this hour. And if this goes down as fast as I think it's going to, we'll need some z's to stay alert and on our feet."

Tessa couldn't deny she was exhausted, but she doubted she'd sleep. Still, if Zy shutting his eyes would mean the difference between saving Hallie and not, she didn't want to regret that she hadn't let him rest. "All right."

"Come with me." He stood and held out his hand.

She frowned at it. "I don't think we should sleep together."

He grabbed her arm, hauling her to her feet. "I mean literally sleep, baby. Nothing else. You're distraught, and I'm exhausted."

"All right. I'll try." She grabbed her phone from the table and let him whisk her away.

He led her to a bedroom at the end of the hall, beside another closed door. Inside stood three walls of hard-core computer equipment —and one small futon.

"You can have the bed. I'll crash on the sofa." She backed out of the room.

"It's like a rock, and it's getting cold enough that Trees will let his guard dog into the house. He'll sleep on that sucker."

And, by process of elimination, there was nowhere else to lay her head. Tessa pressed her lips together. If this was the bed Trees had available, complaining wouldn't change it. At least Zy had somewhere to rest.

"Fine."

He didn't speak again, just started dropping his clothes without an ounce of self-consciousness. When his shirt came off, exposing every ripped, inked, golden inch of his torso, she bit her lip. And when she remembered just how good he always made her feel, an involuntary rush of heat flooded her.

Tessa chastised herself. Yes, he was hot and damn good in bed. No denying that. But they were over. She blamed herself more than him, but they'd both made mistakes. She'd kept secrets. He'd kept secrets. Wishing otherwise changed nothing. All that mattered now was that she had help in rescuing her baby. If there was anything left to salvage between her and Zy, it would have to wait until her daughter came back home…one way or the other.

"I'm going to change into my pajamas. Be right back."

"Sure. Whatever makes you comfortable."

She nodded, then wordlessly slipped into the bathroom down the hall and changed.

Back in the bedroom, Zy had flattened the futon and thrown a couple of big quilts over it. He lifted the corner to invite her in. Tessa dashed under the covers, hating to admit that she probably would have done nothing but shiver miserably on the sofa. Zy had no obligation to her, but he was graciously keeping her warm. She didn't expect to sleep, but at least she wouldn't have to add being half-frozen to her list of problems.

She settled onto the surprisingly comfortable mattress. Since he'd only found one king-size pillow for them to share, Tessa backed against him until her head found memory foam. Zy spooned her as if it was the most natural thing in the world. She stiffened, trying not to notice how instantly he warmed her or how perfectly they fit together.

He tightened his arm around her. "Baby, we can do this easy or hard. I know you have a lot on your mind. But as soon as we rescue Hallie, we're going to hash everything out. That's a promise. I'm not letting this go."

Of course he wasn't. She'd done something truly terrible in his eyes. And he hadn't hesitated to punish her with sex. Granted, amazing sex. Blow-the-top-of-her-head-off sex. But ultimately, he'd used his body as a weapon. And his aim had been perfect. She was almost afraid to ask what else he had in mind, but she'd deal with that later.

"Just stop talking and go to sleep."

"As soon as you drift off." Zy drew her closer against him—for warmth?—and relaxed.

It seemed impossible not to do the same. Despite everything these past few hours, she felt warm, safe, even cared for. Her body started to let go of its starch, and it was so hard not to feel how sleep deprived she was. Her lids got heavy. Her thoughts trailed off.

Next thing she knew, she was opening her eyes to sunshine seeping in between the shutters and Zy behind her, every bit of his body hard as steel, especially the ridge of his cock poking her ass. Morning wood…or actual desire? Not that it mattered. He could clearly want her, even if he hated her.

He lifted the arm he'd thrown around her waist, his hand having drifted breath-stealingly close to her inner thigh. "Sorry."

As he pulled away and slipped from the bed, Tessa wanted to breathe a sigh of relief that they had some space between them, but her wayward body wouldn't cooperate. She still wanted him with an undeniable ache. She probably always would. "What time is it?"

"A little after seven. I set an internal alarm for two hours."

He could do that? "What are we doing first?"

"Let's go find Cash."

"I don't actually know where he is. He went to rehab, and I haven't heard from him since. He should be out by now but…"

"Of course you haven't. Why would he do anything responsible?"

"I could try calling him."

Zy shook his head as he tossed on his clothes. "I don't want to tip our hand until we're in his personal space. It's the best way to control the situation."

"Then I don't know what to do."

"Let me see if Trees can pinpoint him."

Was the guy even awake? "How would he do that?"

"He has ways." Zy smiled. "Follow me."

She'd rather not talk to Trees while wearing her pajamas, and Zy was eyeing her formfitting tank and shorts with an unnervingly intent stare. "Let me get dressed."

She ducked out to the bathroom, tossed on her clothes, brushed her teeth, and secured her hair in a ponytail. She exited to find Zy waiting in the hall. Together they headed to the kitchen.

Trees stood at the coffeemaker, shirtless and huge, his hands braced on either side of the counter. Nothing odd about that, except the petite brunette standing in the cage of his arms, staring up at him with big hazel eyes.

"Talk to me, Laila..."

As in Valeria Montilla's sister?

Tessa glanced Zy's way. He didn't seem at all confused by the woman's identity or the fact she was here.

The brunette shook her head. "I have nothing to say."

"That's bullshit. What happened—"

"Will not happen again." She ducked under his arm to escape—then stopped short, eyes wide, when she caught sight of her and Zy. She wore an enormous T-shirt that clearly belonged to Trees...and nothing else.

"Hello."

Tessa's heart went out to the obviously rattled woman. "Hi, Laila. I'm Tessa."

Immediately, the woman relaxed. Because she wasn't the only woman anymore in a drowning pool of testosterone? They shook hands, and Laila excused herself, all but running past her for the hallway—and her clothes.

Trees turned, and his sweatpants didn't hide how hard he was.

Zy glared at his friend. "What did you do?"

"Zip it."

"Dude..."

"Don't 'dude' me. You're no saint, either." He tossed his head in her direction before pinning Zy with a pissed-off glare.

Zy looked like he really wanted to argue, but he didn't. "Fine. I need your help locating Tessa's ex. We have to find him ASAP."

Trees stared down the hallway where Laila had run, then reluctantly nodded. "Yeah. Let me get dressed."

Once he'd gone, Zy shook his head and made for the coffeepot.

Tessa followed. "What's going on with them?"

"You can't tell? I'm pretty sure they had sex."

She'd guessed that. "Just now?"

"No, but recently. In the past few days."

"Then why is she terrified of him? He seems like a gentle giant."

"He is...mostly. But Trees has a side no one wants to see. Trust me. Not that he's shown Laila. But she was held hostage for nearly seven years at Emilo Montilla's compound...and they weren't at all kind. I wonder if she senses Trees's dark side."

People in the drug trade weren't known for being good people. Just imagining what Laila had endured made her shudder. "If she's afraid, how did they ever..."

"Get close enough to fuck? I don't know. And now he's trying to downshift, but—"

"It's not working."

"That's what worries me."

Trees appeared a few moments later, hair wrangled into place and a fresh T-shirt covering his torso, which hung past his hips and covered his erection.

As if she had a sixth sense, Laila reentered the kitchen, now wearing a pink bare-midriff tank with the thinnest spaghetti straps and a tiny pair of denim shorts.

The big man groaned. "This outfit again?"

Tessa stared. If Laila wanted to be left alone, did she understand that baiting the big, hungry bear wasn't a good idea?

"Nothing else is clean." She crossed her arms over her chest self-consciously.

"I can bring you some things," Tessa offered.

"No, thank you."

"I already tried," Zy said.

"She's too proud," Trees groused.

Laila speared him with a glare. "I refuse to owe anyone anything."

"Can't you consider some different clothes a favor?"

"I did not ask for this favor."

"I'm asking you as a favor to me. Does that help?"

"No."

Trees stepped back with a shake of his head. "You are a stubborn, stubborn woman."

She put her hands on her hips. "I have had to be."

This argument was going nowhere, and Tessa didn't have time for it. "How about as a favor to me, Laila? My baby is missing, time is running out, and Trees can help me. But he needs to concentrate."

The woman turned, and her face softened. "I am so sorry. Of course. I will help in any way I can."

They were about the same size, though she was a bit taller than Laila. Tessa didn't care what she was wearing as long as they helped Hallie, but swapping clothes would take time, too, and she didn't have any other garments in the overnight bag. "Would you be willing to put on a coat or wrap yourself in a blanket for a bit?"

Thankfully, Laila agreed, and Trees found her a sweatshirt that fit her like a sack and hung nearly to her knees. As soon as it swallowed her curves, he heaved a huge sigh and got immediately down to business while Laila made coffee and eggs for everyone.

While Trees tapped away at his laptop, Zy's phone buzzed. "Why is One-Mile calling me on a Saturday morning?"

Trees snorted as he peered at his screen. "I hope all hell isn't breaking loose."

Zy nodded and answered. Tessa held her breath. If something in the business needed immediate attention, would they put Hallie on hold? She had barely twenty hours left to prove their theory and save her baby.

"Hey, Walker..."

Tessa listened to Zy's side of the call with half an ear—until it became clear that he had info about the guy who had threatened her in the parking lot. The man who had taken Hallie.

Her heart leapt, and she shoved herself into Zy's face all but talking into his phone for him. "Does he know this guy's name? Or where to find him?"

Zy wrapped an arm around her and pulled her to his side, away from the device. "Keep going." He paused. "Yeah. And?" Another pause. Then Zy made a motion to Trees for a pen. Tessa saw one on the far side of the table and lunged for it. He scribbled a name. JOHNSON. "Thanks. I'll run with it."

"The man from the parking lot is named Johnson?" she rushed to ask as he ended the call.

"Apparently. One-Mile has been researching. He showed the guy's picture around a police precinct this morning and got a hit. Someone arrested him a few months back for petty possession and remembered the belligerent SOB."

Tessa had no idea how that man had gotten mixed up in a cartel based in Mexico, but now wasn't the time for that question. "That's great! If we can find him…he has Hallie and—"

"Not necessarily. But if not, we'll see what light he can shed as soon as I hunt him down. It would be fucking helpful if we had a first name."

"Got a picture?" Trees asked. "Along with a last name, I might be able to get something while the scan to find your ex-douche is working in the background, Tessa."

"Scan?"

"Yeah, it just takes a while to ping all the cell towers in the state."

She was shocked. "You can do that?"

He grinned. "Well, I'm not supposed to, but…"

Trees was devious. Right.

"How did you get Cash's number?"

He held up her phone. "I was doing a deep dive on it, so it wasn't hard to find."

Of course.

"Look at Tuesday afternoon's security footage of the EM parking lot," Zy insisted.

"On it." With a few clicks, a new screen popped up. Video scrolled in rapid time across his monitor, then froze on the face burned into her memory.

"That's him," she gasped. "The man who stopped me in the parking lot. The man who calls when he has a demand in exchange for Hallie's safety."

"And if she's not with him, he probably knows where she is," Zy said.

Trees nodded. "Now if I just had a fucking first name… He never mentioned it?"

Laila strolled over with steaming plates and glanced at the screen. Her eyes widened, and she gaped, nearly dropping all the food. "Hector."

Tessa helped her set the plates on the table before they fell from her trembling hands. "Mr. Johnson's first name?"

She froze, looking terrified. "I do not know his last name, but in Mexico, in Emilo's compound, he was called Hector. And he was greatly feared and fiercely loyal to my brother-in-law. He is not a man you want to cross."

Trees scowled and rose to take Laila in his grasp. "Did he hurt you?"

"Many times."

The big man's face turned mean. "Then he'll find out I'm not a man to cross, either. I'll make him pay."

Laila looked at him like he was crazy. "You cannot."

"Can't," he corrected. "And oh, yes. I absolutely can."

He pulled up some search engine Tessa had never seen, one far more powerful and secretive than Google. He typed in Hector Johnson's name. Moments later, an address popped up. "Gotcha, you son of a bitch."

Tessa scanned it, wondering what part of town that was when a ding resounded in the background.

Trees flipped to that window, read a few lines of some long string of code, and smiled. "Gotcha, too. Should have known you assholes would stick together."

Tessa's heart caught. "What do you mean?"

"Hector and your ex? They're at the same address."

"Fuck," Zy cursed. "They're in this together."

"Cash helped take his own daughter from me?" Tessa couldn't comprehend it. Cash had never wanted Hallie before.

Of course, he only wanted their baby when she could be used to help him get ahead.

"Yeah. Let's go save Hallie and get the bastard."

"Both of them," Trees growled. "I'm coming with you."

Zy scowled and sent a head bob in Laila's direction. "You're supposed to stay here."

"One-Mile can come protect her for a few hours."

"You'd leave her with that crazy SOB?"

"He didn't hurt her in Mexico when he had the chance."

"True. Then I'll call him and tell him to get his ass out here."

"Tell him to hurry," Tessa insisted. She needed her baby almost more than she needed to breathe. And she was desperate to get over to this address before the men moved—and took her daughter with them. "We need him."

Zy nodded. "You got it."

Chapter Twelve

Zy glanced at Tessa, who looked tense and withdrawn in the passenger's seat of her little sedan. As they sped to Hector Johnson's place, he wished like hell they could clear the air now. But she wasn't in a good headspace, and he was at least half to blame for that.

Why hadn't he shut the fuck up in the bunker when he'd had the chance?

The only good thing he'd done this morning was drop Hunter a text to tell him Tessa's double cross wasn't at all responsible for Kimber's abduction and that he needed a few more hours. After that, he'd explain everything.

"Baby, I know you're worried." Zy was, too…but he didn't want to say that. Even if he didn't share Hallie's blood, that was his little girl, damn it. He knew how ruthless cartels could be. He'd seen the human carnage they left behind firsthand. It fucking killed him to think of that baby in their clutches. "But—"

"How can I not be?"

"If Hallie isn't at this location, we'll keep looking. We'll find her. I'm not giving up."

"We're running out of time." Her voice broke with worry—and broke his heart. "Hector Johnson supposedly lives at this address, but what if he's not there now? Or at all anymore?"

"Cash is. We can physically place him there. He knows something, guaranteed. It's not a coincidence he's at the very address of the man who accosted you in the parking lot. And if that's a dead end, we'll find Aspen. She's somehow involved. She can't be too hard to track down. And she didn't come across as too tough…or too smart. Believe me, I'll do everything in my power to bring Hallie back."

And if he was too late, he would cause every motherfucker who'd had a hand in hurting their baby girl ten times the pain before he ended each one. Not only to rain Hallie's vengeance down on them but to prove to Tessa that he would always be here for her. She didn't believe that now, and if he could take back the hurt he'd caused her in the last few hours, he would. But regrets were like assholes; everyone had one. Lamenting what he couldn't change was pointless. He could only try to move forward from here.

Tessa gathered her knees to her chest, eyes filling with tears. "I'm scared."

She didn't mean for her own safety. The fact she'd insisted on coming along, even though Trees had decided to join this operation, told Zy she wasn't giving a thought about her well-being. She only cared about Hallie's. Zy was both awed and terrified of the lengths she'd go to in order to save her daughter.

He took Tessa's hand in his. "We have a plan. Hector and Cash have no idea we're coming. We'll surprise them. If Hallie is there, I will die before I let anything happen to her."

"Zy..."

She thought he was full of BS and hyperbole, but he straight-up meant that. "I'm going to make it better, whatever I have to do."

Tessa bit at her lip but didn't respond.

Maybe she believed him. Maybe she didn't. That wasn't where he needed to focus now. Time to get his head in this op or there would be casualties...and not just among the enemy.

Zy glanced in the rearview mirror. Trees followed in his Hummer. When they neared Johnson's neighborhood, Trees would take the lead since neither Hector nor Cash had ever seen him, cruise by the house, then report back on activity. From there, they'd finish formulating their plan of attack.

"Seriously," Zy told Tessa. "Trees isn't going to let this go, either."

He had a vendetta to settle, and he was out for blood.

"Trees definitely seems ready to avenge Laila's honor or whatever."

Zy shrugged like he couldn't explain it, but he could. If Trees had stepped over the corporate line to take the skittish woman to bed—Zy still wasn't sure how that had happened—then Trees was feeling something more than passing lust. The man lived by a rigid code of right and wrong. He would only violate that for a cause he considered more important than rule and more sacred than order.

"He's a protector." That was a safe answer.

"You all are. But for him this situation is more."

Tessa was definitely observant. "Yeah."

"When did Laila get here? How?"

Zy hadn't been honest with her about the retrieval mission when it had gone down, but he had no reason not to explain now. He gave her the short version. If they made it through this confrontation, he'd answer whatever questions she had. If not…it wouldn't matter.

"She's had a really rough life."

Since they'd only make her worry about Hallie more, he spared Tessa the grittier details about the terrible things Emilo Montilla's men had done to Laila as a child. "Hopefully, now that she's free of that asshole, she can finally take her first steps to a new future."

Tessa scowled. "You don't have to sugarcoat this for me. I know Laila isn't home free. No one tangled up in this mess is because it's obvious there are different sides warring for the power vacuum left after his death."

Clearly, she was also smart. "You're right. We think Emilo's father, Geraldo Montilla—a legendary drug lord for decades—has Kimber and that he wants revenge on the colonel and the bosses for helping Valeria escape a couple years back. Kane has been asking the woman questions about all the players, but nothing so far. After Laila's revelations today, I'm thinking maybe a group of Emilo's old compadres have banded together to seize control of the territory Emilo used to rule."

"Then why kidnap Hallie? I don't know anything useful."

"But you work for the people who have all the information."

"Not for much longer." Then she shook her head like she couldn't think about that reality now. "But until they fire me, the kidnapper thinks I'm able to learn our next moves. And do what with the information?"

Zy frowned. Trees had never gotten to finish the deep dive on her computer or phone. "I don't know. What did they ask you?"

Tessa filled him in, and that reinforced most of his suspicions—except one thing didn't make sense. "Hmm. I don't know why Hallie's abductor would want to know how Valeria and Laila's safe houses kept getting hit. If he or his buddies wanted her location, why didn't they just ask for that? It's what Emilo himself tortured One-Mile to learn. He wanted that one piece of information every fucking time he had someone spy on us."

"But Hector Johnson only wants to know *how* it's happening." She frowned. "I didn't ask why he wanted the information."

Of course not. That hadn't been her concern or her role. They wouldn't have told her anyway. "Trying to assess our vulnerabilities, see if they could further exploit them? That's my only guess right now."

"This might be a war for a drug cartel, but it's seemingly an information battle."

"Yeah." Later, Zy would see if Valeria could shed any light. It might also be time to move her elsewhere, rotate out her bodyguard. He'd left the new guy with a lot of responsibility, and Kane had handled it well, but the arrangement was starting to make Zy uneasy.

"How much longer?" She fidgeted.

"We're about to turn in. Recognize this part of town?"

"No. I've never come this way."

Zy hadn't, either, and he didn't like flying in blind. Normally, he and Trees would case the place, get schematics, do hours and hours of legwork, and make sure they knew what to expect. *Then* they would go in, using whatever tactic made the most sense. This shit was a wing and a prayer, and he hoped like hell for a miracle, that Hallie would come out of this unscathed.

Just then, his phone buzzed. He scooped up the device. "Talk to me, buddy."

"Why don't you cruise past the entrance? This is a mobile home park. A small one apparently. I'll call you as soon as I've gone in and scoped around. Hang tight."

"You got it." He overshot the entrance to the neighborhood full of newish mobile homes and modest cars, then pulled under a big tree to wait, rolling down the window and pretending to look at his phone as if he was lost.

As they waited, Zy thought Tessa would crawl out of her skin with each moment that ticked by. He wasn't faring much better, gut churning with nerves. He knew how much this meant to her because it meant everything to him, too. He couldn't tell Tessa that she might never see Hallie again or that her daughter might already be dead. He didn't want her crossing that bridge unless Hector Johnson pushed her off of it. But he couldn't pretend the likelihood that this ended in heart-break wasn't high.

"Baby..." He took her hands. "About what happened...what I did in the bunker, I'm sorry."

"We don't have to talk about that now."

"At least let me apologize."

"For telling me how you felt? You can't change that, and we both know I'm not without blame. I don't expect you to forgive and forget anything."

"I love you."

Tessa frowned. "Why would you say that now? You didn't love me in the bunker."

"Yeah, I did. I was mad that I still loved you even when you knew you were sending me to my death."

She bowed her head, looking near tears. "That ripped me up inside. It was the most painful thing I've ever done."

Because she loved him, too? Now wasn't the time to ask, and he was too afraid of the answer. "Just like it ripped me up inside to hurt you."

She gave him a little nod. An acknowledgment? Then she looked out her window. "What's taking so long?"

Trees had been gone less than two minutes. But Zy got it; she wasn't ready for this conversation. She was rightfully focused on her daughter's safety. "He'll call in a minute."

Sure enough, a handful of seconds later, his phone buzzed again. "Whatcha got?"

"Nothing visible from the street. House looks closed up, like maybe they're still asleep. Wait. I spoke too soon. The front blinds just opened. I see..." Trees paused. "Someone's in there. There's too much glare to a make out a face or an outline, but the place isn't empty. And there's a truck in the carport. I'm running the plate now."

"What's he saying?" Tessa demanded.

Zy held up a finger. "I don't want to know how you're doing that, buddy."

"You don't; it's illegal as fuck. Gimme a second. And what do you know? The truck is registered to Hector Johnson."

Good news. "So he's probably there. How do you want to play this?"

Normally, Zy wouldn't question the approach. He'd go in one side, Trees in the other, and flank them so there was no escape. But they didn't know this place, and he had Tessa with him.

"I cased the perimeter of the mobile home park. It's enclosed inside a brick wall. The only way in or out is the entrance you're parked next to."

So Johnson couldn't sneak out the back. "Excellent. That simplifies the situation."

"Yep. I should knock on the door. Neither Cash nor Hector knows me. I'll draw their attention while you slip around the back."

"With Tessa?"

Trees sighed. "I don't suppose she'd wait in the car."

Zy glanced over at her. She looked ready to hurtle herself out of the seat, run to the house, and tear her daughter from the place with her own two hands.

"Negative."

"Fuck."

"Yep." Now that the moment was almost here, he was afraid for Tessa. But they'd already argued about this. She refused to budge. Nothing was more important to her than Hallie. She'd proven that.

"Then put her behind you. Sneak in the back. See if you can find the baby while I keep whoever's inside occupied."

"You going to read their meter? Or sell them insurance?"

"I'll wing it. Something will come to me."

It always did. "You got everything you need?"

"Yep."

"Where should I roll in?"

"The mobile home park is shaped like an *O* so it's a curved street on each side, bisected by a long, straight drag in the middle. At the entrance, take the fork to the right. Go all the way to the end of the street and park just before you round the bend at the back. From there, walk toward the left side of the park. Johnson is along that wall, in the middle. You should be able to pass yourselves off as a couple taking a morning walk."

"Roger that."

After a few more details, they hung up. Zy started the car and followed Trees's directions, stopping between two mobile homes, one with a well-tended fence and planters out front. The other looked like a cookie-cutter shithole.

He double-checked that his Glock was loaded and the blade he'd strapped just under the hem of his pants was secure. Then he stepped from Tessa's sedan, watching as she did the same, and locked it before he walked to the front of the vehicle. "Let's go."

"What are we doing?"

"Take my hand and walk with me. I'll explain."

She did, clasping him tightly. Tension pinged off of her.

"Baby, for this to work, you have to trust me."

"There's no one I trust more with my safety."

Just not with her heart. Zy cursed under his breath. It wasn't as if he could blame her for that. If he'd pulled his head out of his ass long enough to listen to his gut and kept reminding himself that she would never betray anyone without good reason, maybe he wouldn't be worried that even if he rescued Hallie and won this battle…he might still lose the war—and Tessa.

Their shoes made almost no sound in the soft earth as they walked toward the address. When they rounded the corner, Trees knocked on the front door. It took a while, but someone finally answered. A man with a glower.

Hector Johnson.

Trees turned on his most congenial smile. Since the guy's lips rarely curved up unless he got to kill someone who really deserved it, he figured Johnson was as good as dead.

As Trees kept talking—Zy overheard something about extermination services and had to chuckle—he kept his head down and urged Tessa to do the same as they walked past the open door, then veered around the side of the house once they were beyond Johnson's line of sight.

"Follow me. Stay. Behind. Me. Is that clear?"

Tessa frowned. Yeah, she probably didn't like him ordering her around.

"I get it. You hate me right now, but if you want Hallie back alive, you need to listen to me."

"I don't hate you. I just want my daughter back. Until I have her again..."

Nothing else mattered.

"I know, baby." He squeezed her hand.

They rounded the mobile home and found a sliding glass door covered by dark curtains. He released Tessa's hand and tested it. Locked.

Time to get creative.

He withdrew the blade from under his pant leg.

"What are you doing?" she hissed.

"Prying it open."

She looked shocked. "Are you kidding?"

Clearly, Tessa didn't grasp that, in the larger scheme of his job, this was one of the easiest things he did. "No. The door is mounted from the outside. If it had been mounted from the inside, it would be a bitch, if not impossible. But this? Piece of cake. All I have to do is wedge this knife between the door frame and the door itself about six inches from the corner. Here, diagonal from the latch, at the bottom. Now, I'll just pry upward and tilt the door." He demonstrated and heard a faint click, then smiled. "That's all it takes to release the latch from the bracket. And we're in."

Zy tested the door, gratified when it slowly slid open. He stepped inside, motioning her to wait on the back steps. He peeked in and scanned the living room. He saw no one except Johnson, who stood at the open front door, his back to him and Tessa, while Trees gave him an off-the-cuff sales pitch.

"Your neighbors, Jessica and Bill, across the way"—Trees gestured vaguely as he cut his eyes over at Zy with a barely perceptible nod—"you know them, right?"

So as far as Trees was concerned, there was no reason the op wasn't a go.

"No," Johnson grumbled.

"Oh, you should meet them. Nice folks. They started our service last month. Jessica swears nothing else worked before, but their roach problem is practically nil already, and she's seeing far fewer spiders."

"We don't have an insect problem."

"You do. You haven't been here long, right?"

"A couple weeks."

"Then trust me, you do."

Zy had to smile at Trees's schtick, then he turned to motion Tessa inside, nudging her behind a big leather sofa on the right side of the room, where she wouldn't be visible if Johnson turned.

As Trees droned on about the gross habits and unsanitary conditions of roaches—displaying a surprising knowledge of insects—Zy began easing the sliding door shut. It squeaked. He winced and dove behind the sofa, eyes on their target.

"What the hell was that?" Johnson tried to turn around.

Trees grabbed the man's arm, signaling to Hector that this part of the pitch was urgent. "See? Insects. We're half swamp out here, so they're big. If you weren't used to that where you came from… Um, where was that?"

"I didn't say and I'm not interested."

"I don't want you to regret passing up this deal. Have you asked the missus if she's seen any insects? I'll bet she has."

"No."

Zy held his breath as he leaned back and slid the door down the rest of the track without incident before joining Tessa behind the sofa again.

They were safe…at least for now.

"You know how women are these days. Trying to be all independent. My momma would shriek to high heavens every time she came across a spider in her kitchen, but my sisters—I've got three of them—they just whip off one of their ridiculous high heels and whap the spider out of existence. Your wife like that?"

"No. I said I'm not interested."

See anyone else? he mouthed to Tessa.

She pointed to her ear, then to the right.

On the far side of the unit, he saw a sliver of the kitchen. Dishes clanked and a radio pumped out deejay chatter. A vertical half wall dividing the living room and kitchen cut off his sight lines, but clearly someone was in there. Cash?

He would have to get closer for a better vantage point, and that meant moving.

"Listen, Mister…" Trees frowned. "What did you say your name was?"

"I didn't."

Still squatting behind the sofa, Zy edged along its back, holding up a hand to stay Tessa.

She looked breathless and afraid, eyes wide. But she nodded, unmoving, watching nervously as he crept across an open space, then ducked behind a matching black recliner.

Suddenly, Johnson whipped his head around, as if he'd caught movement in his peripheral vision. Zy pressed himself against the back of the chair and held his breath.

"Anyway"—Trees went on—"I'm up for a promotion. If I can sign three people up this morning, that would look real good to my boss. He knows I'm a go-getter, but he wants to see more hustle, so if you could help a guy out…"

Zy tuned out Trees's spiel. He'd heard enough to know they were running out of time. He had to get the lay of the land and figure out how many people were in the house and where everyone was located so they could game plan accordingly.

From his current position, he had a better view of the kitchen, but half of it still wasn't visible. He saw an open cabinet door and heard footsteps, but that didn't tell him who he was dealing with.

Still crouching, he eased into a shadowy corner of the living room, pressing his back to the wall, then craning his head around the remaining obstructions.

Bingo! A woman with long brownish hair swishing down her back and wearing tight black yoga pants emptied the dishwasher, skinny ass swaying to some R and B tune. But that wasn't the only thing that interested him. In the very edge of his view, he caught sight of what looked like the leg of a high chair.

Damn it, another six inches and he'd be able to tell if his eyes were correct and if Hallie was in there.

Suddenly, he heard a baby peal unhappily. His heart leapt in his throat.

"If you want more Cheerios, you're going to have to wait, kid."

So they did have a baby here. He glanced back at Tessa. Her eyes had gone wide. Hope lit them. She trembled, looking anxious, sleep-deprived, and near tears. And he wished like hell he could stop everything, comfort her, and lend her the strength to finish this op. Instead, he had to press a finger to his mouth for quiet.

She flattened her lips together like she was holding in a sob and nodded.

The brunette in the kitchen cracked a little window over the sink and lit up a cigarette, blowing the smoke through the screen. The baby Zy couldn't see let out another howl.

"Shut that damn baby up," Johnson yelled at the brunette across the house, suddenly very tense. "Look, I said I'm not interested. I don't care about your promotion, your sisters, your knowledge of roaches, or your bullshit. Go the fuck away."

When he tried to slam the door in Trees's face, the big guy pressed a palm against the sturdy fiberglass and shoved. The foot he'd already wedged onto the threshold kept Johnson from shutting him out. "C'mon, you don't mean that." Trees laid on the aw-shucks charm. "We're getting to be friends here, I think. We're having a moment."

They weren't, and Zy knew Trees's cover couldn't last much longer. He had to make a move, figure out if the baby in the kitchen really was Hallie and whether he should neutralize the woman while Trees dealt with Johnson on his own terms or abort altogether. But where the fuck was Cash?

"What the hell? The noise level around here..." A man emerged from the other side of the house in a pair of boxer shorts, pulling a T-shirt over his head.

Speak of the devil.

Tessa's eyes widened in panic. Once Cash yanked the dirty tee down and finished rubbing at his bleary eyes, he would be looking right at her.

Fuck.

Zy risked poking his head above the chair to catch Trees's attention and zipped a finger across his neck.

His friend bobbed his head, then sent his widest smile so far to Cash. "You a friend of the family, sir? You've got to tell your pal here that he's missing an opportunity if he doesn't sign up for Pest-Away's platinum-level service."

"I don't fucking want it," Johnson exploded. "Get your foot out of my house."

Trees went on as if he hadn't spoken. "Here. Let me get you my card and…"

As he pretended to dig in his pocket, Cash lost interest in the sales pitch and turned toward the kitchen. He zeroed instantly on her and stopped in his tracks. "Tessa! What the hell are you doing here? Get the fuck out."

When she didn't move, Cash dashed straight for her and grabbed her arm viciously, tugging her toward the back door.

Zy saw red and pulled his Glock.

On the other side of the room, Trees turned back to Johnson—not with a business card but the business end of a Sig. He planted it right in the man's forehead. "Hands up. Just like that. Now step back, motherfucker. Nice and slow."

Hector held up his hands and retreated to the middle of the living room. As Trees kicked the door shut behind him and turned to lock it, never taking his stare off Johnson, Zy stepped out from the corner and aimed his barrel right at her ex's forehead. "Let her go."

"Fuck you." Cash glowered.

"You don't want to give me a reason. I'm already half inclined to blow your worthless brains out."

Wisely, Cash stopped running his mouth and released her.

"Now get your hands up."

Grinding his teeth together, Cash did, muttering curses.

"Tessa, in my back pocket are a couple of pairs of cuffs. Get them out. You"—he told Cash while she did as he'd asked—"get to the middle of the room, by your buddy, Johnson. No. You can walk with your hands in the air."

Trees nudged Hector back toward Cash until they bumped into one another. "Stand back to back. Now!"

Zy motioned Tessa over and took the cuffs from her. Then he handed her his gun. "If either one of them moves, aim in their general direction. This sucker is loaded with hollow points, so whoever you hit, we're talking maximum damage."

"O-okay." She nodded, looking so brave and resolute as she took the weapon and aimed it directly at the two men.

"You're doing great," he told her in a low murmur. "I'm going to cuff them."

Then they could start asking questions. And find out if the baby in the next room was Hallie.

"No, you're not," said the woman from the kitchen. "Let them go."

Zy turned and his heart fell to his knees.

Aspen stood in the opening between the kitchen and the living room with Hallie braced on one bony hip—and a Glock pointed against her defenseless little head.

Chapter Thirteen

Tessa did her best to hold the gun steady and not fall apart, but the sight of that woman threatening to end her daughter with one squeeze of the trigger nearly had her unraveling. Anxiety sat like a thousand-pound boulder, crushing her chest. "Hallie, baby girl…"

Her daughter caught sight of her and started wriggling and screaming, kicking and bowing her back.

"Stop it!" Aspen hissed, shaking Hallie.

If Tessa had any idea how to fire a gun without hitting her daughter, she would have turned it on Aspen.

But she didn't.

Zy came to her rescue, holding up his hands and slowly approaching the other woman. "All right. Let's not be hasty. You don't need the kid. You need information, right?"

Aspen scowled suspiciously. "Yeah."

"Okay, let's make a trade." Zy turned to Trees, who still had Johnson dead in his sights.

What the heck was Zy up to? Tessa didn't know, but she needed to do her part.

She jerked the gun back to Cash. She might not be able to fire on Aspen and risk hitting Hallie, but if it would save her baby she had no compunction about blowing her ex away. He'd obviously had a hand in kidnapping their daughter and he deserved whatever he got.

"What do you mean?" Aspen asked.

"Give Tessa her daughter. A baby doesn't belong in this situation, and I know you don't want to kill her."

The woman screwed up her face like he was an idiot. "I don't give a shit. She's just a whining, crying kid."

Tessa seethed. Her daughter was wonderful and precious. Totally innocent and sweet. It took everything inside her not to stomp over there and beat the shit out of the bitch.

"But Hallie can't give you information. I can. I know everything you want to know. Every. Single. Thing. So let the baby go, and I'll come with you in her place."

Tessa gasped. "Zy!"

Did he know that meant certain death? Was he really willing to do that, sacrifice himself to save Hallie?

"It's okay, baby." He put a reassuring hand over his heart.

Then she understood. He wasn't trading his life for Hallie's simply for her baby's sake. He was doing this for her.

To atone? To prove his love? She didn't understand, but she loved him. Still. No matter how difficult things had become between them. No matter how dark and ugly his interrogation in the bunker had turned. She'd said less-than- words to him in anger, too. But he was the kind of man who'd helped her when she'd been overwhelmed with a newborn. He was the kind of father who had calmed Hallie by letting the baby sleep on his chest. He was the kind of lover who had touched her with his heart as much as his hands the very first time he'd taken her to bed.

And now he was willing to risk his very life to keep her daughter alive.

Against her will, tears welled in her eyes. She couldn't tell him not to trade himself for Hallie, but it was breaking her heart. "Zy…"

"Shh."

"Why should I take that deal?" Aspen grabbed a squirming Hallie viciously and poked the side of her little head with the barrel again, her finger wrapped dangerously around the trigger.

Tessa's heart lodged in her throat and she died a thousand deaths, worrying that Aspen's finger would slip and end her baby girl forever. It was killing her that her daughter was mere feet away, but it might as well have been half a world.

"Because it's a good deal," Zy pointed out. "You let Tessa, her daughter, and my associate"—he gestured to Trees—"go. I'll stay here with you three and tell you all the secrets EM has been keeping."

"Or your two cohorts could simply put down their weapons and I can take all of you prisoner while I extract the information I need from you. If not, I'll off the baby. You've got ten seconds to decide."

"Hey!" Cash piped up. "This isn't what we talked about."

"Shut the fuck up, pip-squeak," Hector growled at him. "You don't get a say in this."

Aspen turned to Tessa then. "Drop the gun. Or the kid loses her head."

She froze. If she let go of the weapon, she had no illusions. These people didn't play by any rules, so Hallie would still die. So would she, Trees, and Zy. But how could she help this situation if she refused?

Tessa turned to Zy with a questioning stare.

"Don't do it, baby."

"You better fucking do it," Aspen shouted. "Five seconds."

The situation was escalating too quickly. Tessa didn't know how to stop it and she couldn't think. A thousand thoughts raced through her head. She swallowed. Shoot Johnson? But what if that startled Aspen and she pulled the trigger? She'd already been over the reasons she couldn't shoot Aspen, and she didn't see how shooting Cash did any good now except to make everything more tense. They talked to him like he was expendable.

"Now, bitch," Aspen insisted. "Five, four, three…"

"No!" Cash stomped toward the woman. "That's my daughter, too."

"*Now* you care? You were the one who suggested kidnapping her."

He stopped in front of Aspen, who gripped a screeching Hallie. "But you promised we'd give her back as soon as you got the information you wanted."

"Are you living in dreamland?" Aspen rolled her eyes. "How the fuck did you think we were going to give back a baby?"

"Y-you *planned* to kill her all along?"

Aspen sighed and glared over at Johnson. "Bringing this idiot in was your worst idea ever."

"Hey, it got us information," he shot back.

Aspen scoffed. "What a pain in the ass…"

Cash lunged in her face. "Answer me. You planned to kill my daughter?"

"Duh."

"The hell you are."

Cash reached for Hallie and tried to yank her from Aspen's grip. The woman didn't let go. A tug-of-war ensued. Hallie shrieked even louder. Tessa's heart pounded. Anxiety for her baby gnawed her stomach.

When Hector tried to break free to help Aspen, Trees cocked his weapon and stepped in his path. "Give me a reason, motherfucker. I would love to pull the trigger."

Finally, Cash's superior strength won out and he pried the little girl from Aspen's grip, holding her tight against his chest. "Don't you dare touch her again."

"Or you'll do what?" Aspen pointed her gun at him. "Never mind. I'll just bury you both together."

Tessa gasped. She had to get her daughter out of the middle of this—somehow. But she wasn't trained for these situations…

Cash's eyes widened, and he finally grasped that Aspen was both totally serious and fully prepared to kill both him and Hallie. Suddenly, he swung the baby onto her feet and started backing away.

"Hallie!" Tessa held out a hand to her daughter, thrilled when she came running, her little arms flailing and her chubby legs chugging. She looked dirty and dehydrated, but she seemed otherwise unharmed. Tears threatened to spill as her baby took the last few steps to reach her.

Then a deafening gunshot filled the air. With her eyes locked on Hallie, she feared she'd see her baby stumble and fall any second, hit and bleeding and dying. But Hallie threw herself against her leg and wrapped her arms around her tightly. It was the sweetest touch she'd ever felt.

Tessa ached to lift Hallie up and hug her tight, but she still held a weapon. The situation was too tense. So she tucked her daughter behind her, then looked up to see Cash on the floor. He lay ominously still, a hole in the middle of his forehead, blood slowly seeping all over the beige carpet.

Cold fear chilled her. These people were every bit as dangerous as she feared.

"Tessa!" Zy held up his hands.

She tossed the gun in his direction. He caught it as she scooped

Hallie into her arms, clutching her daughter's head to her chest and holding her securely while she tried to keep herself together. It felt so good to finally hold her baby…but she didn't know how they'd get out of here alive.

"Go!" he demanded.

But when she reached for the back door, Aspen raised her gun. "You're not going anywhere, bitch!"

Tessa's heart clanged. She turned her body to shield Hallie, hoping it would be enough to spare her baby girl as the next resounding shot echoed in the room.

But the bullet didn't rip through her.

Instead, Zy fired on Aspen, who gasped and recoiled, then looked down at the blood spreading across her pale T-shirt from a wound in her left shoulder.

"Honey!" Hector lurched for her.

"Stop!" Trees growled at him.

The man didn't listen, racing across the room. Before he could tackle Zy, Trees shot Johnson in the back, sending him sprawling face-first into the carpet inches from Cash's lifeless body.

Aspen gasped, crying out in shock and pain as she fell to her knees. But when she lifted her head again, she had murder in her eyes. And she trained her gun on Tessa once more, glaring at Trees. "Drop it or she's as good as dead."

"Stop," Zy snapped, gun pointed her way as he barreled down on her.

"Always did think you were an asshole," she choked out.

Suddenly, Johnson grabbed Zy's ankle mid-stride and held him back. Blood dripped from his mouth. Hate poured from his eyes.

Zy nearly stumbled as he tried to pull free from the other man's grip. Hector refused to let go.

Aspen stood, trembling. Her gun wavered erratically. "Stop. Or I'll kill all of you."

"No, you won't." Trees sounded annoyed.

"Before I kill you, I'll shoot your balls off for shooting my husband."

"Your husband is a rapist," Trees growled. "Let go, Johnson."

He didn't.

"Fuck you," the dying man growled.

"No. Fuck you." Trees took aim. "This is for Laila."

Then he fired again, straight into the back of Johnson's head. The hand around Zy's ankle went limp.

Aspen cried out, launching herself straight for Trees, hobbling and bleeding all over the rug, as she aimed in his direction.

"Final warning!" Zy stepped into her path, weapon pointed.

With a snarl, she came at him and pulled her trigger without even blinking. The shot sounded deafening in the small room. Zy jerked.

Tessa watched in horror as he hissed and gripped his arm. Blood seeped between his fingers as he raised his gun again and fired at Aspen.

He missed.

She laughed. Tessa's heart thudded and chugged as the other woman scowled in concentration and fired again. Zy feinted, making the shot go wide, but he stumbled, tripping over Johnson's body.

His temple struck the coffee table with a sickening thud.

He stopped moving.

"Zy!" Tessa panicked. She couldn't hurdle the sofa and get his gun to shoot Aspen while protecting Hallie. But she didn't dare wait to see what Trees would do. She had to do *something* besides standing here and watching him die. Even if he didn't choose a life with her, she wanted him to live and be happy.

"Now I've got you," the woman cackled at his prone form. "You pricks took from me. I'll take from you. An eye for an eye."

No. Not now. Not like this. Not with so much vengeance and hate.

Tessa grabbed the first thing she could use as a weapon—a big candle in a heavy glass jar—and threw it with all her might at Aspen's head.

The woman didn't see it coming until it was too late. It struck her in the cheek. She grunted in pain and swore before glaring daggers her way. "You should not have done that. I'm going to kill you and your brat. And I'm going to enjoy it."

"Because it's easy, and you can feel like you did something big and bad?" Trees mocked, aiming at her head. "You'll have to kill me first."

"Oh, you're getting yours. After this bitch." Aspen wrapped her finger around the trigger again, her face alive with evil glee.

Before she could fire, Zy, despite being bleary-eyed and shaky, managed to raise his head and pull the trigger.

This time, he didn't miss.

Aspen stumbled back and blinked down at him in shock. "Damn it..."

Then she crumpled to the ground face-first, a gushing hole at her back.

Dead.

Zy fell limply to the carpet again, gun falling from his lax hand.

Had he saved her with his final breath? No, that couldn't be it. She had to help him.

Tessa's calm broke. She trembled uncontrollably as she hugged Hallie, pressing grateful kisses to her head, even as she ran to Zy, tears falling. *Please be okay. Please be okay.*

She dropped to her knees in front of him and applied pressure to the wound in his arm. It looked like a flesh wound. It shouldn't be fatal, so why wasn't he moving? "Zy?"

Nothing.

Vaguely, she was aware of Trees barking into the phone for an ambulance.

She pressed around his neck to feel for a pulse. It seemed fast and faint. He was bleeding—a lot. He wasn't conscious.

Oh, god... Had he saved her and Hallie's lives at the cost of his own?

Hours later, evening shadows began to slant through her windows as Tessa sat in her recliner, cradling her sleeping daughter. Hallie was now clean, well fed, and had been thoroughly checked out by the pediatrician on call in the emergency room. She was fine. She was safe. And Tessa was profoundly grateful.

But she hadn't had much word about Zy since they'd taken him away, and it was killing her.

"I think that takes care of everything, Ms. Lawrence," Matt said, screwdriver in one hand as he settled his signature cowboy hat back on his head with the other.

"Tessa," she corrected automatically. "And thank you. You didn't have to install a new security system for me."

In fact, she really had no idea why he had. He'd asked her out yesterday—it seemed like weeks ago—and she had turned him down. Nicely, but…it had still been a refusal. Now he was helping her?

"Yes, ma'am, I did. Walker told me what happened to your daughter. We can't have that again."

"How much do I owe you?" Tessa didn't have the money for this indulgence, but she needed it for her peace of mind. Too bad her rent was almost due and she was about a hundred bucks short, but she'd figure it out later. Maybe one of the bosses would cut her a final check when they fired her. Then she'd have to start looking for another job immediately, maybe two. And she'd have to find less expensive daycare…somewhere.

But none of those problems were more important than Zy.

"Nothing," he assured. "It's all been taken care of."

Why? And by whom? "I don't understand."

He just smiled. "I see you're cuddling with your little one. I'm glad she's okay. Mind if I help myself to some water?"

"Of course not. I would get it for you, but…" She glanced down at Hallie. She slept like a child who hadn't rested well in days. Probably because she hadn't.

Minutes after the last shot had been fired at the mobile home they'd infiltrated, the police and ambulances had come. The coroner, too. The next while had been a blur—a ride in an ambulance, questions from doctors, questions from the police, the long wait through Hallie's thorough exam before she'd finally received the assurances she'd been holding her breath for. All amazing news that had brought her to tears.

But when she'd asked the hospital staff for word about Zy's condition, they had refused to tell her anything. She understood privacy, but she loved this man. Trees, whom he'd apparently designated as an authorized contact on his medical forms, had come around to say that they were still running tests, but he didn't know much about Zy's condition. That had been six hours ago.

What was going on? Zy was going to make it, right?

"It's no problem. Can I get you anything while I'm up?"

"I'm fine, thanks." Honestly, she didn't feel like eating or drinking right now. Her stomach was in knots. "And thanks for bringing my car back to me."

Moments later, Matt meandered into her living room again and sat in the opposite chair, watching her snuggle her daughter. "My pleasure. I heard you were strong this morning."

Not strong enough since Zy was still lying in a hospital. Why wasn't anyone telling her anything? "If you're all done, you don't have to stay."

"Actually, ma'am, I do. I need to show you how to use the security system before I go."

"Oh, right." With a nod, she clasped Hallie tighter and stood, lifting her daughter against her chest. "I'll set her in her crib."

It made Tessa nervous to take her eyes off her baby, and it would probably be a long while before she'd feel comfortable letting Hallie sleep alone all night in her room, but for a few minutes and with the new alarm system in place, it would be okay. Logically, she knew that.

As soon as she set Hallie down, the baby sprawled out and relaxed into the mattress, her breathing deep and even. With a smile Tessa drew a blanket over her, gave her an affectionate rub, then turned to Matt, who watched from the hall.

She followed him to the new alarm panel near the front door. Her landlord might be mad that she'd cosmetically altered the look of the unit without his permission, but he could kiss her ass.

Within minutes, Matt had shown her how to arm and disarm the system, how to bypass zones, how to enable and disable the motion detectors, and even how to change the time on the pad.

"It looks amazing. I don't know how to thank you."

"You don't have to. I can install these in my sleep. This is one of the best," he assured her. "It's sensitive, hard to tamper with, and I've put extra precautions around your daughter's windows. No one is getting in there again."

That helped set Tessa at ease.

She wandered back to the living room, puzzled when Matt followed. "Well, since that's done, I'll be okay alone now."

Because she'd really love a good shower. And a good cry. She'd tried earlier to nap with Hallie, but every time she closed her eyes, she heard gunshots, saw Zy fall, felt his blood on her fingers…

Matt smiled. "And I'd love to show you that I can take a hint and get out of your hair, but Logan called me earlier. I'm not supposed to leave until someone else who can watch over you shows up to spell me."

Who would that be? Trees had presumably returned home to guard Laila. One-Mile had followed Matt to her place on a motorcycle and left it parked at her curb before hopping into a little car with his fiancée and driving off. Kane was still protecting Valeria. Zy was still in the hospital. And the bosses were certainly still devoting all their attention to recovering Kimber.

"Oh, my gosh… In all the chaos these last few days, I haven't had a chance to ask. Do you have any update on Kimber? Any progress finding her?"

Matt turned somber. "Not enough."

Tessa hated to hear that. Deke must be going out of his mind. Their children must be missing their mother, and they had a baby even younger than Hallie… It broke Tessa's heart to think of them, not to mention what Kimber herself must be enduring. "I'm praying something breaks in the case soon."

"You and me both, ma'am."

The silence that fell was awkward. Sure, he'd more or less propositioned her—politely—but she didn't feel uncomfortable around him. In fact, she got the feeling he was full of something she wished she could soothe. Sadness? Loneliness? She couldn't quite put her finger on it.

"So…you're from Wyoming?"

A little smile pulled at his lips. "Yes, but you don't have to be polite and pretend you care after the day you've had."

"I do care." He seemed genuinely nice. "I know you said no yesterday, but I really do know this amazing girl…"

He tried to hide his grimace. "Maybe another time."

That was his pride talking, and she wished it wouldn't. He really was a hunk, and Madison would be incredibly good to him if he was even half as good to her as she suspected he could be. "If you change your mind..."

Thankfully, they were both spared continuing the conversation by a knock on the door.

Tessa leapt up from her seat. "I'll get it."

Matt stood, too, and pulled out his keys. "And I'll be going. I left my cell number near the primary keypad, in case you have any questions. You ladies have a good evening."

He pulled open the door before she could and blocked whoever stood on the other side of the portal. An instinctively protective gesture, she supposed.

Then Matt relaxed, tipped his hat to her, and walked out. "Evening."

"Bye."

She saw the colonel filling her doorway now. He looked haggard, like he hadn't shaved or combed his hair in days. His clothes looked limp. He was at the end of his rope.

Tessa's heart went out to him, and she rushed over, wrapping her arms around him. "Oh, my goodness. I'm so sorry for everything you're going through. I wish I could do something helpful. But I'd be happy to get you some food or coffee or..."

He hugged her tightly, and she could tell this strong man, this pillar of his family, needed to draw strength from her.

"No, but thank you," he said, his voice tight and gruff.

"Come in." Honestly, she didn't know why he'd stopped by, but if he needed to talk or needed an ear, she would always be here.

"I just came by to check on you, maybe sit with you a spell. That okay?" He tried to give her a smile, but she could tell the effort was costing him. "The fact you got Hallie back today gives me hope. I need that."

Of course he did. Her heart broke for him. "Don't lose faith. I'd half given up ever getting my daughter back, but I'm glad I kept trying."

But in the back of her head, Tessa knew that if the people who held

Kimber were as horrible as the ones who had taken Hallie, her friend's safety was in serious jeopardy. She didn't want to say that out loud, though. Especially now. But the colonel had been around the block more than a few times. He knew.

"How is your daughter?"

"Sleeping." She led the older man back to Hallie's bedroom, as much because she needed to set eyes on her daughter and reassure herself that her baby was okay as she did to give the colonel a sliver of hope.

"She looks good."

"After a checkup, a good bath, and a couple of meals, she seems almost like her old self." The baby had been a little cranky and anxious at first, but she was young. She would have no memory of this incident, thank goodness.

Her former boss nodded. "I'm glad to hear it."

Together, they backed out of Hallie's room and returned to the sofa. "Are you okay, sir?"

He let out a long sigh. "I won't bullshit you. I don't know. I'm trying to put on a brave face for my boys and my wife, for my son-in-law and my grandkids. But I'm losing hope of recovering Kimber. It's wearing on me."

"What do they want?"

"Valeria."

"And you can't give her up." If EM Security Management surrendered their client, it would ruin their reputation forever. They would have to shutter their business, give up their livelihoods, and find a whole new arena to thrive in.

"No. Even if we did, we don't negotiate with drug dealers and terrorists. They're notorious for not keeping their end of a bargain."

She understood that now. After Aspen had made it clear she'd always intended to kill Hallie, no matter how cooperative Tessa had been, she realized she should have gone straight to people who could help her after her daughter's abduction, not tried to handle everything on her own.

"I know."

"But maybe we have a ray of hope on the horizon. Laila has agreed to act as bait to try to draw Kimber's kidnappers out, so we're working on that. Hopefully soon."

Tessa knew exactly how Trees would feel about that, and she felt sorry for the guy. He wasn't going to be able to protect or keep her from this, no matter how hard he tried.

"Yeah. By the way, I'm sorry for mixing you up with Aspen when I went on maternity leave."

He gave her a reassuring smile. "You didn't know."

"But I knew Cash was a jerk. I should have at least considered the fact that any contact of his wasn't a good idea." And now they were both gone. The brief conversation she'd had with Craig had been heartbreaking. The man was not only crushed to lose his son but stunned to learn he'd helped drug dealers kidnap his own daughter *and* spied for Emilo Montilla before his demise—all for money. Despicable, but she was sorry for Craig that Cash's greed had led to his death.

"You always want to believe the best about people. Don't lose that quality."

Tessa wanted to assure him she wouldn't because it seemed important to him, but after the last week, she didn't know if she'd ever look at the world the same again.

Instead, she just patted his hand. "Have you received communications with pictures of Kimber or anything that gives you hope?"

He nodded. "We've received some proof of life. I just don't know how much longer they'll have patience. We're going on day six. I thought we'd be a lot further in tracking down these assholes. But so far? We don't have a lot to go on. They're good."

"I'm sorry."

He gave her a tight smile just as his phone buzzed. Then he stood. "That's my cue. I need to get back to the safe house and sleep. It's been over twenty-four hours."

That poor man... While the colonel was sharp, fit, and robust, he wasn't young anymore. And he looked like his daughter's absence was killing him.

Tessa stood and dropped a hand on his forearm. "It was so kind of you to drop by to see me. I'm sorry for the way everything happened.

I'm under no illusions that your family will consider me a friend after what's happened, but if I can do anything—"

A knock interrupted, and to her surprise, Hunter poked his head in the door. "We got this, Dad. Go on. Grab a hot meal and a bed."

The colonel patted her arm. "I'll let you know. Take care of that baby."

Tears stung her eyes. It had been an emotional day—and it wasn't getting any easier. Her heart ached for him. She knew what it was to worry about a daughter's safety. And with every silent hour that passed, she wondered if the news about Zy from the hospital would be agonizing.

"I will," she assured. "Goodbye."

The older man nodded as he let himself out. Hunter filed in, followed by Logan and Joaquin. None of them looked as if they were faring any better than their father, but dread filled Tessa's belly. If they were all here on a Sunday in the middle of their own personal crisis, they weren't here for a glass of sweet tea.

They were here to fire her.

Tessa didn't blame them. They'd trusted her, and she had betrayed them. With good reason…but that probably didn't matter to them.

"Come in." She motioned them into the living room.

"Sorry to barge in, but this can't wait."

Tension gripped her, squeezing her chest. "Of course not. But before you say anything, let me first tell you I'm sorry. I feel horrible for what I've done. I-I didn't expect to be the target of anything. I didn't know what to do. And I didn't handle it well. I understand that you have to do what you need to. I have no hard feelings, and I wish you all the absolute best."

Hunter frowned. Logan swore.

Joaquin just shook his head. "We're not firing you."

Had she heard that right? "Y-you're not?"

With a tired sigh, Hunter leaned in. "None of us ever imagined this war that's embroiled our family would come to your doorstep. You didn't ask for your daughter to be abducted. You probably never even imagined it was possible."

"No, but—"

"Should you have told us?" Logan prompted. "Yeah. But we understand why you didn't. Trees explained. I hate to make you promise that you will next time, because I hope like hell there isn't one…"

"I don't think I could handle it, to be honest."

"I wouldn't expect you to. And if you don't think you can come back to work and feel safe after what you've endured, I understand, but I want you to know we're going to send you help."

"Help?"

Joaquin jumped in with a nod. "The alarm system is your first line of defense. It should feel safer whenever you find yourself here alone."

"Y'all arranged that?"

"Yeah." Hunter grimaced. "Trees reamed us out. We promised we'd do what we could to protect you in the future."

Bless Trees. She hadn't known that having so many protective men as friends would feel like having brothers. It warmed her. "Thank you. I know you have your own problems to worry about, so the fact you took care of me, despite everything I've done…"

Tessa couldn't help it. Tears fell. After the day she'd had and the fact she'd barely slept in thirty-six hours, they never seemed far away.

"Hey." Logan took her hand and squeezed. "Don't cry. I know it's been a long, horrible day. But Hallie is safe, you're safe, and—"

"What about Zy?"

"What about him?" Hunter asked, but he looked at her as if he already knew the answer.

She was in love with him. But that wasn't what he wanted to hear.

"I'm worried. I haven't heard anything in hours. I didn't think his injuries were life-threatening, but no one will tell me anything. My head is spinning with all kinds of possibilities. Did he have internal bleeding they couldn't stop? Did he hit his head so hard that his brain swelled? Is it a concussion or a coma…or something worse?" Tessa tried, but she couldn't carry on without breaking down.

If something had happened to Zy, one of the most joyous moments—rescuing Hallie—would be tainted by one of the most crushing, tragic events ever. She didn't know how she'd ever recover. Honestly, she didn't think she would. She would probably spend her life alone, rather than settle for less than the love she'd shared with him. She certainly couldn't stay in Louisiana. She'd probably pack Hallie up, return to Tennessee, and start over. Or hell, maybe move out west, get away from all her memories—good and bad—of the past.

Logan cocked his head at her. "Are you in love with Zy?"

Tessa hesitated. They didn't want to know simply because they were curious. These three never did anything without a reason, and less than a week ago, she had been strictly forbidden from touching Zy at all. Maybe they'd rewritten the contracts, never imagining that one of their operatives would ever fall in love with the office receptionist… but they'd probably frown on that.

"I don't know what you want from me," she demurred.

"I want the truth, baby," said a deep, heartbreakingly familiar voice.

Tessa gasped and looked up. Zy stood in her front door, bandaged and battered but otherwise gorgeous, healthy, and alive. She could hardly believe her eyes.

She stood, her heart thundering. "You're here?"

He nodded and sauntered in. "Yeah. And I'm waiting for you to answer that question. Do you love me?"

Chapter *Fourteen*

After a teeth-gnashing game of twenty million questions with the local police at the hospital and a seemingly never-ending battery of tests demanded by the ER doctor over nine fucking hours, Zy finally pushed his way out of the hospital and marched for the taxi he'd called. He was free—and he had an agenda.

It sucked big, hairy balls that the colonel had been forced to pause his efforts to save his daughter to make the local cops see reason, but finally after some coaxing and good-ol'-boying, the police had let Zy go. Apparently, his statement had matched Trees's and Tessa's almost to the last detail. The preliminary forensics, too.

His buddy had hung with him for a while, but Zy hadn't needed hand-holding. Since he couldn't do it himself, he'd needed Trees to do him a few favors, including bending the bosses' ears about everything Tessa had suffered, then checking on her.

Zy wished like hell she had come to see him. But she had Hallie to worry about, of course. After all she'd been through, she needed time with her daughter. But he'd hoped she would poke her head in to check on him. The fact that she hadn't sent disquiet sludging through him.

Had he hurt her so much in the bunker that she was ready to turn her back on him—on them—for good?

If she was, he had no one to blame but himself.

One thing he couldn't put off another second? Calling his father. People were fucking dying because Phillip Garrett was a greedy asshat. He was going to put a stop to that shit once and for all.

Once he settled into the backseat of the taxi that smelled like old leather and butt sweat and ensured the plexiglass divider would give him some privacy, he pressed the contact on his phone he hated most to tap and waited.

His father picked up quickly, but his greeting sounded almost reluctant. "Chase?"

"Yeah."

"This is a surprise. We don't talk for months, then twice in the same week?"

"I thought you might want to know that your son—granted, the throwaway and not your beloved Ivy-League carbon copy—almost died this morning in a shitty mobile home in BFE, Louisiana, because you're so fucking unscrupulous that you're willing to take cash or favors or whatever the fuck you're getting from drug dealers so they can use Abuzz to communicate. I'm sorry for you that they failed to off me, but it was close. Better luck next time."

"Wha… I don't… Someone almost killed you? This morning?"

"What the fuck do you think I do for a living? I take down bad guys. Every. Single. Day. And you've been enabling them for a buck. But not anymore. I'm stopping it. They also kidnapped my girlfriend's daughter. They put a gun to her head. She's an infant. And it was all coordinated on your fucking app. Won't that look good in the press, especially after you banned people so publicly for merely talking about government overreach because you thought they *might* get violent? These people *are* violent—and they're criminals. Give me a fucking break."

"Son…"

The emotional appeal in that one word pissed him off. "Don't call me that."

"But you are."

"In blood only. If you don't want me to go to the press with everything I have—accounts, screenshots, secret groups that clearly violate your terms of service—you ban every one of those motherfuckers and you live up to your promise of a safe platform. If you don't, in twenty-four hours everything I have will be public. And since it resulted in three deaths just this morning, not to mention another man's torture a few months back and a woman's abduction—who's still missing, by the way—won't that make you look good?"

"Don't do that. Please. If I ban them and cut off their communication, they'll come after me. They'll kill me."

Zy shook his head. His father probably hadn't seen self-risk in taking money from criminals. Now he was about to get a harsh lesson in reality, and Zy couldn't feel sorry for him at all. "If you didn't understand who you were getting into bed with, that's your stupidity. But you can afford to hire bodyguards. My job is to protect people who can't, and I'm going to fucking do it. Twenty-four hours or I talk."

"Wait!" his father jumped in, sounding desperate. "I'll give you ten million dollars to keep this quiet. Cash. In a Swiss bank account. Today."

That was a lot of fucking money, but money didn't motivate Zy. He had enough to be happy and take care of Tessa—if she would have him. He didn't need more. "Ten million isn't enough to buy my principles."

"Fifteen."

"You can't buy me off. No amount of money will ever be enough to make me look the other way."

"You don't know what that much money could do for you..."

Yeah, he did. Make a shitload of problems he didn't need. "Pass. I'm serious. You have twenty-four hours."

"What if I sold the company?"

And divested himself of his fiefdom and Theo's inheritance? "Elaborate."

"Your mother and I are going public with the divorce day after tomorrow. It would be the logical time to announce that I'm selling the business, too."

So he could supposedly give her half. The fact he hadn't needed to do that in order to settle with his mother said he had another plan... but the public didn't know that.

"Who would you sell it to?" Because they might be as bad or worse.

"I had an offer last week from an investment group. I haven't actually replied yet. I wasn't interested at the time, but I wanted to see how high I could drive them."

Of course the asshole had. Zy wasn't even surprised that he'd toyed with people for an ego stroke.

"But I could take them up on it...and let them know there are some security problems on the platform," Phillip rushed to add.

"The sale needs to get announced by five p.m. Pacific."

"That's awfully fast. These things take weeks, sometimes months.

"Get it done today. Or else."

His father hesitated, and Zy could feel him fuming. Finally, he huffed. "Fine."

That was one hurdle down, but Zy had other provisions. Even if his father and the investment group agreed to a deal today, the actual close of the sale would take a while. "Two more things: first, you have an 'outage' or a 'glitch' or whatever you need to have to not piss off these cartels, but disable, throttle, or delete their accounts until the company changes hands. Be all apologies for the technical problems, but get it done."

His dad sighed. "All right."

"And you give ten percent of the sale of the business to helping others. Women's shelters, food banks, halfway houses. Not through your buddies and their tax shelters or pet projects. And not to your investment guy to line your pockets later. Actual people in need. Don't buy another fucking Lamborghini or whatever overpriced phallic symbol you drive these days. Be a human being."

Phillip turned very quiet. "You're right."

Zy didn't kid himself. His dad's sudden change of heart and self-enlightenment wouldn't last, but if it protected the people he loved for now, he'd done what he could. "And one more thing. I know you're going to dive back into the tech pool, and I'd be an idiot to think you don't already have something working, but you don't do business with these criminals again. Ever."

"Fine." His dad paused. "I don't even know who you are. How are you so not like the rest of us?"

More than once, Zy had wondered the same thing. He still didn't know why he'd never been a fortune chaser like his father, lazy and worried only about appearances like his mother, or a budding tycoon more concerned about his own pleasure than actually contributing to society like his brother. "I grew up with three examples of what not to be. That was all I needed."

That and the fact he'd been determined to be his own man.

"Are you still in Louisiana?"

"Why?"

"It's...backward and mostly full of bumpkins and—"

"The 'bumpkins' are great people who care about each other and their community. They're turning into the kind of family I've always wanted and never had."

"Ouch."

"You never spared my feelings as a kid. I'm just returning the favor. Oh, and when you announce the divorce tomorrow, my name better not be anywhere on that press release."

"I'll have it removed." His father sighed. "Will I ever hear from you again?"

"I don't know." Then the taxi driver pulled into Tessa's neighborhood, and his patience with this conversation ended. "That all depends on you. I have to go."

"I'm sorry."

Zy knew his dad wasn't merely apologizing for this latest fiasco but a lifelong host of disappointments. "And I'm sorry it's come to this. Maybe someday."

"Goodbye, son." His father actually sounded choked up.

And Zy didn't have the energy to decide whether he believed the man or not. The taxi was stopping in front of Tessa's place, and *this* was the future he needed to focus on. "Goodbye."

With that, he hung up, paid the taxi driver, then hauled ass out of the car—well, as much as he could in his banged-up condition. Then he hobbled up Tessa's walkway. On the other side of the door, he heard familiar male voices. The bosses were here? They fucking better not be firing her…

"Are you in love with Zy?" That was Logan.

Exactly what Zy wanted to know. His heart caught in his throat as he eavesdropped, waiting for her reply.

"I don't know what you want from me," Tessa said. Her voice was so soft, but he heard the catch in it.

Zy frowned. What kind of answer was that?

He pushed the door open and took in the scene, Tessa surrounded by all the bosses, looking exhausted and worried and put on the spot by the three bastards they worked for. "I want the truth, baby."

She stood, clearly shocked. "You're here?"

Had she thought he wouldn't come as soon as he could? Or was she simply wishing he hadn't?

He nodded and entered, shutting the door behind him. "Yeah. And I'm waiting for you to answer that question. Do you love me?"

"And that's our cue to leave." Hunter stood.

The other two followed suit, Logan frowning as if he wasn't quite ready to rush out the door.

Good. Since Zy was on a roll, cleaning house and sweeping out the shit, he might as well continue. "After you three apologize for lying to her and manipulating her."

She gaped. "I'm the one who owed them the apology. I passed on company secrets. I didn't do what I should have when Hallie went missing and—"

"You've already owned up to it," Hunter put in.

"And that's good," Zy added. "But what they're not telling you is why they suddenly removed the restrictions in our contracts keeping us apart."

Tessa frowned and turned to the trio.

Hunter grimaced. "When we suspected you or Trees of being our mole, we assigned Zy to investigate you both. He was pissed and he resisted. After weeks of almost no progress, we decided to change the contracts, which, as you know, we finalized on Monday. Then we told him he had two weeks to prove which of you was our mole. If he didn't, we planned to fire you all."

She gaped, then lifted trembling fingers over her pretty pink mouth. "You put Zy in a terrible position."

He nodded. "The worst, and I'm sorry for my part, baby. I should never have suspected you."

"I gave you reasons to." She looked down contritely, then turned to the bosses. "I understand why you did what you did, but I wish you'd come to me directly instead of putting Zy in the middle."

Logan sighed and elbowed his older brother.

Hunter looked grumpy but nodded. "Yeah. In hindsight, we should have. So we're apologizing to both of you."

"And we'll try to be less asshole-ish in the future," Logan added.

Joaquin rubbed at the back of his neck. "This management thing is still new for us. We're, um…feeling our way through and sometimes we're a little blind."

"I understand," she murmured. "And I hope you find your sister soon. If there's anything I can do, let me know."

"You'll be in the office next week?" Hunter asked.

"Maybe not first thing on Monday." Of course she needed more time with her daughter. But then she looked up at him, a silent acknowledgment that they had unresolved issues. "But soon."

"Same here," Zy cut in. "I'm not medically cleared for the next forty-eight hours."

"Concussion protocol?"

He nodded. "If I have one, it's mild. I lost consciousness at the scene and woke up with a bitch of a headache. But it's getting better. They monitored me for hours, even after all the tests. But they still want me to be cautious."

"Gotcha. Apology accepted? You're coming back soon?" Logan asked like it very much mattered to him.

"Yeah." They might have fucked up, but they meant well. After dealing with his dad, he knew how critical that distinction was.

"Thanks. We don't know when or if we'll return to normal, so… um, keep on being in charge."

"All right. But we should spell Kane. He needs a break."

"Yeah. Call us later. Jack and Deke are willing to loan us one of theirs. We haven't met Trevor except in passing, but he's got to be a good guy if his nickname for One-Mile is Serial Killer."

They all forced a laugh at the joke, but the truth was, after everything they'd been through, nothing felt light or humorous. And if they didn't recover Kimber, Zy didn't know if anything ever would again.

After that, the trio filed to the door. Tessa shut it behind them. Zy followed her and locked it.

They were alone.

She set the alarm that hadn't been there before, and he wondered who had installed it and when, but that was a question for later, not the one burning hottest through his brain.

He braced his hand against the door, above her head, caging her close to him. "Where's Hallie? Is she all right?"

She turned to him. "Yes, thank goodness. The doctors at the ER could hardly find a scratch on her. She's sleeping now. She was exhausted."

"I'm glad she's okay. I worried like hell about her."

She sent him a little smile. "I could tell. You risked your life for her. Saying thank you doesn't begin to express how grateful I am."

"You don't have to thank me. I think of her as my own."

That choked Tessa up. "I worried about you. I waited hours today without any word… I asked, but no one would tell me anything, even where to find you. I hoped you'd call but—"

He pulled the phone from his back pocket. "It died shortly after we reached the ER."

She placed a soft hand on his arm, and even that touch was enough to send a shudder through him. "Are you okay? Really?"

"Better now that I'm here. With you."

"I'm better now that you're here, too. Can you stay?" Her soft entreaty gave him hope.

"That depends on you."

"Me?

"You never answered my question, you know."

She shook her head, her body so close he couldn't resist cupping her cheek. "What are you… I don't… Zy, if there's even a chance you have a concussion, you should sit and rest and—"

"After we've talked."

Tessa looked away. "You don't have to say anything. The bosses explained why you investigated me. I'm still so sorry I betrayed everyone—but especially you. The guilt will eat at me for a long time. I hope you can forgive me—"

"Baby, I absolved you the second I heard why you'd done it. You put Hallie first. You had to. I understand. And you're right that you didn't handle things the way I would have, but you had no way of knowing how to deal with a situation like that. I've been trained to. You haven't. I just hope you can forgive me. What I said and did in the bunker—"

"I understand."

"But if you hate me for it..." Goddamn it, the thought nearly ripped him in two.

"No." She lifted her stunned gaze to him. "I don't. I couldn't."

"Okay, I can work with that. I know we have a lot to figure out and a lot of trust to repair—"

"I trust you." She bit her lip, her face full of regret. "But I should have trusted you more."

"Just like I should have. Let's not fuck up again, huh?"

She laughed. "Let's not. Let's agree to talk anything out in the future."

"Absolutely. Now I'm dying to ask you a question, baby." He took her by the hand, never breaking her soft, blinking gaze as he urged her to the sofa, then knelt at her feet, pulling the box from his pocket Trees had dropped off earlier. When he lifted the lid, she gasped as he pressed a kiss to her hand. "Marry me."

She looked absolutely stunned as she trembled against him. "Y-you mean that? Really?"

"Of course. You know I love you. I bought this ring four days ago. I want you to be my wife. I want to be a father to Hallie. I want to grow a family with you. I'd like the answer to my first question, too, but if that's a no—"

"Zy, I love you." Tears filled her eyes and spilled down her cheeks. "I love you so much."

His heart caught and lifted. He'd waited forever to hear those words, and having her say them now was way more than he'd dared to hope for today. Hell, maybe for weeks or months. As long as Tessa had agreed to be his, he'd been prepared to do or say whatever he needed to win her over. But if she already loved him...

She sniffled and looked at him with such an earnest gaze, he melted. "In fact, I've loved you for a long, long time, since shortly after you first walked through my door."

"Baby..." He gripped her shoulder. "Is that a yes? You'll marry me?"

More tears fell, but she gave him a watery, heartfelt nod before throwing herself against his chest. "Yes. I'd be thrilled and honored to marry you."

"Oh, thank fuck. I want this ring on your finger before you have a chance to change your mind." He slid it on, surprised to find his own hand shaking.

It fit perfectly.

She gave him a tearful giggle and looked down at the diamond winking on her finger, then back up at him. "Oh, my gosh. I'm going to be Mrs. Garrett."

"Damn straight." Zy couldn't resist another second. He kissed her —for the first time finally knowing he could claim her mouth every day for the rest of his life. "The sooner the better."

"I can't wait. My life is complete now because I have you."

"Same, baby." He cupped her face. "And you better not ever stop looking at me like that."

She grinned, beaming with joy and love. "Like what?"

"Like you want me to peel off your clothes and take you to bed as much as I'm dying to."

"I'll never stop, I promise. I just want to know what you're waiting for."

"Nothing. I'm done waiting. You're mine now—forever."

Epilogue

February 2
3 a.m.

Forest Scott, known to most everyone as Trees—because what else was someone supposed to call a gawky-as-fuck, six-foot-eight dude?—jolted awake to the nagging whine pealing from the alarm panel and sat straight up in bed.

Someone unauthorized had opened one of his doors or windows.

His first thought was of Laila Torres.

Had someone come to take her from him…or was she trying to escape?

Again.

It didn't matter which scenario he was facing, someone was getting interrogated tonight.

Trees vaulted out of bed and disengaged the alarm before hopping into his sweatpants and steel-toed boots. Without bothering to lace up, he grabbed the Benelli he kept propped beside his bed and a pair of cuffs from his nightstand, then pocketed the nearby flashlight.

Trees prowled across the house quietly—a skill acquired from years at war in both urban dogfights and desert shitholes—until he reached Laila's bedroom. He wasn't surprised to find the door closed. She shut it every night. Locked it, too. Apparently, she thought that would save her from him if he was the kind of asshole who would force his way into her bed. She had known men like that most of her life, so he'd let her keep the illusion. Trees hated to screw with her peace of mind now, but…

He had her door open in less than ten seconds.

Her bed was empty, her window tightly shut. But it was chillier in here, as if someone had recently let the winter night into her room.

Son of a bitch.

He doubled back, charging to the front door, plucked his coat off the nearby hook, and shoved it on over his bare torso as he hauled ass onto the porch. Thank god he still had a pair of thermal night-vision binoculars in his pocket.

Trees lifted them to his face and found Laila in seconds.

She was alone.

He grunted, wanting to be grateful that someone hadn't taken her from him, but he was just too pissed. Did the woman not understand that her life was in danger? Or did she simply not value her goddamn safety?

Cursing, he bounded off the porch and ran after her. He would catch up to her quickly for four reasons: First, she had nothing on her feet but flimsy flip-flops. Second, it was thirty-seven degrees, and she was covered only by a tank top and short shorts. Third, his height advantage meant he had hella long legs, and her soft curves proved that, unlike him, she didn't run a few miles a day. Fourth—and most important—she might want to leave him badly enough to brave nature and the elements at three o'clock in the morning, but he was far more determined to keep her under his roof.

Hell, if he could, he'd keep her in his bed. But ever since he'd heaped a trio of orgasms on her and shared the most mind-blowing fuck of his life, she'd done nothing but try to escape him.

Time to drag her back, put his foot down, and tell her exactly how things were going to be.

It didn't take him long to catch her. He could see the flash of her sleek, naked legs in the moonlight, along with the puffs of her breaths in the cold.

Laila had no idea he even chased her until he was practically on top of her.

She whipped her gaze over her shoulder just as he hooked an arm around her waist and lifted her from the ground. He yanked her kicking, writhing form into his arms and against his body. Her flip-flops went flying.

"Let me go!"

"Nope." He retrieved her shoes and shoved them in his pocket, despite her struggles.

She did her best to punch and kick him, even bit him once. But, as his mother would have said, bless her heart. Every attempt to get free was both ineffectual and pointless.

"You cannot keep me here against my will."

That's where she was wrong. EM Security Management was paying him for just that.

"I can," he said as he headed back toward his house.

"My sister needs me."

"Your sister has her own protection. We've ensured that, and you know it. That's not why you're trying to run, and you know I'm right."

Laila went stubbornly mute—a response he was well used to.

She didn't want to talk? Fine by him.

Trees contained her still-wriggling form, bypassed the front door, then headed around to the back, before flipping on his chipper shredder.

"No!" she screamed in terror, scratching and clawing, scrambling to get away from him as if her life depended on it.

What the hell did she think he intended to do, feed her into it?

One look at her face told him she did.

Fuck.

"Hey, calm down, honey. It's all right. I'm not going to hurt you."

She looked at him with wary eyes. "Then what?"

He didn't need words to explain. Instead, he took her flip-flops from his pocket and fed them into the machine, watching a pile of pink rubber emerge on the ground, then he turned it off.

"Are you crazy? Those are my only shoes!"

"Were. They're not shoes anymore. Let's go." He hiked her up against his body, thick arm around her middle.

Instinct won out, and she wrapped her legs around him to ensure she didn't fall. "Why would you do this?"

Trees didn't answer until he climbed the front porch, made his way inside, and set her on her feet. By the ambient security lights—most would call them nightlights—he watched the fear and anger war across that face of hers, which still had the power to take his breath away. It didn't matter that he terrified her or that he hadn't touched her in days. He hated the fact that she hated him. They were a fucked-up tangle, but he refused to let anyone hurt her.

"Because now you can't go anywhere," he pointed out.

Laila fumed. Oh, she tried to hide it, but he was learning her tells. She might be a gorgeous Latina, but she didn't have the stereotypical spicy temper to go with it. Nope. Laila wasn't the sort of woman to get mad. She got even.

Trees was pretty sure she was plotting some really shitty revenge right now. That didn't worry him half so much as her insistence on escaping.

He took her by the arm, hauled her to the kitchen table, and thrust her into the first chair, then wrapped his hands around her shoulders. It didn't escape his notice that his grip covered most of her upper arms. "What we have here is a failure to communicate."

"I understand your English. Though it may shock you as a man, I have my own thoughts and I disagree with you."

"I'm not shocked at all. I'm just making it incredibly clear that you're not getting your way. You and your sister are under our protection. As long as either faction warring for control of the Tierra Caliente cartel is after you, it's my responsibility to keep you alive. You can't fight them alone and you've got to know that. But since you don't seem to and I'm not getting through to you, we're going to make some changes around here until you grasp the concept."

Without waiting for a response, he began patting her down. It was fucking hard not to notice her soft, lush breasts when he had to cup them. Impossible not to remember having them in his mouth or watching them bounce when he'd gripped her hips and she'd ridden him hard and fast. But now wasn't the time for this trip down memory lane—or his erection. He needed to find her phone.

Laila pushed at his hands and turned her body away protectively, but he finally felt his way from her chest to her ass—and pulled the phone from her back pocket.

He saw three messages from her sister, which was no surprise. And one from Hunter Edgington.

That shocked the hell out of him.

"What are you up to?"

Stubbornly, she pressed her lips together, crossed her arms over her chest in a way that made her tits look even more luscious, and jerked her stare out the window.

Damn it. How the fuck could he get her to talk? Turning her ass red and stripping the starch from her attitude sounded great. But she'd made it clear she never wanted him touching her again, and she didn't trust him even a bit, so she'd never volunteer for any sort of consensual spanking. Even if she needed it.

So Trees did the next best thing. He waved her phone in front of her face until it unlocked, then started prowling through the device.

"No!" She lunged out of her chair and reached for the phone.

Trees merely held it level with his face, kind of amused as he watched her jump for it. There were occasional benefits to being freakishly tall.

Finally, he found the message string he'd been looking for, scanned and scrolled, then nearly lost his fucking mind. "Why were you planning to have a conversation with one of my bosses?"

With a frustrated huff, she plopped in her seat again. Because she realized the jig was up?

"It is none of your concern."

The hell it wasn't.

With a sigh, he flipped on the overhead light and headed to the coffeepot. If he was going to interrogate her, he needed some damn caffeine. Days and days without a full night's sleep were catching up to him.

The instant he turned his back, she shoved out of her chair, legs scraping across the tile, and sprinted for the door. She'd barely reached it and pulled it open when he caught her around the waist again, lifted her petite curves, kicked the door shut, then carried her back to the kitchen. He pulled out the cuffs.

Her eyes widened. "What are you doing?"

He ignored her, managing to slap one cuff around her wrist before she started fighting like a hellcat. But she was too late. He'd already looped the chain around the rungs of the chair and grabbed her free hand.

"You cannot do this."

He clicked the second cuff into place. "I just did. Now we're going to talk. Want a blanket?"

He hoped like fuck she said yes because he was getting a full frontal of her under the kitchen lights, and it was impossible to miss her thick, beaded nipples.

Fuck me.

He loved tits, and she had a great pair. And that really wasn't the number one subject on his brain. Well, it shouldn't be.

"What will I owe you for it?"

For a fucking blanket? "Nothing."

She hesitated. "Fine. Then yes. Please."

He nodded as he grabbed a quilt from the corner of his bed. When he draped it over her, they both breathed a sigh of relief.

Then Trees turned the nearby chair backward and straddled it, resting his arms over the top. "Let's start over. Why were you asking to talk to my boss?"

Laila proved once again she was as strong-willed as she was beautiful when she refused to answer.

"You want to tell him we fucked? See if that will get me in trouble? Are you hoping he'll assign you a guard you can slip past?"

But as soon as the words were out, Trees realized he was wrong. She'd had days to throw him under the bus. For some reason, she hadn't. And if she thought for a minute she'd be able to slip past someone else on the EM Security team, she would already have done her best to swap him out. But she'd met enough of them by now to know better.

So what was her angle?

Laila wouldn't meet his gaze, so he took her chin in his grip and forced her to look at him. As always, her soft hazel eyes undid him—not to mention that pouty, fuck-me mouth he remembered kissing feverishly in the dark.

How many times had he jacked off to that memory?

"Why would you want to talk to Hunter without me knowing?"

Her white teeth bit into that pillowy lower lip, and he stifled a groan. She had no idea what she was doing to him, and he couldn't let on. She'd already used his desire against him once. Trees wouldn't let it happen again.

Since she still stubbornly refused to say a word, he'd have to puzzle the answer out himself.

If Hunter, Logan, or Joaquin had an issue with the job he was doing, based on her complaints, they would have called his ass on the carpet by now. If it wasn't about the sex he'd once stupidly taken her up on and it wasn't about the fact he was keeping her "captive" at his isolated compound, he could only think of one other thing.

And it fucking pissed him off.

"Were you arranging to use yourself as bait to catch whoever's after your sister?"

Laila glared at him as if debating the wisdom of answering with anything close to the truth. Finally, she yanked her chin from his grasp. "Don't touch me."

"Then answer me."

"Yes. And you cannot stop me."

That's what she thought. "Were you planning to run to Hunter's place? Maybe get clear of my property, then call him to come get you?"

It wasn't anything she did that told him he'd hit the nail on the head, but he knew. "Oh, that would have made me look really fucking good. Then again, you don't care about that, do you?"

"I have no wish to hurt you, but my sister—"

"Will be fine."

She shook her head. "They will come. They will keep coming. They will never stop until they kill her and take her son. I know these people. They are animals. They will never give up."

"Then neither will I. I can be an animal, too. And I'll prove it."

The End

Thank you for reading Wicked and True! If you enjoyed this book, please review and/or recommend it to your reader friends. That means the world to me!

Dying to know how Trees and Laila's fiery collision started? Brace yourself.

WICKED AS SEDUCTION
Trees and Laila, Part One
Wicked & Devoted, Book 5
By Shayla Black
(will be available in eBook, print, and audio)

Coming March 15, 2022!

If you missed One-Mile and Brea, catch up with the sexiest bad boy meets good girl story. Wicked as Sin kicks off the addictive, suspenseful Wicked & Devoted series!

WICKED AS SIN

One-Mile & Brea, Part One
Wicked & Devoted, Book 1
By Shayla Black
NOW AVAILABLE!

The good girl wants a favor? She'll pay in his bed.

Pierce "One-Mile" Walker has always kept his heart under wraps and his head behind his sniper's scope. Nothing about buttoned-up Brea Bell should appeal to him. But after a single glance at the pretty preacher's daughter, he doesn't care that his past is less than shiny, that he gets paid to end lives…or that she's his teammate's woman. He'll do whatever it takes to steal her heart.

Brea has always been a dutiful daughter and a good girl…until she meets the dangerous warrior. He's everything she shouldn't want, especially after her best friend introduces her to his fellow operative as his girlfriend—to protect her from Pierce. But he's a forbidden temptation she's finding impossible to resist.

Then fate strikes, forcing Brea to beg Pierce to help solve a crisis. But his skills come at a price. When her innocent flirtations run headlong into his obsession, they cross the line into a passion so fiery she can't say no. Soon, his past rears its head and a vendetta calls his name in a mission gone horribly wrong. Will he survive to fight his way back to the woman who claimed his soul?

SNEAK PREVIEW

Sunday, January 11
Sunset, Louisiana

Finally, he had her cornered. He intended to tear down every last damn obstacle between him and Brea Bell.

Right now.

For months, she'd succumbed to fears, buried her head in the sand, even lied. He'd tried to be understanding and patient. He'd made mistakes, but damn it, he'd put her first, given her space, been the good guy.

Fuck that. Now that he'd fought his way here, she would see the real him.

One-Mile Walker slammed the door of his Jeep and turned all his focus on the modest white cottage with its vintage blue door. As he marched up the long concrete driveway, his heart pounded. He had a nasty idea how Brea's father would respond when he explained why he'd come. The man would slam the door in his face; no maybe about that. After all, he was the bad boy from a broken home who had defiled Reverend Bell's perfect daughter with unholy glee.

But One-Mile refused to let Brea go again. He'd make her father listen…somehow. Since punching the guy in the face was out of the question, he'd have to quell his brute-force instinct to fight dirty and instead employ polish, tact, and charm—all the qualities he possessed zero of.

Fuck. This was going to be a shit show.

Still, One-Mile refused to give up. He'd known uphill battles his whole life. What was one more?

Through the house's front window, he spotted the soft doe eyes that had haunted him since last summer. Though Brea was talking to an elderly couple, the moment she saw him approach her porch, her pretty eyes went wide with shock.

Determination gripped One-Mile and squeezed his chest. By damned, she was going to listen, too.

He wasn't leaving without making her his.

As he mounted the first step toward her door, his cell phone rang. He would have ignored it if it hadn't been for two critical facts: His job often entailed saving the world as the people knew it, and this particular chime he only heard when one of the men he respected most in this fucked-up world needed him during the grimmest of emergencies.

Of all the lousy timing…

He yanked the device from his pocket. "Walker here. Colonel?"

"Yeah."

Colonel Caleb Edgington was a retired, highly decorated military officer and a tough son of a bitch. One thing he wasn't prone to was drama, so that single foreboding syllable told One-Mile that whatever had prompted this call was dire.

He didn't bother with small talk, even though it had been months since they'd spoken, and he wondered how the man was enjoying both his fifties and his new wife, but they'd catch up later. Now, they had no time to waste.

"What can I do for you?" Since he owed Caleb a million times over, whatever the man needed, One-Mile would make happen.

Caleb's sons might be his bosses these days…but as far as One-Mile was concerned, the jury was still out on that trio. Speaking of which, why wasn't Caleb calling those badasses?

One-Mile could only think of one answer. It was hardly comforting.

"Or should I just ask who I need to kill?"

A soft, feminine gasp sent his gaze jerking up to Brea, who now stood in the doorway, her rosy bow of a mouth gaping open in a perfect little *O*. She'd heard that. *Goddamn it to hell.* Yeah, she knew perfectly well what he was. But he'd managed to shock her repeatedly over the last six months.

"I'm not sure yet." Caleb sounded cautious in his ear. "I'm going to text you an address. Can you meet me there in fifteen minutes?"

For months, he'd been anticipating this exact moment with Brea. "Any chance it can wait an hour?"

"No. Every moment is critical."

Since Caleb would never say such things lightly, One-Mile didn't see that he had an option. "On my way."

He ended the call and pocketed the phone as he climbed onto the porch and gave Brea his full attention. He had so little time with her, but he'd damn sure get his point across before he went.

She stepped outside and shut the door behind her, swallowing nervously as she cast a furtive glance over her shoulder, through the big picture window. Was she hoping her father didn't see them?

"Pierce." Her whisper sounded closer to a hiss. "What are you doing here?"

He hated when anyone else used his given name, but Brea could call him whatever the hell she wanted as long as she let him in her life.

He peered down at her, considering how to answer. He'd had grand plans to lay his cards out on the table and do whatever he had to —talk, coax, hustle, schmooze—until she and her father came around to his way of thinking. Now he only had time to cut to the chase. "You know what I want, pretty girl. I'm here for you. And when I come back, I won't take no for an answer."

Don't forget to grab the gripping conclusion of this unforgettable couple…

WICKED EVER AFTER
One-Mile and Brea, Part Two
Wicked & Devoted, Book 2
By Shayla Black
NOW AVAILABLE!

The good girl is keeping a secret?
He'll seduce it out of her until she begs to be his.

WICKED & DEVOTED WORLD

Thank you for joining me in the Wicked & Devoted world. If you didn't know, this cast of characters started in my Wicked Lovers world, continued into my Devoted Lovers series, and have collided here. During Zy and Tessa's journey, you've read about some other characters and you might be wondering if I've told their story. Or if I will tell their story in the future. Below is a guide in case you'd like to read more from this cast, listed in order of release:

WICKED LOVERS

Wicked Ties

Jack Cole (and Morgan O'Malley)

She didn't know what she wanted...until he made her beg for it.

Decadent

Deke Trenton (and Kimber Edgington)

The boss' innocent daughter. A forbidden favor he can't refuse...

Surrender to Me

Hunter Edgington (and Katalina Muñoz)

A secret fantasy. An uncontrollable obsession. A forever love?

Belong to Me

Logan Edgington (and Tara Jacobs)

He's got everything under control until he falls for his first love...again.

Mine to Hold

Tyler Murphy (Delaney Catalano)

His best friend's ex. A night he can't forget. A secret that could destroy them both.

Wicked All the Way

Caleb Edgington (and Carlotta Muñoz Buckley)

Could their second chance be their first real love?

His to Take

Joaquin Muñoz (and Bailey Benson)

Giving in to her dark stranger might be the most delicious danger of all…

Falling in Deeper

Stone Sutter (and Lily Taylor)

Will her terrifying past threaten their passionate future?

Holding on Tighter

Heath Powell (and Jolie Quinn)

Mixing business with pleasure can be a dangerous proposition…

DEVOTED LOVERS

Devoted to Pleasure

Cutter Bryant (and Shealyn West)

A bodyguard should never fall for his client…but she's too tempting to refuse.

Devoted to Wicked

Cage Bryant (and Karis Quinn)

Will the one-night stand she tried to forget seduce her into a second chance?

Devoted to Love

Josiah Grant (and Magnolia West)

He was sent to guard her body…but he's determined to steal her heart.

As the Wicked & Devoted world continues to collide and explode, you'll see more titles with other characters you know and love, so stay tuned for Trees and Laila's story, as well as duets about Kane, Matt, Trevor, and more!

I have so much in store for you on this wild **Wicked & Devoted** ride!

Hugs and Happy Reading!

Shayla

LET'S GET TO KNOW EACH OTHER!

Shayla Black is the *New York Times* and *USA Today* bestselling author of about eighty novels. For twenty years, she's written contemporary, erotic, paranormal, and historical romances via traditional, independent, foreign, and audio publishers. Her books have sold millions of copies and been published in a dozen languages.

Raised an only child, Shayla occupied herself with lots of daydreaming, much to the chagrin of her teachers. In college, she found her love for reading and realized that she could have a career publishing the stories spinning in her imagination. Though she graduated with a degree in Marketing/Advertising and embarked on a stint in corporate America to pay the bills, her heart has always been with her characters. She's thrilled that she's been living her dream as a full-time author for the past eleven years.

Shayla currently lives in North Texas with her wonderfully supportive husband and daughter, as well as two spoiled tabbies. In her "free" time, she enjoys reality TV, reading, and listening to an eclectic blend of music.

TELL ME MORE ABOUT YOU.

Connect with me via the links below. The VIP Readers newsletter has exclusive news and excerpts. You can also become one of my Facebook Book Beauties and enjoy live, interactive #WineWednesday video chats full of fun, book chatter, and more! See you soon!

Connect with me online:
Website: http://shaylablack.com
VIP Reader Newsletter: http://shayla.link/nwsltr
Facebook Author Page: http://shayla.link/FBPage
Facebook Book Beauties Chat Group: http://shayla.link/FBChat
Instagram: https://instagram.com/ShaylaBlack/

TikTok: www.tiktok.com/@shayla_black
Book+Main: http://shayla.link/books+main
Twitter: http://twitter.com/Shayla_Black
Amazon Author Page: http://shayla.link/AmazonFollow
BookBub: http://shayla.link/BookBub
Goodreads: http://shayla.link/goodreads
YouTube: http://shayla.link/youtube

OTHER BOOKS BY SHAYLA BLACK

CONTEMPORARY ROMANCE

MORE THAN WORDS

More Than Want You

More Than Need You

More Than Love You

More Than Crave You

More Than Tempt You

More Than Pleasure You (novella)

More Than Dare You

More Than Protect You (novella)

Coming Soon:

More Than Possess You (novella) (Sept 28, 2021)

More Than Hate You (Fall 2021)

WICKED & DEVOTED

Wicked as Sin

Wicked Ever After

Wicked as Lies

Wicked and True

Coming Soon:

Wicked as Seduction (March 15, 2022)

THE WICKED LOVERS (COMPLETE SERIES)

Wicked Ties

Decadent

Delicious

Surrender to Me

Belong to Me

Wicked to Love (novella)

Mine to Hold

Wicked All the Way (novella)

Ours to Love

Wicked All Night (novella)

Forever Wicked (novella)

Theirs to Cherish

His to Take

Pure Wicked (novella)

Wicked for You

Falling in Deeper

Dirty Wicked (novella)

A Very Wicked Christmas (short)

Holding on Tighter

THE DEVOTED LOVERS (Complete Series)

Devoted to Pleasure

Devoted to Wicked (novella)

Devoted to Love

FORBIDDEN CONFESSIONS (Sexy Shorts)

Seducing the Innocent

Seducing the Bride

Seducing the Stranger

Seducing the Enemy

Seduced by the Bodyguard

Coming Soon:

Seduced by the Spy (June 1, 2021)

Seduced by the Assassin (July 13, 2021)

Seduced by the Mafia Boss (August 17, 2021)

DOMS OF HER LIFE

(by Shayla Black, Jenna Jacob, and Isabella LaPearl)

Raine Falling Collection (COMPLETE)

One Dom To Love

The Young And The Submissive

The Bold and The Dominant

The Edge of Dominance

Heavenly Rising Collection

The Choice

The Chase

Coming Soon:

The Commitment (2021)

THE PERFECT GENTLEMEN (COMPLETE SERIES)

(by Shayla Black and Lexi Blake)

Scandal Never Sleeps

Seduction in Session

Big Easy Temptation

Smoke and Sin

At the Pleasure of the President

MASTERS OF MÉNAGE

(by Shayla Black and Lexi Blake)

Their Virgin Captive

Their Virgin's Secret

Their Virgin Concubine

Their Virgin Princess

Their Virgin Hostage

Their Virgin Secretary

Their Virgin Mistress

STANDALONE TITLES

Naughty Little Secret

Watch Me

Dirty & Dangerous

Her Fantasy Men (Four Play Anthology)

A Perfect Match

THE HOPE SERIES

Misadventures of a Backup Bride

Misadventures with My Ex

Coming Soon:

Untitled (2021)

SEXY CAPERS (COMPLETE SERIES)

Bound and Determined

Strip Search

Arresting Desire (novella)

HISTORICAL ROMANCE STANDALONES

The Lady and the Dragon

One Wicked Night

STRICTLY SERIES (VICTORIAN DUET)

Strictly Seduction

Strictly Forbidden

BROTHERS IN ARMS (MEDIEVAL TRILOGY)

His Lady Bride

His Stolen Bride

His Rebel Bride

CPSIA information can be obtained
at www.ICGtesting.com
Printed in the USA
LVHW051612080421
683869LV00012B/1337